LOVE AND LEPRECHAUNS

A BALLYBEG ROMANCE

(BOOK 3)

ZARA KEANE

Beaverstone Press LLC
Switzerland

LOVE AND LEPRECHAUNS

Published 2014 by Beaverstone Press GmbH (LLC)

Cover Design © 2014 by Kim Killion.

Cover photographs: The Killion Group, Inc. and Patryk Kosmider Photography at iStock

Beaverstone Press
CH-5023 Biberstein
Switzerland
www.beaverstonepress.com

Book Layout © 2014 BookDesignTemplates.com

Ordering Information:

Quantity sales. Special discounts are available on quantity purchases by corporations, associations, and others. For details, contact the "Special Sales Department" at the address above.

Love and Leprechauns/Zara Keane. -- 1st ed.

ISBN 978-3-906245-08-9

For all the special kids in the world.
May you thrive and prosper!

CHAPTER ONE

BALLYBEG, COUNTY CORK, IRELAND

Olivia was a devout Catholic in two circumstances: on planes and at the dentist. Right now, she was praying for deliverance from the dentist's drill.

Hail Mary, full of..."Ouch." Vicious pain jolted through her jaw.

The dentist stood back and flexed his aged shoulders. "You need a filling on the lower right."

A trickle of sweat slithered down her spine. *Feck.* Not today of all days. She *had* to get to the meeting with her bank manager on time. She needed to convince him to loan her the money to start her café. Without the café, she couldn't move out of her estranged husband's guest room. And until she lived on her own, she couldn't rescue her brothers from the lunatics they called parents.

The irony of it all was that their parents' debt to Aidan was what tied Olivia to her farce of a marriage. Being this close to getting the bank loan, she could practically taste freedom. She couldn't let anything derail her plans.

"Can't you do the filling another time?" Her clammy hands gripped the arms of the leather reclining chair. "I'm in a rush this morning, and– "

Dr. O'Shea chuckled with good-natured chastisement. "Now, now, Olivia. That's what you get for leaving it two years between checkups. Didn't I teach you better?"

This sort of condescension was part and parcel of going to the same dentist since childhood. Knowing from experience that arguing with him was futile, she swallowed her frustration, slumped back in the chair, and shut her eyes.

If only the bank hadn't changed her appointment. She'd been scheduled to go by next week, but they'd called while she was in the waiting room to change the day. *Inconsiderate sods.* It was too late to cancel the dentist and too early to have her papers organized for the loan application. At this rate, she'd have to use whatever material she could find in her briefcase and hope for the best. She took a shuddery breath and visualized rosary beads.

"It shouldn't be too deep." The dentist was oblivious to her rising panic. "Shall we try the filling without an anesthetic?"

Olivia's eyes flew open. "Absolutely not. If you intend to come near me with a drill, I want drugs. Lots of them."

The old man's mustache bobbed in amusement. "I'll get the syringe."

The whirring of the drill soon catapulted her piousness from visualizing rosary beads to contemplating life in a cloister. There were certain drawbacks to the plan– neither fasting nor celibacy had ever been her forte. Although becoming a nun would solve the Aidan problem, wouldn't it? Not to mention the bank. *The bank...Oh, blast.* The thumping in her chest increased in tempo. At this rate, she'd never make it on time.

"All done." The dentist beamed. "That wasn't so bad, was it?"

That, Olivia surmised, was a matter of opinion. She poked her new filling dubiously, noting her numb jaw and the lower lip that felt like it had been stuffed with foam.

"The numbness will wear off within an hour." He removed his rubber surgical gloves and discarded them in the rubbish bin.

She swung her legs over the side of the chair and stood with caution, wobbly as day-old jelly.

The dentist held the door. "I'll see you in six months – and no later. Julie will give you an appointment. In the meantime, take good care of your teeth."

Olivia emerged from the dentist's torture chamber to the melodic chime of the grandfather clock in the reception area. Ten o'clock. She had a decent chance of getting to the bank on time. *Major whew.* Whether or not she'd be coherent for the meeting was another matter.

"How did it go?" Julie Jobson sat behind the reception desk, sporting a smug smirk. Her blouse was at least two sizes too small, making her ample bosom more prominent.

Olivia scowled at her erstwhile classmate and childhood tormentor. She'd like to add an expression of haughty superiority, but that was rather difficult to achieve when one half of her face was immobile. Instead she settled for an arched eyebrow. "I need another appointment in thix months."

Fabulous. She was woozy, numb, and drooling. Now she had a lisp to complete her humiliation.

"Oh, dear," Julie said in mock concern. "Had a filling? I suppose you'd better make sure you brush and floss regularly from now on, hadn't you?"

Olivia gave her the evil eye.

The other woman took no notice. "Still ginger-haired, I see." Her scarlet-lacquered talons clicked over the keyboard.

At least I don't look like I stuck my head in a bucket of toilet cleaner. As for ginger-haired...certainly not. She used the best dye on the market. When one's natural hair color was carrot, one did what one must.

She tossed her long "Titian Tresses" over her shoulder and wrapped a peacock-blue scarf around her neck. It was one of her own creations, and she wore the scarf with panache. She took every opportunity to look her best. Aidan had always insisted upon it, and old habits were hard to break. With this morning's imminent appointment at the bank, she needed the veneer of confidence lent to her by a coordinated outfit and perfect makeup.

Julie slid an appointment card across the counter. When Olivia reached for the card, her phone began to vibrate to the tinny opening chords of "It's Raining Men". Her fingers, tingly and uncooperative after her almost panic attack in the dental chair, refused to cooperate. She fumbled in her handbag, making futile attempts to grasp the phone. *Blast.* At last her fingers maintained their grip on the phone, but by the time she got it out of the bag, the caller had hung up. The display glowed with the uninformative message that the call was from "Unknown" and that the person hadn't bothered to leave a message.

She shoved the phone into her bag along with the appointment card. She had zero time to waste wondering who'd been trying to contact her. If the matter were that urgent, the person would call again. She gave Julie a curt nod and went to the coat stand to grab her coat. Bracing herself for the bitter chill outside, she gripped the door handle.

Before she could push it, the door swung open, bringing in a gust of wind and Jonas O'Mahony. Olivia staggered back. A strong arm grabbed her wrist, breaking her fall. His fingers sent heat searing through the layers of clothing. Blood hummed in her veins. She blamed the Novocain. Breathing hard, she yanked her arm free.

For years, she'd managed to avoid him. Easy enough to do– he didn't exactly run in the same circles as Aidan. Since his best friend had hooked up with hers, they'd crossed paths more frequently than she liked.

"Olivia." His gravelly voice broke the silence, as deep and rough as single-cask whiskey.

"Jonath," she lisped. *Silly anesthetic.*

He gave her a cool once-over, his indifferent expression indicating he wasn't impressed with what he saw.

She returned the favor. Jonas's broad frame was encased in leather and biker boots. His overly long black hair had a wild look that she suspected was caused by the recent removal of a motorcycle helmet. His dark eyes riveted her in place. She sensed the leprechaun on her behind burning a hole through her skirt. What had possessed her to commemorate her eighteenth birthday by getting a leprechaun tattooed on her arse? Her erratic heart thumped an extra beat. She knew the answer to that question. It wasn't *what* but *who,* and she was looking right at him.

"Jonas," Julie cooed from the reception desk. "How are you? How's your adorable little boy? Luca, isn't it?"

Blech. Clearly, Julie laid on more than makeup with a trowel.

"Hey, Julie." He treated the receptionist to a warm smile– treacle hot and sickly sweet. "Luca's grand. Adjusting to his new environment, but he'll get there. Should I take a seat in the waiting room?"

The receptionist's face registered disappointment that her flirting had failed to have the desired effect. "There are a few people ahead of you. You might have to wait for a bit."

"No problem." Jonas strode past Olivia without sparing her another glance. She caught a whiff of his aftershave– spicy and exotic. It sent her whirling back in time to the heady days of their love affair– intense, passionate, cut short by tragedy.

The vibration of her phone jolted her back to the present. *Shite.* Why was she still at the dentist? She needed to get moving. Holding the phone to her ear, she pushed open the door and stepped out into the blustery gale. She'd have to talk while she walked, and she'd better do both fast.

"This is Mary McDermott..." The woman's voice trailed off in an ominous ellipsis.

Not a positive sign. Please let this not be bad news about her bid for the cottage. "Yeah?"

"I'm afraid circumstances have changed. The cottages on Curzon Street are no longer available to rent. I'm sorry."

Sorry? The hell she is. Olivia was temporarily bereft of speech. "We had an agreement," she said finally, forcing herself to remain calm. Now was not the time to lose her cool. "You said I could have one of the vacant cottages if I paid the deposit by the end of the month. It's only the sixteenth." Courtesy of the anesthetic-induced lisp, each "s" came out as "th".

"We discussed you renting one of my properties, but we never got around to signing a contract." Mary's tone was defensive, bordering on peevish.

"I emailed you a reminder about the contract last week. You never replied."

"A landlady needs to know her prospective tenant will pay the rent on time and stay longer than a handful of months."

Whoa...that was way out of line. "Which prospective tenant proved solvent enough to get more than an oral agreement out of you?"

"You know I can't reveal that information. It's confidential."

"As was *my* bid for the bigger cottage. That didn't stop you from telling half the town. I'll ask you again: who?"

Mary's hesitation echoed down the phone. "He's not a tenant, exactly. My nephew– "

"Not Jonath?" Olivia stumbled to a halt, her head whipping round in the direction of the dental practice. But who else could it be? Niall O'Mahony was away at university, and he and Jonas were Mary's only living nephews.

"Jonas is a good lad. When he moved back to Ballybeg with his son, he had trouble finding a place to live. Curzon Street was the obvious solution."

"Surely he doesn't need *both* cottages. Why can't I have the other?"

"You know the answer to that question." Olivia could visualize Mary's Gallic shrug. "If you want to negotiate a deal with him, go for it. He's responsible for renting out the second cottage and he's unlikely to want to live next door to you. I'm sorry, but you'll have to look for somewhere else to open your café."

She began to formulate a cutting response, but Mary had already hung up, leaving her staring at the phone clutched in her hand. *Unbelievable.* Had Jonas engineered this reversal in her fortunes? Did he hate her that much after all these years? She wasn't having it. Pivoting on her heel, she stalked to the dental practice and barged in the door.

"Something wrong?" Julie batted her false eyelashes.

Olivia ignored her and marched straight through the reception area and into the waiting room. Three heads swiveled, but she was only interested in one. She directed the full force of her glare on Jonas. "You thcheming thcumbag."

Jonas regarded her coolly. "Had a filling?" His deep voice dripped condescension.

Olivia uttered an oath.

He laughed.

The rat bastard.

"What have I done to warrant being called a 'thchumbag'?"

His exaggerated air quotes made the other waiting room occupants snigger. Olivia itched to wipe the smug expression off his face.

"You knew I wanted one of the cottages for my café. Mary and I had a deal. You played the family card and poached it from me."

"Indeed?" His expression was inscrutable. "All's fair in love, war, and business, right? There'll be other premises. It simply wasn't meant to be."

"Could you be any more patronizing?"

He gave a slow grin. "I'm sure I could if I cared enough to try."

Olivia bit her lip in frustration, then registered the acrid taste of blood. *Fantastic.* Now she was going to arrive at the bank sporting a split lip, a lisp, and no prospective business premises. Perhaps it was time to change tack and use her feminine wiles to persuade Jonas to do the right thing. The notion galled her, but that simpering crap worked for other women, didn't it?

"Jonath," she began in what she hoped was a husky tone. "I'd planned my grand opening for the beginning of June. I'll never find alternative premises in time."

His lips twitched. "Wasn't planning your 'grand opening' before you'd inked the deal premature?"

So much for her feminine wiles. Her fingernails bit into her palms. "You're despicable. I pity your son being stuck with you as his lone parent." She regretted the words the moment she uttered them. *Drat.* She should have left the kid out of this, but it was too late to backtrack now.

Jonas's eyes narrowed, his expression turning to granite.

She refused to be intimidated. She held his icy stare.

"Suck it up, Olivia," he said in glacial tones. "The cottages are mine. Find another place to open your café."

She cast him a look of loathing and stormed out of the waiting room.

"Best of luck with your search," Jonas called after her retreating form.

Ignoring Julie's gleeful expression, Olivia shoved open the front door and marched out into the gale force wind.

She was blown down Patrick Street. Ballybeg was famous for its brightly colored buildings, but the cheery facades were an insult to Olivia's black mood.

Jonas had done this deliberately. She'd known he disliked her, but sabotaging her plans for the café seemed extreme. That cottage was hers, goddammit. She'd spent months planning the layout, knew exactly what would be positioned where. To come so close and have her dreams implode...*Feck Mary McDermott and her toad of a nephew.*

Olivia checked her watch. She had minutes to spare to reach the bank in time for her appointment, but it would suffice. It had to. The droplets of rain she'd noticed when she'd first exited the dentist's office were growing more insistent. More often than not, Irish drizzle was a polite warning before an imminent deluge. She rummaged through her handbag and located her umbrella. The stupid thing likely wouldn't work in this wind, but she'd have to take the chance. She opened her umbrella and ran.

CHAPTER TWO

By the time Olivia entered the bank's dim lobby, she was wet and bedraggled.

"Terrible downpour out there." Mairéad Moran, the manager's longtime PA, stood to greet her.

Shivering, Olivia removed her dripping coat.

"I'll hang it up to dry." Mairéad bustled over to her and took the wet garment. Olivia had always had a soft spot for Mairéad. The woman was as wide as her sunny smile and exuded a maternal warmth Olivia's mother would do well to cultivate.

She pushed tendrils of damp hair out of her face and peeled off her hat and scarf. The soft wool was soaked. Eau de wet wool was *not* her fragrance of choice. Her cunning plan to make a positive impression on the bank manager by looking her professional best was well and truly smashed to smithereens.

"Sorry for rearranging the appointment," Mairéad said. "Paddy will be out of town for a couple of weeks. His mother took a tumble and broke her hip. We're trying to get through a mountain of paperwork before he leaves."

"No worries," Olivia lied. She'd promised Aidan she'd be gone from the office for no more than an hour. He'd been on edge ever since a fellow investor in a new shopping center project had absconded with the cash, and his mood this morning was particularly foul. Judging by the ashtray on his desk, he'd smoked half a packet of cigarettes before she'd brought in his morning coffee.

"I'm afraid your meeting will have to be short. Paddy's booked solid the entire morning. I know you're keen to get your business started, and I slipped you onto the list."

"Thanks, Mairéad. I'll be out of his hair in no time, I swear." A vision of Paddy's straggly comb-over appeared. Perhaps a poor choice of words.

"He's on a call, but I'll let him know you've arrived." Mairéad already had the phone to her ear. "Why don't you take a seat?"

While she waited, Olivia scrutinized the information booklets on the table before her. They depicted a frothy Irish fantasy that had evaporated when the so-called Celtic Tiger had met its dramatic demise. Happy couples standing in front of spanking new homes; men in business suits roaring off in fancy cars; young people sporting backpacks and maps. All the dreams and aspirations that had turned to ash when the Irish economy collapsed. Yet here she was, hoping to beat the odds.

Fifteen minutes passed before Paddy O'Neill approached with an insincere smile and an outstretched hand. He wore a gray suit that might have fit had he been fifteen kilos lighter.

"Olivia." He took her hand and gave it a hearty pump.

The patently false jollity grated on her nerves.

"Delighted to see a determined entrepreneurial spirit, especially in these hard times." He paused in his perusal of her body. "Did something happen to your face? It looks puffy."

"I had a filling." She enunciated the words with care, but the numbness had worn off.

"Ah, fillings. Nasty but necessary. Well, come along to my office and we'll have a chat about your little café."

Her little café...*Nice.* Gritting her teeth, she grabbed her briefcase and followed Paddy down the narrow hallway that led from the bank's dim lobby to his office at the rear of the building. The room was small and cramped. Cheap air spray did little to conceal the pervading smell of damp.

Paddy pulled out a worn leather seat and indicated she should sit. "Tea?" he asked. "Or would you prefer coffee?"

"Nothing, thanks."

The bank manager sat at his desk across from her, affording her an excellent view of his comb-over and flaking scalp.

"Mairéad told me about your mother's fall. I hope she'll be all right."

"Ah, she'll be fine, thanks. She took a tumble down a flight of stairs. Doesn't care for the idea of going into a nursing home when she gets out of the hospital. Can't say I blame her, but it's awkward for me. The perils of being an only child, I suppose. Now," he said, adjusting his girth. "Let's have a look at your loan application for the café."

"To be precise, it's a café-cum-gift-shop," she corrected. "In addition to the food and drinks offered in the café, I'll house an assortment of Irish woolens, soaps, and jewelry."

"Both a café and a gift shop are risky business at the best of times, and we're in the middle of a recession."

"The current situation won't last," Olivia insisted. "People are scared right now, and the local businesses are feeling the pinch. Nevertheless, customers still gravitate toward quality, and that's what I intend to provide. In addition to a lunch menu, I'll offer a variety of freshly baked goods throughout the day. The coffee will be the best in town, and there'll be a selection of teas to satisfy everyone. My motto is quality over quantity, and I'll also apply that to items I stock in the gift section."

The bank manager had an odd expression on his face. She couldn't tell if it was incredulity or respect. "You're gambling the economy is going to turn around fast enough for you to make a go of it, but we're not seeing any evidence of that so far."

"I know I can make it work." Olivia extracted a slim blue folder from her bag and slid it across the desk. "I've saved for years and taken courses with the local enterprise board. They've approved my start-up grant with the proviso I raise the remaining fifty percent of the capital. My recipes are good. More than good, if I do say so myself." She tapped the folder. "You can see examples in here. Plus I have plenty of contacts with suppliers and local artisans. I've listed the company from whom I'll rent the kitchen equipment, and the farmers who've agreed to supply me with fresh produce. Bridie Byrne has already promised to hire me to supply the Book Mark café with baked goods."

The bank manager leafed through the file. "Your talent isn't in question. I'm not convinced you have the business know-how to run your own café, especially in today's tough market."

"I realize it's a risk, but it's one I'm prepared to take."

"That's clear. The question is whether or not the bank is willing to take a risk on you." Paddy flicked through the papers in front of him. When his brow furrowed, Olivia's palms began to sweat. "Did you bring a copy of the lease?" he asked. "I don't see it here."

She swallowed. "About that..."

"Yes?"

"There is no lease," she admitted. "The deal fell through."

"Ah," Paddy said, betraying no flicker of surprise. "That is a problem. You see, your venture is what I would classify as high risk. The one thing you had in your favor was the prospect of premises in a central location. Do you have alternative rooms sorted out?"

She shifted uncomfortably in her seat. "No, not yet. I only found out this morning."

"Is there no chance of Aidan giving you the start-up capital? Or your parents?"

"None whatsoever." A tinge of bitterness flavored her words. If it weren't for Aidan and her parents, she wouldn't be in this desperate situation.

The bank manager made a noise of regret. "In that case, I'm sorry, but I'll have to decline your request for a loan at this time."

Her stomach churned. "Can't I at least have the chance to look for another location before you turn me down? I found out about the cottage a few minutes ago, and I don't want to waste time going through the application process again. Besides, I wasn't expecting to see you until next Friday."

Paddy steepled his fingers. "I'll be back from my mother's in a couple of weeks. Do you think you can secure your premises by then?"

"I'll give it my best shot," she said, willing her left foot to cease its nervous tapping.

Even as he nodded, the manager's attention drifted from her. She imagined he was thinking about his next appointment, probably with someone wealthier and more business savvy than she was. But she hadn't come this close to realizing her dream to quit.

The bank manager shook his head in resignation. "All right. Come by in two weeks. Mairéad will e-mail you with the exact time. If you have a viable alternative location for your business, I'll take it into consideration before I give you my final decision."

"Thanks, Paddy. I appreciate it."

She stood and extended her hand. He shook it with noticeably less enthusiasm than when she'd arrived and made halfhearted small talk while escorting her to the exit. It was clear he couldn't wait to get rid of her. "I'll see you after the holidays. Best of luck with your search."

I'll need it, she thought, and she stepped outside. In the short time she'd been in the bank, the wind and the rain had whipped themselves into a ferocious frenzy. Olivia stood on the pavement, letting rain and dejection wash over her. She took a deep breath, expanding her core as her Pilates teacher advocated, held it briefly, then exhaled. The self-pity party was canceled. She had too much to lose if the café fell through, not least of which was her sanity. Time to figure out a Plan B.

Damn Mary McDermott and her shameless display of nepotism. And damn Jonas O'Mahony and his arrogance. May he be struck down with an incurable case of crotch crabs.

CHAPTER THREE

Luca's screams echoed off the kitchen walls. "Come on, mate. Calm down." Jonas aimed the flyswatter at the catalyst of the chaos. The bluebottle circled Luca's head one more time before coming in to land on his glass of milk.

The screams turned to hysterics. The boy flailed with such force that he sent the milk flying, knocked over his chair, and landed on the kitchen tiles with a crash.

Jonas knelt on the floor and took his son in his arms. "It's okay, mate. I've got you." Luca's dark curls were soft underneath his touch. He bent to give him a kiss. "I'm betting that fly's more scared of you than you are of him."

Actually, he bet no such thing. The bluebottle had led Jonas in a merry dance these past fifteen minutes. It took a perverse delight in teasing him into thinking he'd finally got the fecker, only to buzz off at the last millisecond.

"You're not to kill it, Dad," Luca said between sniffs. "Put the fly outside where it belongs."

"What?" He drew back in surprise. "You want me to *catch* the fly, not kill it?"

The boy's small face was tear-stained and blotchy. "Flies live outside. He's not *supposed* to be in here. It's not right."

Jonas rummaged in his pocket for a clean tissue and came up empty. His mother had a never-ending supply about her person– yet more proof he was not cut out for this parenting lark. "Um, okay. Not sure how I'll manage that, but– "

"What's the fuss?" Mam stood in the doorway, laden with shopping bags.

"A fly," said Jonas and Luca in unison.

Jonas's mother surveyed the chaos with a benign expression. After dumping the grocery bags on the kitchen counter, she strode to the back door and threw it open. As if on cue, the bluebottle made its exit.

His jaw slackened. *Unreal.* How did she do that?

"Now stop your messing and tidy up while I get the sandwiches ready."

"Right-o."

"And for heaven's sake, give that poor child a tissue." A packet of tissues materialized from the depths of her handbag.

While Jonas righted the fallen chair and mopped the spilled milk, Luca set the table.

"How does ham and cheese sound?" Mam sliced the fresh loaf of bread into thick slices. She didn't hold with buying pre-sliced and had reacted with horror when Jonas once offered to buy her a bread slicer for Christmas.

"Add a pickle to mine and I'll love you forever."

A small smile hovered on her lips. "You're a slick talker, boy. You remind me of your dad when he was younger. What was all the fuss about that fly?"

"Luca isn't fond of insects indoors. They– " He glanced at his son, but Luca's concentration was focused on aligning the cutlery on the table. "They set him off."

"Right." She handed him a plate laden with sandwiches followed by a large bowl of salad. "Let's pray there are no creepy crawlies lurking in there."

Luca's knife sliced with expert precision. Once he had four identical squares, he proceeded to eat the sandwich in his usual fashion: clockwise, starting with the piece at the top right. A stab of fear pierced his gut. Fatherhood had never featured in his life plan. Yet here he was, lone parent to a little boy with special needs. The man upstairs had an odd sense of humor, that was for sure.

His mother poured tea into pottery mugs and handed him one. His glance strayed to the kitchen clock. In another twenty minutes, he could escape to his home office and lose himself in a world of make-believe.

"Did you know Mary had promised to rent one of the cottages to Olivia Gant?" he asked between bites of sandwich. "I met her this morning at the dentist's office. She's pissed about the deal falling through." Pissed was an understatement. He was still reeling from her verbal onslaught. How in the hell was he supposed to know his aunt had promised her a lease? Mary hadn't mentioned a prospective tenant when she'd offered to deed him the properties on Curzon Street.

Mam snorted. "Let her be annoyed. What was my sister thinking? Why would she rent one of her houses to that woman?"

"Mary's a businesswoman. I'd say she was thinking of a tenant to pay rent."

"Regardless, I was relieved when Mary told me she'd decided to deed the cottages over to you instead of renting them out."

"My good fortune is Olivia's bad luck. She seemed genuinely upset." Despite everything that had happened between them, he didn't wish Olivia ill. Once upon a time, they'd loved one another. Had it not been for Bry's death, perhaps they still would.

His mother pursed her lips. "Why should it matter to Olivia if she rents Mary's cottage or another? Let her rich husband pull strings and find somewhere else to launch her little hobby business."

"That's a bit harsh."

"But true." His mother waved a hand in a dismissive gesture. "Enough about that silly woman. Will you be working late again?"

Mam didn't do subtle. The rebuke in her voice was impossible to miss. He refused to rise to the bait. Instead he took a sip of his tea, wincing when the hot liquid burned his tongue. "I'll collect Luca at the usual time. Around seven."

She snorted. "I'll believe it when I see it. Even if you do come at seven, it's late to be collecting a small boy."

A dull ache pulsed behind his temples. She was right. She was always bloody right. But he had mounting bills and a deadline, not to mention the stress of waiting for his agent to call about the book he had out on submission.

Mam's mug met the hard wooden table with a clatter. "Since you finally deigned to drag yourself away from your desk and show up for lunch, there's something I need to discuss with you."

"Yeah?" He bit into his sandwich. Her voice was a distant buzz. He'd grown used to tuning her out when she started in on one of her harangues. Instead, he focused on the peeling wallpaper in his parents' small kitchen. It was orange with a black geometric design. The wallpaper had been ugly when they'd first hung it in the eighties, and time hadn't enhanced its aesthetic appeal. Apart from the clock, the only ornamentation was a huge crucifix framed by a painting of the Virgin Mary and a photo of Pope John Paul II.

"Jonas, are you listening to me?"

He lowered his sandwich and met his mother's disapproving stare.

"You haven't heard a word I said."

"I'm sorry. My mind is on other things at the moment. Luca's fees for the next quarter are due, and I'm a couple of months away from my next royalty payment. If I don't meet my next deadline, I'll be even more pressed for cash. I need to devote my full attention to finishing the book. Working late is part of the deal." Plus he and Mary had an appointment with the solicitor at two o'clock tomorrow. That meant yet more writing time gone from his week.

"That boy needs at least one of his parents spending time with him. Now that Susanne has left, that means you."

"Can we please discuss this another time?" He cast a significant look in his son's direction. Luca was eating his lunch with intense concentration, but Jonas knew he was absorbing every word.

"All right. I was just saying." His mother poured herself another cup of tea and sat back with a sigh of martyred resignation.

He was sick of her "just saying" things about Susanne in front of Luca. His mother adored her grandson, but she seemed to think the boy was too stupid to understand what was going on around him. Despite what some so-called experts would have him believe, Jonas was convinced that was far from the case.

"Anyway," she continued, "I was trying to tell you..."

His phone vibrated violently, sending his pulse into overdrive. His agent's number glowed on the display. "Sorry, I have to take this call." Ignoring her protests, he retreated into the hallway and shut the kitchen door behind him. "Hey, Kate. What's the story?"

"An apt choice of words." Kate's tone was dry. "Bad news, I'm afraid."

Jonas's fingers tightened around the phone. "Not the deal?"

"I'm afraid it's a no-go. Both editors passed on *Trial by Blood*, and they were the last two on my list. I'm sorry, but we're going to have to shelve this project for a while. In the current market, this book is not going to sell."

He stared at his white fingertips. They were leached of color. It was his personal stress detector. *Goddammit.* "I guess I can scrap the outline for the sequel," he quipped.

"Don't do anything rash. Put it away for now and concentrate on meeting your deadline for the next Detective Inspector Brady mystery."

"I poured my soul into that proposal," he said in a morose tone.

"I know. Therein, I suspect, lies the problem."

"How do you mean? Those chapters are my strongest work to date. If I get the opportunity to finish the book, I know it's going to be great."

"They're tightly written, yes, but that's not the point. It's my responsibility to see the big picture. *Trial by Blood* doesn't reflect the brand you've created. When readers buy a Jonas O'Mahony mystery, they expect a character-driven, action-packed read that doesn't stint on humor. In contrast, *Trial by Blood* is slow, introspective, and–frankly– deeply depressing. It doesn't reflect the tone of your other books."

"There's no chance of selling it? I believe in this series, and I know I can make it work."

"You could try selling the book under a pseudonym," she said, "but I wouldn't recommend it. If you were a faster writer, maybe, but you're stretched producing one book a year as it is. The Brady mysteries are hugely popular. Pursuing this new and very different series at the expense of D.I. Brady is inadvisable."

Jonas pressed his forehead against the cool paneled walls of his parents' hallway. She was right, of course. Kate was always right. Which was why he was lucky to have her for his agent. "Thanks for trying."

"No problem. My news isn't all doom and gloom. The TV execs loved your new crime series script. Perhaps we'll have better luck there."

"Fingers crossed."

"Now take a brief breather and get back to work on Detective Brady's sixth adventure."

Jonas gave a rueful laugh. "Yes, boss. I'm almost finished. Expect it in your inbox by Saturday."

He disconnected. *Damn.* He'd been convinced they'd nail that deal. *Trial by Blood* was as unlike the Brady mysteries as it was possible to get, but that was the whole point. He'd wanted to stretch himself, write something completely different. Despite the success of Detective Inspector Brady, most of his money came from the TV adaptation of the series and from the two TV miniseries he'd cowritten.

Dazed, he wandered into the kitchen.

Luca was on his third quarter of sandwich. His mother was red in the face. *Shite.* Sliding into his chair, he prepared himself for a lecture on his litany of failings as a father, a son, and a member of the human race. He didn't have long to wait.

"Since you don't have time to listen to what I have to tell you," his mother snapped, "I'll keep it short and simple."

That'd be a first. He checked the clock. In five minutes he could retreat into his fantasy world of murder and mayhem.

"Mary and I are going on a cruise. You'll have to find someone else to look after Luca."

He started violently. "What? For how long?"

"Two months. We're going on an extended holiday. We leave next week."

His lungs deflated in a whoosh. "What am I going to do with Luca?"

"That, my boy, is your problem," she replied tartly. "You're his father. It's your responsibility to organize childcare for while you're working. Instead you assume I'll always be available."

"I thought you *liked* looking after Luca."

"I do, but not every day. I didn't mind helping out for a few weeks while you looked for a place to live, but I never agreed to be his full-time babysitter." Her shoulders slumped. "Look, son, I've raised three children and buried one. I love being a grandmother, but it shouldn't mean I'm responsible for Luca's welfare. That's your job."

He regarded her across the table, took in the shadows under her eyes and her gray complexion. *Aw, shite.* "I didn't mean to make you feel that way. You know that. I've been busy and– "

A surge of panic hit with the force of a tidal wave. What the hell was he going to do? After Susanne had left, he'd floundered in Dublin. He'd barely muddled through with the help of an au pair– until she'd quit, unable to deal with Luca's night terrors. Jonas couldn't blame her. When he moved back to Ballybeg. he'd envisioned his parents' house being Luca's place to go after school and during holidays, leaving him free to write during the day. He didn't have a contingency plan. Frankly, he hadn't realized he needed one.

He swallowed past the lump in his throat. His mother was right. It was unfair of him to expect her to shoulder the lion's share of the childcare. She was Luca's grandmother, not his mother. "Why didn't you mention the cruise before now?"

"Mary surprised me with the tickets. Your uncle Martin's first anniversary is next month, and she wants to escape Ballybeg for a while. You know your father's not one for travel, and Martin was too ill for a trip like this. We've talked about going on a cruise together for years, but lack of time on her part and money on mine got in the way. Now that Martin's dead, there's nothing stopping us from going."

Except Luca. The words remained unspoken, yet the implication resonated off the orange kitchen walls.

Jonas regarded his son across the table. He was paralyzed by love and angst. Luca was his mini mirror image. You'd think it would make it easier for him to connect with the kid, but it didn't. Luca's lack of eye contact and repetitive gestures were unnerving. Having a child on the autistic spectrum was definitely *not* what he'd signed up for. His stomach twisted into knots of guilt even thinking those words. He worried about Luca's future; he worried about people being mean to his boy; he worried about every damn thing. Right now, he worried about coping with Luca's night terrors on his own for two months.

Mam reached across the table to pat his hand. "You're an adult and a parent. You can sort this out. In the meantime, I'm going into town to look for travel guides. Knock on your father's door before you leave. He'll watch Luca until I get home."

He nodded, dazed by the enormity of what lay ahead. Most days, he chose not to dwell on it, trusting he'd get by with the help of his parents. Today...well, today that safety net was gone. "I'm glad for you." And he was, despite the hassle of finding a babysitter at short notice. "You'll have a great time on the cruise."

His mother's careworn face split into a tired smile. "Thanks, love. I'll see you later."

The kitchen door clicked shut behind her. He and Luca were left alone to finish their lunch. The formerly delicious sandwich turned to sawdust in his mouth.

CHAPTER FOUR

"What the hell is this?" Aidan snatched the sketchpad from Olivia's desk. His nostrils flared, and his chiseled features were mottled with rage. Cigarette fumes warred with egg sandwich– he must have snuck out for another smoke. In the background, Brona– Aidan's part-time junior solicitor– scuttled into her office and shut the door.

Olivia struggled to suppress a wave of nausea and maintain her cool. "They're patterns for autumn scarves." She kept her voice bland and hoped she exuded a calm she sure as hell wasn't feeling.

Her boss– and soon-to-be ex-husband– loomed closer, pressing his palms against the edge of her desk. "Olivia, what do I pay you to do?"

"To do your job for you while you watch porn online in your office?"

Aidan's eyes bulged.

She sighed. "Fine. Let me rephrase that. To answer the phones and perform other administrative tasks?"

"Right. How does designing scarves fall under that definition?"

She nibbled on the top of her pen. "It doesn't."

"So do the job I'm paying you to do." Aidan slammed his fist onto her desk with sufficient force to make its contents dance. In one fluid movement, he ripped in two the designs she'd spent hours creating. The pieces floated to the floor. Her throat constricted. Wasn't it typical of Aidan to choose that moment to emerge from his lair? "Now get back to work," he snarled. He turned to leave.

She let out the breath she hadn't realized she was holding. As soon as he was gone, she would discreetly gather the remnants of her designs and tuck them in her handbag. Ripped in two was good. She'd been afraid he'd go for the shredder.

Her phone chose that moment to ring. Aidan halted midstride. Olivia removed the top of her pen from her mouth, transfixed by its ragged edges. She braced herself for the inevitable temper tantrum.

"Why is your mobile phone on during working hours?" His voice exuded an arctic chill that clashed with the fury blazing in his bloodshot orbs.

"I'm expecting a private call."

"Why can't this 'private call' use your work number?"

Because it's confidential and I don't want you eavesdropping. Particularly not on a call with an estate agent. She adopted a bored tone. "You've told me on more than one occasion not to take personal calls on my desk phone. I thought it made sense for the person to call me on my mobile, and I'd return the call when I had an opportunity."

"You thought, did you, Olivia? I don't pay you to think. I pay you to do the tasks I assign."

Her heart rate kicked up a gear. Patience wasn't a trait she had in abundance. Dealing with Aidan took every ounce she possessed. "In that case," she said through gritted teeth, "I'll continue staring at the computer screen. My e-mail inbox is empty, and I've finished the filing. Until the new election campaign brochures arrive tomorrow, there's not much for me to do."

Irritation flickered across his face before he reined in his temper. Aidan was even less patient than she was. The problem in their situation was that he held the power cards and they both knew it. While he was powerless to prevent her from leaving him, he'd make certain she upheld her side of their devil's bargain.

Finally he snorted, farted, and then returned to his office. She waited for the slam. Yep. Of course he wouldn't forget that part. She rooted in her desk drawers for scented candles.

She was on the verge of lighting a match when a heavy tread sounded on the stairs that led from the ground floor to Gant Solicitors. That would be Aidan's two o'clock appointment. She looked up, expecting to see George Quinn's fleshy features.

Instead Jonas O'Mahony stood on the threshold– tall, dark, and sinfully sexy. Her stomach flipped. He'd exchanged the biker gear for a suit. She wouldn't have expected him to wear a suit well, but this one molded his frame to perfection.

His dark brows drew together when he registered her presence. "Olivia."

"Jonas."

The room quivered with tension. It was hard to tell if Jonas's expression of revulsion was caused by the stench left by her boss or the sight of her.

She cleared her throat. "Are you here to see Aidan?"

His expression was inscrutable. "Yeah. My aunt and I have an appointment with him at two."

She exhaled in a whoosh. Aidan had lied about George Quinn's appointment. This meeting had to concern the lease to the cottages. Aidan knew how much she wanted one. No doubt he was anticipating her reaction with glee.

As if on cue, Aidan reemerged from his office, sporting a self-satisfied smirk. "Jonas," he boomed as he crossed the reception area. "Delighted you could make it. Why don't we step into my office while we're waiting for Mary? In the meantime, Olivia will bring us coffee."

Jonas muttered something indecipherable and followed Aidan into his office, leaving a tantalizing whiff of aftershave in his wake. Honestly, that stuff ought to be outlawed. She couldn't stand the man, yet his scent was making her feel like a sexually frustrated spinster.

"Olivia." Aidan's voice interrupted her reverie. "The coffee?"

Their eyes met. That she hated him was clear to both of them. That she was stuck in this stinking job for the time being was equally apparent. Quelling her resentment, she stood from behind her desk and went to the small kitchen that contained a crappy excuse for a coffee maker.

She watched brown sludge drip and contemplated murder. As soon as she had the loan for her café secured, she'd be out of here. No more living a half life in one of Aidan's guest bedrooms. No more plastering on fake smiles and playing the role of Mrs. Politician. And no more lying– not to her friends, not to strangers, and not to herself. She'd have to work her notice, of course, and see her deal with Aidan through until after the election. But the knowledge that her days here were numbered would help her survive.

In the background, she registered Mary's arrival and Aidan's fawning greeting. His insincerity made her teeth ache. She added a plate of stale shortbread biscuits to the coffee tray and approached the office. After she'd knocked on the door three times, Aidan finally bid her enter. He did love his little power trips.

Aidan's office wasn't large to begin with, and Jonas dwarfed it with his presence. He leaned his elbows on his knees while his left foot tapped a restless pattern on the carpet. Mary's designer-clad form appeared equally uncomfortable. She sat ramrod straight and refused to make eye contact with Olivia. As always, she was impeccably dressed and accessorized, just like Aidan's mother. Being a wealthy widow had its perks.

Olivia kept her hands steady as she poured the coffee. Aidan's gaze bored into her while she performed the task, willing her to spill.

"Mary, would you care for a cup?" Her voice was as steady as her hands.

"No thanks," Mary muttered.

She placed a cup before Aidan.

"Add sugar."

She paused. Aidan hated sugar in his coffee. Yet another one of his games. He loved putting her to the test when they were in public and punishing her in private when she failed. She envisioned a field of Friesian cows, mooing softly. Cows soothed her for some bizarre reason. Fine, she'd play along. With a bit of luck, he'd soon bore of the game and leave her in peace.

"How many spoonfuls?" She gave him a tight smile and held his gaze.

"You know how much sugar I take in my coffee."

She bit back a scream of frustration. If she said he usually took no sugar, he'd say she'd made him look a fool in front of his clients and take his revenge later. If she put in...*Oh, hell.* It was a no-win situation. She dumped four heaping spoonfuls into his cup. Let him try to swallow that.

Jonas's somber dark gaze sent prickles down her spine. Hurriedly she handed him a cup of black coffee and turned to leave.

"Olivia." The sound of Aidan's voice was akin to being doused with ice-cold water. *Drat.* She'd fallen into the trap. "Aren't you going to ask Jonas how he takes his coffee?"

The words hung in the air like icicles.

Jonas's deep drawl broke the silence. "No worries. I can help myself to milk."

Milk. Good save. Aidan wouldn't like the idea of his wife remembering how her first boyfriend took his coffee eleven years after they'd broken up.

She continued in the direction of the door, not breathing until it clicked closed. At the rate her day was going, she would be seriously oxygen-deprived come evening. Her mobile phone began to sing once more, and she sprinted to her desk. *Feck.* She'd meant to switch it off earlier, but she'd been distracted by Jonas's arrival. Her eyes darted in the direction of the office door. She could quickly take the call and switch off the phone before Aidan finished his meeting. She pressed the green button.

"Olivia Gant?" The woman's tones were cool and clipped. Not a voice Olivia recognized.

"Speaking."

"This is Louise Cavendish from Glencoe College. I've tried calling your parents, but I've been unable to reach them."

She groaned inwardly. Her father had called in sick that morning, fueling Aidan's bad mood. No doubt he and her mother were indisposed after another marathon drinking session. Goodness knew where they were now and in what state. She gazed out at the gray sky outside. "What's Kyle done this time?"

"Actually, both Kyle and Ronan are in my office at present, as are two members of *An Garda Síochána.*"

The police? She exhaled sharply. This did *not* sound good. "What the hell happened?"

Olivia heard disapproval in Louise Cavendish's voice. "From what I could ascertain, your brothers were the ringleaders in a fight that broke out during the afternoon recess. One boy had to be taken to hospital with suspected concussion, and another has a split lip. I needn't tell you that this behavior will not be tolerated."

She rubbed her temples. "Who did they allegedly attack?"

"James Jobson and Robert Boyle."

Julie Jobson's brother. Fantastic. His father, the town councilor, would freak. She didn't know Robert Boyle, but there was a Reverend Boyle in a neighboring village. It would be typical for her brothers to pick an ordained minister's kid to bash.

"I'm suspending Kyle and Ronan for two weeks. The police have taken statements, but much depends on whether or not the injured boys' parents decide to press charges."

"What do you need me to do? Should I collect them?"

"Yes, Mrs. Gant, that would be much appreciated. You're listed as the boys' emergency contact should your parents be unavailable."

Olivia massaged her temples and glanced at the clock. "Okay. I need to get my stuff together, but I should be at the school within a half hour."

After she hung up, Olivia stared out the window at the torrential rain. If the boys had wanted to get her out of the office, they could have picked a day with better weather.

She ran a fingernail down Aidan's schedule. He'd listed his fictitious appointment with George Quinn as a long one, followed by dinner with a client at a restaurant in Bantry. *Client my arse.* More like dinner and a shag with Moira Keating, his campaign manager and latest fling. She grabbed her handbag from underneath the desk and stood. With a bit of luck, she could nip to the school and be back before Aidan noticed her absence.

She glared at the glossy brochures on the display rack next to the entrance. Aidan's rictus was reproduced in triplicate. He was pictured standing in front of a brand new house, shaking hands with a cheery homeowner. Probably someone whose elderly relatives he'd helped fleece.

Olivia tasted bile. How could she have been so foolish? In a bid to better her circumstances, she'd married the devil himself.

CHAPTER FIVE

As was typical for an Irish April, the weather morphed from torrential rain in the morning to blistering sun in the afternoon. By the time Jonas and Mary returned to his parents' house after their appointment with Gant, it was warm enough to sit in the garden and watch Luca play with his toy cars.

He handed his aunt a cup of black coffee and slumped into the seat opposite. In his memory, Gant's smug expression loomed large, as did Olivia's downcast gaze. "Why would anyone stay married to that pig?"

Mary folded her long legs and adjusted her sunglasses. Despite her prim appearance, she was anything but stuffy. Childless by choice and wealthy by marriage, she reveled in being an aunt. "Marriage to Gant has its advantages. Money, for one. What's a little public humiliation in return for a platinum credit card?"

He snorted. "You don't believe that."

"It doesn't matter what *I* believe. Who knows what goes on in other people's relationships? Perhaps they get off on the bickering. Some couples do."

A vision of Olivia's pale face rose unbidden, its beauty marred by stress lines around her startling blue eyes and rosebud mouth. No, she definitely didn't "get off" on Gant's goading.

Mary peered at him over the rim of her coffee cup. "How does it feel to be a man of property?"

"A huge relief. Luca loves living in the cottage. I can't thank you enough."

"I'm glad you're settling into your new home." She smiled the twenty-four-carat smile that had once broken half the hearts in Ballybeg. "But you might not be thanking me on the first of the month. Remember what Gant said. In order to keep the transfer of ownership above board and away from the tax man, you'll need to give me a sum of money every month."

"All the same, it's a fraction of what I was paying to rent my flat in Dublin. I'm getting a great deal."

His aunt regarded him with a thoughtful expression on her well-preserved face. "I'd rather you and your brother get your inheritance now while you're young and need it most. Besides, what do I need six houses for? There's only one of me."

"Even so, you're very kind to do this. I'd never get a house for that price, let alone two."

"It's always good to have a little something to fall back on. It's up to you whether you want a permanent tenant for the next door cottage or tourists on weekly rentals. Both options have their advantages and disadvantages."

He toyed with his coffee cup. "Which do you recommend?"

"I went the tourist rental route for years, but I was considering a regular tenant around the time you moved to Ballybeg and were looking for somewhere to live. You can charge higher rent for short-term leases, but there's more work involved. You're responsible for cleaning the house between visitors, for example. There's also the possibility that the house will be vacant for long periods of time during low season, and you'll need to remember to heat and air the place regularly."

"So you'd suggest I opt for a long-term tenant?"

"It's less hassle on a day-to-day basis. Barely any admin work." Mary drained her cup and stood. "I'd better get back to the dogs. Ludo will be ready for his walk."

Jonas's chair scraped against the patio tiles as he stood. "Thanks again, Mary." He gave her a hug.

She patted him on the arm. "No worries. I'm happy to help. What's the point in being an aunt if you can't spoil your nephews?"

"Even when we're both taller than you?"

"Even when you're older than I am now and I'm tottering around a nursing home." Mary bent to kiss Luca's soft cheek. "Bye to you, too, little man. See you soon."

After his aunt left, Jonas fingered his smart phone. Luca was playing on the small path that wound through the flowerbeds, each car aligned precisely behind the one before. Although the garden was small, his parents kept it well tended. He liked the greenery, but his father had gone way overboard with the flowers. In the summer months, every spare centimeter was covered in lush blooms.

His gaze dropped to the phone, feeling its weight in his hand. Clenching his teeth, he dialed the number he'd intended to delete a few months ago.

"I'll be right back," he said, pausing to ruffle his son's dark curls. The boy made no response, nor any indication he'd heard him speak. He'd barely closed the kitchen door behind him when the call connected. "Susanne?"

"No. It's Theresa. Who's this?"

His ex's sister. They'd never had much in common, but she wasn't a bad sort.

"Hey, Theresa. It's Jonas. Can I speak to Susanne?"

Her cigarette-tinged rasp followed a brief silence. "Susanne's not here."

Jonas took a deep breath. "I need to get in touch with her. Do you know her new number?"

"Is Luca okay?"

"He's fine, but a situation's arisen. I need Susanne to help look after him for a couple of months."

Theresa sighed. "Good luck with that. She's on her honeymoon."

His grip on the phone tightened. "Honeymoon? She's married?"

"To Barry Brennan."

Barry Brennan. One of Ireland's most revered and feared barristers. Father of the guy Susanne had left him for. She was keeping it classy, as per usual.

"When was the wedding?" The words came out in a croak.

"Last weekend. They held it at Dromoland Castle."

One of Ireland's premier hotels– Susanne had gone up in the world.

"How long will she be away?"

"Six weeks, I think." From the other end of the line, Theresa took an audible drag on her cigarette. "I don't see her opening her five-star heart and home to Luca. Do you?"

No, frankly, he couldn't. He'd called Susanne because he was desperate and because he couldn't bring himself to believe she was serious about cutting ties with him and Luca. What parent did that? Yes, Luca could be hard work. Yes, his diagnosis and its ramifications brought a lot of stress and strain. But the boy was her child, goddammit. You didn't quit on your kid.

"You still there?"

"Yeah. Thanks for telling me, Theresa. Keep in touch. You know you're always welcome to visit."

"I'll come down to Cork soon, yeah? Give Luca a kiss from me." She paused. "I'm sorry about Susanne. Frankly, you and Luca are better off without her in your lives."

By the time Jonas returned to the garden, Luca was packing his cars neatly into a play box. Despite the warm weather, a chill snaked down Jonas's back.

He gave the little boy a peck on the cheek. "I have to go write. Granddad is going to look after you until Nana gets home. Be a good boy, okay?"

Luca considered his request. "Yes, I think I can be good today, Dad. I'm not feeling naughty."

Jonas suppressed a laugh. At times, Luca's literal interpretations drove him crazy, but they could also be highly amusing. "Bye, mate."

Liam O'Mahony barely glanced up when Jonas entered his workshop, intent on the wooden chair he was carving. He was a few centimeters shorter and wider than his son, but otherwise his spitting image. "Off already?"

"Yeah. I need to get back to work."

A smile lurked on Liam's lips. "I don't know how you stick it. I'd be bored out of my skull if I had to type words all day."

Jonas laughed. "I'd have no hands to type *with* if I attempted to use a saw."

"True enough." His father's smile faded into a frown. "Did your mother tell you about her cruise?"

"Yeah, she did. I'll find a solution for Luca." *How,* he didn't know, but he'd have to come up with something.

"You know I'll help out in whatever way I can, but I can't take Luca with me on a job. Having him here in my workshop is one thing. Out on a building site is another."

"I know, Dad. No worries. You and Mam have been great since we moved to Ballybeg." He hesitated, weighing his words. "I called Susanne."

His father glanced up from his work. "If your expression is anything to go by, that didn't go well."

"She wasn't there. Her sister answered. Apparently, Susanne got married a few days ago."

Liam flexed his shoulders. "Your mother said you're meeting Gavin for a drink this evening. Sounds like you'll need it."

"Only a quick drink. I have to put in a couple more hours on my book tonight, so I'll be back for Luca by nine."

"Why don't you leave him here overnight? Have a proper evening off."

"Are you sure?" He was tempted. It would give him the option to work late without the disruption of Luca's nightmares.

"I wouldn't offer if I wasn't. Come and collect him after breakfast tomorrow."

"Okay. Thanks, Dad." He paused in the doorframe. "For everything."

When he left his father's workshop, guilt gnawed at his stomach. His mother was right. He'd been relying too much on his parents. They should be in a position to make a spontaneous offer as his father had just done, not be Luca's regular babysitters. Why hadn't this occurred to him before? He'd been complacent and had taken advantage of their good nature. Not only did he need an interim childcare solution effective immediately, he needed to look for someone permanent.

CHAPTER SIX

Olivia fumed silently on the drive home from Glencoe College. Louise Cavendish proved as stiff and proper as her telephone manner implied. While charges hadn't yet been brought against the boys, Olivia figured it was only a matter of time.

She slapped the steering wheel in frustration and took a sharp right turn into a narrow country lane. Trees, bushes, and fields passed in a blur of various shades of green. Her ancient car might not be the most powerful vehicle on the roads, but she made the most of her accelerator, much to the delight of the local police.

"What were the pair of you thinking?" If her stress levels rose any higher, she'd spontaneously combust.

"We weren't," quipped Kyle. His short hair was gelled into spikes, and he reeked of cheap aftershave. If only he'd pay as much attention to his schoolwork as he did to his appearance.

"Smart arse. Why couldn't Mum or Dad collect you?"

"Mum's swanned off to an art show– date of return unknown. Dad's gone sailing with the local deadbeats," Ronan said from the backseat. These were the first words he'd uttered since they'd left the school.

Olivia swore beneath her breath. "Why didn't you tell me?"

Kyle shrugged. "You didn't ask. Besides, you know Mum. She always shows up– eventually."

Taking another sharp turn and narrowly missing an overgrown rhododendron bush, she pulled up in front of her parents' ramshackle home. It had once been a picturesque two-story country house complete with a thatched roof and limestone walls. These days, its only redeeming feature was the seaside location. The thatch had long since been replaced by slates, many of which were missing. The walls were more grimy gray than pristine white. In short, the place was a shambles.

Once she'd slammed the car door shut, she marched across the weed-infested driveway. The front door was unlocked. When she nudged it open, the warring smells of unwashed clothing, peat smoke, and cigarettes assailed her nostrils. Her father, Jim Dunne, was seated at the kitchen table, playing cards in one hand and a beer in the other. Flanking him on either side were his partners in crime.

"How're ya, Olivia?" Buck MacCarthy's speech was slurred, and he squinted at her through his one good eye. The other was covered by a patch, pirate-style. The story of how Buck had lost an eye varied on the teller and ranged from the prosaic (shot out during a fight with the local gypsies) to the mundane (injured during a drunken encounter with a fishing hook).

John-Joe Fitzgerald, her father's second drinking companion, treated her to a lascivious once-over. John-Joe worked– if one could call it work– as an Elvis impersonator-cum-stripper. That was one show she'd pay *not* to see. "Looking good, lass," he leered.

She fixed him with a hostile stare. "Wish I could say the same for you lot." She crossed her arms over her chest and regarded the debris with disgust. Dirty plates were piled in the sink, a line of empty beer bottles decorated the sideboard, and overflowing ashtrays were in every room. "The place is in an even worse state than the last time I was here."

Kyle and Ronan trooped in behind her and slung their schoolbags on the floor.

"Ah, don't fret," Jim said with breezy unconcern. "The lads and I will tidy up later."

And pigs might fly. "Where's Mum?"

Her father's cheery face brightened. "Gone to London for an art show. We're on our own for the next few days."

Olivia spied the phone by the sink, off its stand and out of juice. No wonder Louise Cavendish hadn't been able to get through. "You'll have plenty of time to hang with the lads. Kyle and Ronan are out of secondary school for the next couple of weeks. They got suspended for fighting." Her father's expression remained impassive. "I need to get back to the office, but I'll call round again after work. Do you need me to bring anything?"

"Ah no, love. We have a few things in the fridge."

She yanked open the fridge door and peered inside. Its contents caused her to recoil. "When did you last go shopping? Apart from a beer run, I mean. There's meat in here that is literally crawling."

"Don't worry." Her father was concentrating on his hand of cards. "We'll get takeout."

She'd buy a couple of bags of groceries after work. The boys needed proper nourishment. "Aidan wants you back at work tomorrow. I can't keep covering for you. The campaign brochures will need to be stuffed into envelopes and sent out by the evening post."

"Yeah, yeah. I'll be there tomorrow. Tell him I've got the flu."

If her father kept flaking on the job, her parents were never going to pay off the debt they owed Aidan. "Tomorrow would be good day to return," she said encouragingly. "Aidan will be attending the Gnome Appreciation Society luncheon in Cork City."

"Jaysus." Her father shuddered. "How many garden gnomes does he own?"

"He had fifteen when we married eight years ago. He now has over one hundred and fifty."

"Wow." John-Joe blinked his beady eyes. "Even marriage to my Nora hasn't driven me to such depravities."

Olivia laughed. "At least the gnomes keep him busy. Does anyone want anything from the supermarket?"

Ronan shook his head. "Nothing for me."

"Deodorant," Kyle said.

She made a note of it on her phone, adding a variety of basic groceries to the list. She eyed her youngest brother speculatively. He was scratching his left arm and looking tense. "Do you have enough asthma meds?" she asked. "You sound chesty."

"It'll pass."

Hmm...She wasn't convinced, but there was no point in pressing the issue. At fifteen, Ronan was old enough to manage his medication. "When did you two last see Mum?" she asked, keeping her voice low.

"A couple of days ago," said Kyle at the same time Ronan said, "Early last week."

Her breath caught. "Last week? She's been gone that long?"

"So?" Ronan's tone was surly. "It's not like we see much of her when she is home. She's always in her bloody studio."

Olivia's hand flew to her temple. "Did she say anything before she left? Give any indication where she was going, or with whom? London's a big city."

Kyle gave a bitter laugh. "Sis, you've been out of here too long. Mum doesn't hold herself accountable to anyone, least of all her husband and children. She simply up and left. Good riddance in my opinion. She destroyed the sofa before she left. She needed feathers for her art. Now I can't play my Xbox in comfort."

"What?" She went to the living room door and stepped inside. A thick layer of dust covered every surface. No wonder Ronan's asthma was bad. The sofa had been ripped apart violently. Alarm bells clanged in her ears. When she saw the blood on the knife, she gasped. "Boys, come quick."

Kyle popped his head round the door and regarded the knife dispassionately. "Dried paint."

Olivia sagged against the ruined sofa. *Thank goodness.* For a moment there, she'd thought...

"Get a grip, sis. We're a sorry lot, I grant you, but we haven't stooped to murder."

"Cheeky sod." Regaining her composure, she opened the patio doors and stomped through the garden toward her mother's studio. It made the house look tidy in comparison. She had no idea how her mother moved in here, never mind created art.

Canvases were stacked willy-nilly, paint-dried brushes lay discarded on the floor, and the smell of paint stripper pervaded. She held her nose as she picked her way through the debris, searching for any sign her mother might have left behind her. A note, anything. As she advanced through the room, she checked behind paintings and in her mother's old-fashioned school desk. There was nothing save the inescapable scent of lilac, her mother's signature perfume. How that scent managed to assert itself against the paint fumes, she'd never know.

She picked up an old paintbrush and examined it. Bright blue paint was dried into the bristles. Her mother or Kyle could have identified the exact shade. She caught sight of a particularly hideous painting featuring an orange sun with burning cherubs. Charming. Her mother's imagination was even more macabre than her own. There were a few gallery owners and art collectors who fawned over her work, but Olivia suspected it was her cleavage they were admiring, not her art. She tossed the paintbrush onto the desk in disgust.

Back in the house, Ronan was sitting on the ripped sofa, reading a sci-fi book. Kyle was eating a Nutella sandwich. Goodness knew what state the bread was in. Nutella, at least, could survive a nuclear war.

"I'll be back later with real food."

"Whatever," Ronan said. Kyle merely smirked. How had her beautiful baby brothers turned into surly teenagers? They'd been little boys when she'd left home eight years ago. Leaving them was gut-wrenching, but she'd craved freedom, and she'd thought Aidan Gant was the answer to her prayers. Her mouth twisted into a grimace. How wrong she'd been.

Once she opened the café and had somewhere to live besides one of Aidan's guest bedrooms, she'd ask the boys to move in with her. Her parents might not agree to the scheme, but she owed it to the boys to at least offer.

Outside, the strong Atlantic wind propelled her to her car. All she wanted to do right now was curl up in bed with an escapist book. Instead her agenda consisted of an afternoon spent dealing with Aidan's smug satisfaction and barbed comments. Thank goodness she had drinks with Jill– her old pal from cookery school– to look forward to this evening. A rant to a friend followed by a good laugh was exactly what she needed to decompress after her crappy week.

CHAPTER SEVEN

When Jonas strode through the door of MacCarthy's pub at eight o'clock, the place was packed. The economic downturn hadn't prevented the folk of Ballybeg from going out for a pint, that was for sure.

He muscled his way through the heaving throng, nodding to people as he passed. Despite the hard rock music blasting through the speakers, MacCarthy's had the appearance of a typical traditional Irish pub, complete with a snug in the corner and the requisite portraits of Ireland's fallen heroes adorning its wood-paneled walls. Although Jonas had been in MacCarthy's a thousand times, the incongruity of the alternative music and the pub's old-fashioned appearance never failed to amuse him.

Ruairí MacCarthy, the pub's owner and manager, stood behind the bar. He was a bear of a man. Quiet and gruff and just the sort of bloke you'd want on a rugby field or to have your back in a fight. The recent arrival of his estranged American wife had been the talk of the town. As Jonas approached, Ruairí caught his eye. "The usual?"

"Yes, please." He hung his jacket on a peg beneath the counter. "How's Jayme doing?"

The other man's face split into a smile. "Grand. She's started working at a hospital in Cork City."

"Life in Ballybeg hasn't sent her running back to New York?"

"Not yet." Ruairí's grin widened. "I'm doing my best to persuade her to stay."

"Tell her I said hi." He slid onto a free bar stool and let his fingers run over the newly polished counter. "This place looks great after the renovations, but I kind of miss the scratched counter. The grooves told a tale or two, you know?"

The corners of the barman's mouth quirked. "I do know. Still, Gavin and your dad did a top notch job."

"That they did." He settled onto his barstool and observed the soothing ritual of the barman pulling his pint. It was a sight to behold. Ruairí did it nice and slowly, letting the drink sit for a while to allow the head to form before adding more. Most barmen these days rushed the process, especially when there was a queue of thirsty customers waiting to be served. Finally Ruairí pushed the pint across the counter.

"*Sláinte.*" Jonas clinked his pint against his friend's water glass, then took a sip of the thick black liquid. As he licked the froth from his lips, a memory flickered. A vision of dark red hair and soft skin. He gulped down his drink. Today was bad enough without his mind playing tricks on him.

"Penny for them– or do I want to know?" A familiar voice broke through his reverie. He turned as his best friend claimed the bar stool next to his. In marked contrast to Jonas's dark hair and tanned skin, Gavin was fair-haired and pale-complexioned. Not even his recent trip to Australia had done more than add the barest hint of gold to his cheeks. "I'll have a shot of Jameson, Ruairí."

The barman reached for a tumbler.

"I've been expecting to see you in here licking your wounds since Wednesday." Gavin pulled a tenner out of his wallet.

Jonas slid him a look. "News travels fast."

"Ballybeg, *baile beag*. In a small town, gossip travels faster than gonorrhea." Gavin's grin was sly. "Actually, Olivia filled Fiona in on the lurid details."

"Mary reneging on their deal had nothing to do with me. Besides, Olivia's rich enough to buy her own cottage. Don't know why she's making such a fuss about not being able to rent Mary's."

"I don't have the particulars, but I believe Gant controls the money in that household. Fiona said he didn't want Olivia to open a business."

"So she takes her domestic spat out on me? She needs to grow up and stop acting like everyone in this town is at her beck and call."

"Never got that vibe from her myself," Gavin said, "and I've seen her regularly since Fiona moved in."

Ruairí placed a whiskey on the counter.

Gavin slipped him the money. "Thanks, mate. Keep the change."

"What's new with you and Fiona?"

His friend raised an eyebrow at his not-so-subtle attempt to steer the conversation in another direction. "Nothing new. Fiona is splitting her time between assisting her aunt at the Book Mark and helping me with admin stuff for the business. It's nice being able to spend time together. I'll miss her when she starts her new teaching job in August."

Jonas felt a pang of envy at his friend's newfound happiness but quashed it. "Sounds like you two aren't regretting how things worked out last year."

"Hell no. Best life implosion ever," Gavin said cheerfully. "But enough about me. You've had a sour puss since I arrived, and I don't think it's solely to do with your fight with Olivia. What's up?"

"Childcare crisis." Jonas took a fortifying sip of Guinness. "My mother's off on a cruise with Mary."

"Hey, good for them." Gavin's handsome face split into a smile. "They've been talking about a cruise for years. When do they leave?"

Jonas cast him a black look. "Next week."

"Ah...hence your crappy mood. I take it you haven't found a babysitter for Luca?"

"No," he said sourly. "Who'll want to look after a kid with special needs and a slew of appointments each week?"

Gavin twisted his long-and-lean form around on his stool. "Why don't you look after him yourself? About bloody time, if you ask me."

"Which I didn't."

"All right. No need to bite my head off. I'm just saying you've been leaving him with your parents an awful lot since you moved back to Ballybeg."

"Only because I've had one deadline after another. If I don't hand in my books on time, I don't get the next installment of my advance, and I need every penny to put toward Luca's therapies."

"Doesn't that defeat the purpose of getting an advance?"

"Tell me about it. That's the publishing industry for you."

Gavin took a swig from his whiskey glass and swirled the amber liquid pensively. "When's your next book due?"

"In two days. That's why I have to make tonight's drink a quick one."

"Why don't you send Luca to us tomorrow night? You can power write all night if you want to. Then we can swing by your house on Saturday morning to collect you for the Easter parade. I don't see Luca wanting to miss that."

Jonas frowned. "Are you sure? I don't want to put you and Fiona out."

"Course I'm sure. Gotta do my godfatherly duty. But apart from us helping out the odd time, the way I see it, you're in the ideal working situation to cope with this. You can write mornings in your home office while Luca's at school or therapy, take the afternoons off to be with him or ferry him to appointments, then write again in the evenings. Seems perfect. That's how Fiona and I juggle looking after Wiggly Poo."

Jonas wavered between irritation and amusement. "I hate to break it to you, mate, but looking after a kid– even one without autism– is *not* the same as caring for a labradoodle. If you want to see what it's like trying to concentrate on work with a kid running wild in the background, feel free to borrow Luca for a day."

"Aw, come on. Surely it can't be that bad. Luca just happens to be a bit different from the rest of us."

Jonas stared at a portrait of Michael Collins and willed patience. Gav meant well, but he didn't get it. "Luca's autistic. That's more extreme than a bit different. He's also a six-year-old boy. Getting into mischief is what he does. I can't shut myself into my office and leave him to his own devices."

Gavin threw his arms up in a gesture of surrender. "Okay, man. Don't bite my head off. You know I adore the little fella."

"I came out tonight to have a quiet pint, not to get into an argument with you. Let's drop the subject, okay?" Gav didn't understand how precarious his financial situation was at the moment. If it hadn't been for Mary's generosity, he'd be well and truly screwed. He needed every second of writing time he could get.

"Fair enough," Gavin said. "I'm hoarse from shouting over the music anyway."

Jonas's mouth quirked. Blaring music or no, Gavin managed to carry on a conversation in any environment if he had a mind to.

"Have you found a tenant for the second cottage?"

"Not yet. I'm putting an ad in the newspaper next week."

Gavin tapped the side of his glass. "I'm guessing renting it to Olivia is out of the question?"

"Nah. It's a no-go." The very idea made his stomach twist.

"Why?"

He shot his friend a look of exasperation. "You know why. My mother would have a conniption if I did Olivia a favor."

"Way I see it, she'd be doing *you* a favor. You need to rent out the place, and not many people are looking to rent a cottage this time of year. Besides, Mary didn't have a problem with the idea of having Olivia as a tenant until you showed up."

"I didn't ask my aunt to turn her down, if that's what you're implying." He hadn't needed to. Mam had taken care of that. "If I offered her the lease, it would cause major friction with my mother. She's not reasonable on the subject of Olivia."

"After all this time? Surely she knows what happened to Bry wasn't Olivia's fault."

"She must on some level, but blaming Olivia has become a habit. My dad definitely doesn't hold her responsible."

"Speaking of which...how does it feel to be a house owner?"

Jonas pondered the question for a beat. "Weird. I know I should be delighted. Mary is doing me an enormous favor."

"But...?" Gavin prompted.

"The atmosphere at Gant's was off. I can't put my finger on what the problem was. I figured it would be awkward with Olivia working there, but he's been Mary's solicitor for years. Oddly enough, it wasn't so much the tension between us and Olivia that felt wrong, but her interaction with Gant."

Gavin chuckled. "My friend, you are behind in the times. It's common knowledge that Aidan and Olivia hate each other's guts. I don't need to be privy to her conversations with Fiona to know that."

His jaw dropped. "Are you serious? Why are they still together?"

"I don't know. Not even Fiona knows. My guess is that they'll stay together until after the mayoral election at the very least. Ballybeg is old-fashioned enough to want a male politician to have a wife, and Gant intends to be the next mayor."

"It's all a sham?" He shook his head in disgust. "No wonder the tension in Gant's office was at boiling point." No doubt his and Mary's presence had made matters worse. "Did Gant know Olivia planned to rent the cottage from Mary, I wonder?"

"Aidan Gant doesn't miss a trick. It must have caused him no end of pleasure to see that deal take a dive. I suspect her plans to open a café are a bid to gain financial independence from Gant so she can afford to move out when the election is over."

"Dammit. There's no love lost between me and Olivia, but I don't wish her harm."

"I know you don't," his friend said. "Perhaps this info will make you reconsider renting the cottage to her."

"I wish it were that straightforward. My mother will see it as a betrayal. She was livid when she found out Mary had been thinking of renting the cottage to Olivia." He paused for a moment, searching for an excuse. "Besides, Olivia's a snob."

"That's crap, and you know it. Olivia doesn't suffer fools gladly, but she's no snob. And you know she's not responsible for your brother's death. It's not fair to tolerate your mother blaming her after all these years."

"Tell that to Mam. The fact remains that Olivia and I rub each other up the wrong way. Can you seriously see us surviving next door to one another?"

"Depends on what you'd be surviving," Gavin said with a sly smile. "She's a good-looking woman."

Jonas snorted. "If you like snotty redheads."

"Which you once did, and I suspect you still do." Gavin grinned. "Not that you'd ever admit it."

Heat crept up his cheeks. His short-lived relationship with Olivia was the stuff of Ballybeg legend– and not in a good way. No way he'd want to revisit those dark days, but he had to admit that he had a grudging respect for the way she'd stood up to him at the dentist's. The memory of her flashing eyes and flushed cheeks lingered. "She's not my type." The words sounded lame even to his ears.

"No offense, but after Susanne, you should change your type."

Jonas narrowed his eyes.

"Sorry, mate," Gavin said. "Guess that was out of line."

"Forget it."

"Will you at least consider making that offer to Olivia? Opening the café is important to her."

"Lay on the guilt, why don't you? Oh, all right. I'll consider it." With a bit of luck, Olivia would balk at the notion of working next door to him, and that would be that.

Gavin smiled and drained his whiskey. "Good on you, mate. Listen, Fiona's expecting me for a late dinner. Will I see you on the beach for our morning run? Say about six o'clock?"

"You're determined to get me fit, aren't you?"

His friend grinned. "I'm determined to do well at Ballybeg Sports Day."

"Torturer. Go home to your dinner. I'll see you tomorrow." Tomorrow...when he had to figure out what do with Luca for the next two months.

He finished his pint and stared morosely at the play of light through the glass. God, how he loved that little boy, but he felt utterly inept in his presence. He was terrified of letting his son down, of falling behind on his therapy payments, of the lingering sensation that Luca deserved better than he could offer.

He pushed back his barstool. Right now, what he needed to do was get home and squeeze in another couple of hours of writing time.

***

Jill shook her head, and her beaded dreadlocks jangled. "If looks could kill, Jonas O'Mahony would be deader than the victims in his crime novels."

She and Olivia had cornered the last free table in the pub, affording them an excellent view of Jonas's denim-clad derriere. Did he still have the matching leprechaun tattoo? Olivia wondered. Or had he run to the nearest dermatologist after Bry drowned and their relationship imploded? Pulling her gaze from Jonas's broad back, she faced her friend. "That scheming fecker poached my cottage."

"Don't be daft. Mary is Jonas's aunt. Of course she gave him priority."

"We had a *deal.*"

"You had an oral agreement. Worthless without a written contract to back it up." Jill screwed up her nose, making her coffee-colored freckles stand out against her light brown skin. "I stuck with my legal studies long enough to learn that much before I dropped out."

"It still stinks of nepotism." Olivia took a swig of her tonic water, deliberately restraining herself from looking in *his* direction. "What's more, Jonas now *owns* the building."

"Eh?" her friend said in surprise. "I didn't see that one coming."

"Nor did I. When I returned from dropping off my brothers, Aidan wasted no time imparting that nugget of information. To avoid inheritance tax, Mary signed over a few of her properties to Jonas. I highly doubt he'll want me as a tenant, do you?"

"Probably not. Any luck finding another place to rent?"

"Not so far. I have less than two weeks to find one." She'd checked a few places online, but they were either too small or too big for her needs, and they were all out of her price range. The cottage had been perfect: great location, right size, and affordable.

In spite of herself, her gaze was drawn back to Jonas. He hadn't moved a centimeter since she'd arrived. He appeared to be lost in his own world and oddly morose for a man who'd just acquired a valuable piece of real estate. What did he have to worry about? He had a place to live and a successful writing career. Was it something to do with his kid? Fiona had said the boy was autistic.

"We can go somewhere else if you prefer," Jill said, cutting through her ruminations.

"Where? This is the only place in town with decent music...unless you're in the mood for techno-filled fun at O'Dwyers."

"Perish the thought. I'd rather go to bingo night at the town hall."

Olivia laughed. "You're on your own if you do. My grandfather and Bridie Byrne are regulars."

"If we are staying here, you need to stop glaring daggers into Jonas O'Mahony's back."

"All right. Point taken. I was hoping I'd be able to tell Aidan to stick his job and his stinking guest room where it hurts. If I have to work with that man much longer, I swear I'll kill him." A couple of people at the next table turned to gawp at her in horror. She ignored them but lowered her voice a notch. "The tension between us is unbearable. He's been in a foul mood ever since the shopping center project folded. He should have had more sense than to invest money in anything involving Bernard Byrne. At least Fiona and Bridie got the money Bernard owed them before this happened."

Jill put down the beer mat she'd been shredding. "Aidan's an arse, but at least you still have a way to pay the bills until you get the café up and running. That's not to be scoffed at."

"Is something up?" Olivia eyed her friend questioningly. "You've been on edge since we got here."

Jill hunched her shoulders. "I lost my job."

"What? That's terrible."

"It wasn't unexpected. I got through the first two waves of layoffs. Figured I wouldn't survive a third."

"Have you decided what you're going to do?"

"There's not much out there at the moment in the food production industry, and certainly not around here. I'll admit that being a cheese quality controller wasn't my life's ambition, but the job paid the bills."

"Gosh, that sucks. It seems like most of my friends have either left Ballybeg or are planning to. Fiona bucked the trend by moving back."

Jill twisted a dreadlock tight around her index finger. "I want to stay in Cork, but you know how it is. I might not have a choice."

"If I ever manage to open my café, *I'll* give you a job. When we were at cookery school, you were always better at making savories than I was."

"And you rocked at cakes and pastries. Hey, if I don't find a new position fast, I might take you up on the offer, albeit on a temporary basis."

"In that case, I'd better find new premises for the café fast."

"My faith in the Irish job market is such that I have a feeling you'll find a place for the café before I find a new job. Unfortunately, my side gig doesn't generate enough money to cover my rent."

"Not enough demand for dildos in Ballybeg?" Olivia asked with a chuckle.

"Not this time of year. Racy lingerie and sex toys sell well around Christmas and Valentine's Day. In a few weeks, the pre-wedding parties will start up again. I should get a few bookings then." Jill rooted through her handbag. "Our area sales manager just sent me a copy of the new catalogue."

Olivia flicked through the glossy pages that depicted the latest product range of Passionate Pleasures. "Good grief. Please tell me I'm hallucinating. Padded leopard print thongs?"

"Give your crotch some extra oomph," Jill quoted with a sly grin. "You should get a pair for Aidan."

"Ugh." Olivia gave an exaggerated shudder. "I try very hard to excise all memories of Aidan's crotch."

"Now there's a man who has no need for padded underwear." Jill nodded at someone approaching from the bar.

Olivia whipped round. Jonas O'Mahony was weaving his way through the crowd. He paused when he reached their table, his gaze dropping to the catalogue in her hand. Heat seared her cheeks when she realized the catalogue had fallen open to reveal a selection of anal plugs.

Jonas flashed her a wicked grin. "I didn't have you down for that sort of caper."

She hated the tingling effect his gravelly voice had on her body. Why couldn't he have developed a paunch? Or a bald spot? If anything, the years had enhanced his good looks. There was no justice in the world. She itched to close the catalogue but refused to give him the satisfaction of seeing he'd embarrassed her. Knowing he'd witnessed this afternoon's scene with Aidan was sufficient humiliation for one day. "What do you want, Jonas? Come to gloat over the cottage?"

His grin faded. "I'm sorry for the way things worked out with the lease."

"Why would you be sorry? You always said you'd get even with me one day. Is this not part of your Screw Over Olivia master plan?"

He flinched and took a step back. "No. It wasn't like that."

"Wasn't it?" She sounded haughty. Not quite the effect she was aiming for, but he had a knack for bringing out her worst side. "Now that you've schemed to get the cottage, you feel you can be magnanimous?"

His tanned cheeks flushed. "Pardon me for trying to bury the hatchet. I'll leave you ladies to your drinks."

His leather-clad frame melted into the crowd.

Jill radiated disapproval. "Did you have to goad him?"

"What?" Olivia said, thrusting the catalogue at her friend. "I thought that went well."

Jill gave a snort of disgust. "You'd better hope you find premises soon."

"I will," Olivia said with more self-assurance than she felt. "Just watch."

CHAPTER EIGHT

Jonas woke on Saturday morning to pounding on his front door. The rhythmic beat of fists on wood was in sync with his throbbing headache. Pulling a coffee-fueled all-nighter to finish his book always left him a wreck the next day. He groaned and pulled the duvet up to his chin.

"Hey." Gavin clambered up the ladder to his loft bedroom.

Jonas supposed he'd forgotten to lock the front door last night. He mumbled a greeting and buried his head under the pillow.

"What's the deal?" Gavin demanded. "We need to get going. Luca doesn't want to miss the start of the Easter parade."

"What?" He sat too quickly, making his head spin and his stomach heave. "What's the time?" He groped for his alarm clock, but he must have knocked it off the nightstand.

"A quarter to eleven." His friend strode to the wardrobe and rifled through the clothes with an air of intent, eventually throwing a clean pair of jeans and a sweatshirt at Jonas.

"I need a shower, Gav. I can't go out like this."

"Make it quick." Gavin surveyed the room. "Guess you haven't finished unpacking."

"Not yet." He and Luca had been living in the cottage for almost a week. Most of the rooms were habitable, but his bedroom resembled a storage unit. No doubt it offended Gavin's neat-freak tendencies. Standing carefully, he padded across the floor to the ladder. "Where's Luca?"

"Waiting in the garden with Fiona and Wiggly Poo."

"Did he behave himself for you last night?"

"He was good as gold. Slept like a log too."

Didn't that figure. Why was he the only one plagued by Luca's night terrors?

"Any luck finding a childminder?" Gavin asked.

"Not so far. I'm interviewing a couple of people next week."

He made for the bathroom and stripped. The hot, sharp needles of the shower provided a welcome relief. If he'd had the time, he'd have stayed under the water for ages. Instead he soaped and shampooed with as much speed as he could muster in his coffee hangover. Yeah, that sixth espresso had been a lousy idea, but it had helped him to blast through to the end of Detective Inspector Brady's latest mystery.

He dried himself off and dressed with as much speed as his groggy state permitted. He fingered his stubble. It would have to do– there was no time to shave.

When he emerged from the bathroom, Gavin was sprawled across the sofa bed, reading one of Jonas's favorite fantasy novels. Luca sat beside him, studying a picture book on dinosaurs. He didn't make eye contact when his father dropped a kiss on his cheek. In contrast, Wiggly Poo greeted Jonas in an ecstasy of delight, tail wagging and tongue lolling.

"Did you have fun at Gavin's last night?" he asked Luca as he stroked Wiggly Poo's golden fur.

Luca shrugged. Still no eye contact.

Jonas stood and tousled his hair. "Come on, mate. You know I had to work late."

"Granddad says writing books isn't proper work. He told Nana you should get a real job like everybody else. If you got a real job, you wouldn't need to worry about paying the bills."

Jonas bit back the retort that sprang to his tongue. He loved his father and he'd never been in any doubt that his father loved him, but Liam had never– and probably would never– understand his passion for storytelling. As far as Liam was concerned, the only proper work for a man involved manual labor. This was yet another instance of his parents discussing stuff in front of Luca and assuming he didn't understand. Maybe having Luca go there less wasn't such a bad idea after all. "Granddad and I are different. He likes making things with his hands, and I like telling stories."

Gavin tossed the book aside. "Fiona's gone on ahead to get us a good spot for the parade. We'd better get moving or she'll be mobbed."

"Okay," Jonas said. "Let me pop a painkiller, and we'll hit the road." Late or not, he needed something to take the edge off his headache before facing the crowds. The

Ballybeg Easter parade was one of the major events of the year. The whole town turned out to watch the floats as did people from neighboring areas.

He strode toward the kitchen. Yeah, the bare look had to go. Luca's room was the one room he'd made an effort to decorate. He needed to transform the rest of the place into a home worthy of the name.

Wiggly Poo danced around his legs, whining.

"Are you looking for food?"

The labradoodle panted and stared at him beseechingly through large doggy eyes.

"Don't give him anything," Gav yelled from the living room. "He's on a diet. The vet says we're feeding him too much. I say it's more likely to be the quantity of shoes and slippers he consumes between meals."

Jonas laughed and rifled through the makeshift medicine box in one of the kitchen cupboards. "Not to mention wedding suits. I'll never forget the expression on your face when we walked in on him regurgitating your trousers."

"Ha," said Gavin. "Don't remind me. I still haven't recovered from the horror of that bloody rental suit I ended up wearing."

Finally Jonas located a packet of painkillers. He popped a couple of pills, washed them down with tap water, and returned to the living room. "Luca, do you have your hat?"

"No."

"Where is it?"

The kid shrugged, still absorbed in his book. "Dunno. Maybe I left my hat at school."

Great. Did the boy have a spare? If he did, it was probably at his grandparents' house.

"You can wear mine." He rooted through an unpacked moving box and located an ancient woolen hat. He plopped it on Luca's head. *Problem solved.*

The hat slid down over Luca's nose. *Or perhaps not solved.* "This is way too big, Dad."

"It'll do for today," Jonas said, trying to sound cheerful.

"I can't wear this. It doesn't fit. It has to fit, Dad." The boy's voice quavered.

Gavin and Jonas exchanged looks. Luca got stressed if things weren't perfect. The last thing they needed was him freaking out before they even got to the parade.

He turned to his son. "Have you any idea where it is? Let's check your room."

Luca's bedroom was immaculate. He definitely hadn't inherited his organizational skills from his father. A search of the wardrobe proved fruitless. Jonas scanned the room in desperation, his gaze resting on the dress-up box. He rummaged through it and struck gold. "How's this?" He held up a pirate cap. "It's an unusual look, but it's a hat, right?"

He plopped it on Luca's head and gave him an encouraging smile. Luca regarded his reflection in the mirror dubiously. He opened his mouth as if to protest, but Gavin cut in.

"Why don't we put this pirate sash on Wiggly Poo? That way, you'll match."

Luca's face lit up. "Cool. You're the best, Uncle Gav."

Gavin beamed in delight. The familiar twist in his gut made Jonas nauseated.

Wiggly Poo and Luca bounded out the door and down the short path to the gate.

Jonas's head throbbed. He had the feeling it was going to be a long day.

***

On the corner of Delores Street, Olivia stopped to let her mother-in-law catch her breath. They were late. *Very* late. Aidan would have apoplexy.

The last-minute offer to look at potential premises in Clonakilty had seemed a godsend, especially with the bank appointment looming. Unfortunately, the rooms were dingy and cramped– utterly unsuitable for the café. Courtesy of heavy holiday traffic, she was late collecting her mother-in-law– a fact for which she was currently being berated– and now late to meet Aidan for the Easter parade.

"This is simply too much," Patricia gasped, clutching her Gucci handbag to her voluminous fur coat. "You can't expect me to walk for miles in these shoes."

"We circled the town several times. That was the only parking space I could find."

"If you'd collected me at the time we'd arranged, I'd already be sitting in the comfort of Colette Buckley's front room, sipping tea and watching the parade from a safe distance. Instead I'm traipsing through litter and the hoi polloi."

"Oh, put a sock in it," Olivia snapped. "If you hadn't insisted on wearing those ridiculous shoes, you'd be able to take more than a few mincing steps at a time."

"Well, really." The older woman's jowls wobbled in indignation. "Other women treat their mothers-in-law with respect."

"Perhaps other women don't have mothers-in-law who lose their licenses for drunk driving. I'm not your personal taxi service."

Patricia drew herself up to her full height, her heavily made-up eyes wide. "I had *one* glass of champagne. One glass of *vintage* champagne."

Olivia laughed. "Breathalyzers don't distinguish between five-euro plonk and expensive bubbly."

"Apparently not," sniffed Patricia. "Why were you so late collecting me, anyway?"

"I told you. The traffic back from Clonakilty was a nightmare."

"I don't understand why you're so determined to open your own business. Why can't you be content working for Aidan?"

"You know why," Olivia said through gritted teeth. "Once the election is over, we're filing for a legal separation."

"How absurd." Patricia pursed her lips into a scarlet slash of disapproval. "If you'd taken my advice and had a baby, you wouldn't be in this mess. Children cement relationships."

Ironically, the decision not to have children was one of the few topics on which Olivia and Aidan were in complete agreement. "Given that we're separating, I'd say it's fortunate neither he nor I felt any inclination to reproduce."

"I'd hoped you'd tame him. It's hard watching my friends become grandmothers. Colette already has three."

"If you're that desperate to bounce a baby, borrow one of Colette's grandchildren."

Patricia withdrew a cigarette from her handbag with shaky hands and lit up as if her life depended on it. "What happens when Aidan becomes mayor? He'll need a wife at his side then."

"*If* he becomes mayor, that wife won't be me."

"You make too much fuss about Aidan's little indiscretions," she said between puffs. "Men will be men, you know. His father was no different."

Olivia flexed her jaw. Aidan's "little indiscretions" were the least of her worries in her marriage. His bullying tongue and menacing fists were more pressing concerns. Her mother-in-law wasn't a stupid woman, but when it came to her son's faults, she was obstinately obtuse.

"Look," Olivia said in relief, "there's Colette." She dragged Patricia across the street and deposited her on her friend's doorstep.

"We had to walk all the way into town," Patricia said in tragic tones, collapsing into her friend's arms. "My feet ache and I'm absolutely parched."

"The kettle's on. Or I can offer you something stronger if you prefer." Colette gave Olivia a conspiratorial wink over Patricia's shoulder. "Let's get you inside."

"Have fun, ladies." Olivia checked her watch. *Drat.* She was due to meet Aidan over an hour ago. Dodging a passing float, she waded into the throng.

CHAPTER NINE

Patrick Street was a pulsing mass of humanity. Squealing babies were accompanied by laughing adults, some none too steady on their feet despite the early hour. Older children and dogs roamed the colorful street, their guardians apparently unconcerned by the prospect of them being flattened by a passing float. The stench of spilled beer wafted from the littered pavement, warring with the sounds and sights for dominance over Jonas's embattled senses.

He groaned inwardly. He loathed parades. Always had. That he was attending this year was solely for Luca's sake. He glanced down at his son. If only the little guy would show more enthusiasm. Luca stood beside him with his eyes resolutely shut and his hands over his ears. *Ah, hell.* The boy was noise sensitive at the best of times, not to mention wary of strangers. He should have known better than to subject the child to this sensory overload.

"If it gets too loud, we'll leave," he promised, giving the boy an awkward pat.

Luca stiffened at his touch, but didn't say anything.

The procession wound its way through the narrow streets of Ballybeg, each float more garish than its predecessor. The parade was a raucous affair. Most of the spectators were well lubricated with alcohol, and many on the floats were no better.

Jonas held tight to Luca's hand as they weaved their way through the crowd. The smell of spilled beer and vomit turned his stomach. They'd lost sight of Gavin, Fiona, and Wiggly Poo, but they'd catch up with them later.

When they finally squeezed their way to the edge of the street, he hoisted Luca onto his shoulders, just as his father had done with him and his younger brothers when they were kids.

"It's too high, Dad. I'll fall," Luca protested.

"Nah, you'll be fine. I'll hold on tight."

Luca's complaints ceased once he realized how much more he could see from his new elevation. The music throbbed; people sang. Someone's beer trickled down Jonas's arm but he ignored it. There was no point in challenging anyone in this crowd, especially not the bunch to his right. He recognized a few local thugs from the nearby housing estate, lager louts one and all.

A leprechaun leapt out in front of them, wielding a shamrock. All thanks to bloody *Darby O'Gill and the Little People*. Jonas hated that film. It was a faux Irish freak fest, and Sean Connery's terrible accent grated. Yet it was shown on TV around Easter and St. Patrick's Day every year without fail. People had no taste.

His eyes wandered over the crowd. And froze. Across the street, Aidan Gant was holding court with a bunch of local bigwigs. Olivia stood beside him, expressionless but beautiful as always. His gut twisted at the sight, and the familiar longing made its presence known.

"Dad, it's too loud," Luca whined.

"All right, mate. Let's head away from the crowd."

"Can I get a lolly first?"

"You haven't had your lunch yet."

"I won't need lunch. I had an extremely enormous breakfast at Uncle Gav's."

Jonas smiled. In many ways, Luca was an odd kid, yet in others, he was like every other little boy. "I suppose you want one of those hideous green shamrock lollies."

"They do look yummy."

"Okay. One revolting mass of green sugar coming right up."

They crossed the road to the lolly stand. Jonas set Luca down and purchased an overpriced green monstrosity. As he was slipping his wallet into his pocket, he saw Olivia barreling down the road. Her snug green pullover and tight jeans drew his attention to her slim curves. Not that he needed any help in noticing them– more was the pity.

She stumbled to a halt in front of him, blinking as though surprised to find an obstacle blocking her path. Neither of them spoke for a beat, letting the sea of background noise wash over them.

After a long moment, she tore her gaze away from his and shifted her focus to Luca. "Are you okay?"

Luca opened his eyes and regarded her solemnly.

"Does the noise hurt your ears? Or is it an infection? I see you're pulling at your earlobes."

Luca glanced up at his father, then back to Olivia.

"You have an earache?" Jonas inspected his son's ears but couldn't see inside. The possibility of Luca having an ear infection should have occurred to him before. Luca's case manager had mentioned acute hearing and other sensory issues, and that's what he'd assumed was the problem. He slipped his hand down the neck of the boy's pullover. The kid's skin was burning with fever.

Shite. How had he missed this? What did one do when a kid had an earache? Take him to the doctor straight away? Wait to see if he improved? Mam would know. Unfortunately, she was somewhere in the Caribbean.

"Should we go home?" he asked Luca.

The boy shrugged. "No, just away from the noise."

"You could take him to the beach." Olivia's voice was bland but he was acutely aware of her watching him. "I don't see anyone down there. It will be quieter than here."

Jonas peered over the wall and down to the strand. The tide was out, exposing a vast expanse of wet sand. "Okay, Luca, what do you say? Will we go and build sandcastles?"

"We have no bucket and spade."

"We can improvise," he said with false jollity. "We can find shells big enough to dig with, and we can use our hands."

The boy was dubious. "I guess we can try."

"Great. Let's go." Jonas nodded to Olivia, the movement as stiff and awkward as their entire interaction over the past decade. "Thanks for noticing his ears."

She shrugged. "My brother Kyle always had ear infections when he was small. I got used to noticing the signs."

As he edged past her to the flight of steps, the familiar electricity between them crackled. She licked her pink-tinged lips, and his tangle of emotions tumbled to the fore. For an insane moment, Jonas had the urge to kiss her.

"Dad?"

He whipped round at the sound of Luca's voice. "On my way."

Without looking back at Olivia, he followed his son down the steps to the beach.

***

Olivia leaned against the wall and watched Jonas and Luca walk along the sand. Her reaction to Jonas was unnerving. Why did he, of all men, possess the power to get under her skin?

Above the surface of the sea, two seagulls took flight, flapping their way toward the Atlantic Ocean. She envied them their freedom. Heaving a sigh, she hurried across the road to where Aidan was standing with her family and his political cohorts.

Her father was his usual jolly but vague self. He disliked large public events, particularly those that required him to wear a suit. The sole reason he was present today was out of loyalty to Aidan– his employer, creditor, and oldest friend. *Oldest, not best. There's a distinction, Dad, even if you don't see it.*

Olivia glanced around the group. Kyle had disappeared with friends, but Ronan stood to the side of the group, his thin shoulders hunched. Her mother had poured herself into a clingy, thigh-length dress and was in full-flirtation mode with various male members of the town council– including John Jobson, father of Julie and James, the boy Kyle and Ronan had allegedly punched. Although flirting was more natural to Victoria than breathing, it rarely went further than that. Nonetheless, it was bloody embarrassing to witness, particularly when she was loud and tipsy.

"Olivia, darling. You're finally here." Victoria gave her an air kiss. "Why aren't you smiling? It's the start of the long weekend. You should be happy."

Happy...right. Happy to have to spend three long days traipsing around after Aidan while he schmoozed his future constituents and made a token appearance at church? She thought not. "When did you get back from London?"

"Yesterday. The art exhibition was simply divine."

"Did Dad tell you about the boys' suspension?"

"Oh, yes." Her mother giggled. "Kyle is delighted to have time off school."

"Given how close Kyle is coming to failing several subjects, he should use the time to study."

Victoria waved her hand in breezy unconcern. "You're such a stick-in-the-mud, darling. I don't know how I produced a daughter like you."

Aidan was standing beside Julie Jobson, who was tittering at one of his off-color jokes. His eyes turned to slits when he registered his wife's presence. He plastered a rictus on his face and grabbed her arm, yanking her away from the group. "Where have you been?" His fingers dug into her skin, making her wince. "You should have been here an hour ago."

"Your mother's Jimmy Choos and Ballybeg's cobblestoned streets had a disagreement."

"Why aren't you talking to the other town councilors? You're supposed to be playing the role of my devoted wife, remember?"

How could she ever forget? "Why would they want me to talk to them?" she asked in exasperation, trying to wrench her arm free. "I'm not on the town council. I doubt they want to hear my views on what should be done in Ballybeg."

"Of course they're not interested in your opinions," he snapped. "Be sociable. Mingle, for heaven's sake. Why can't you be more like your mother?"

Why, indeed? Aidan chose to forget Victoria's frequent social lapses and disappearing acts. As far as he was concerned, she was his first crush and his oldest friend's wife. Olivia had always wondered if Aidan's rose-tinted affection for Victoria was part of the reason he'd chosen to marry the woman's daughter.

"Kyle is the only one of my children to inherit my artistic talent," Victoria was saying loudly to the elderly councilor at her side. "Ronan tries, but the poor boy simply hasn't a hope."

Ronan's cheeks turned red with shame.

Olivia yanked herself free from Aidan's grasp. Her arm ached. She'd have bruises. It was unlike Aidan to be so careless, but he probably thought it didn't matter in this weather when she wouldn't be wearing short-sleeved tops. She moved beside Ronan. "Don't mind Mum," she whispered. "You know what she's like. Always needs to be the center of attention."

"I don't know if I can take much more," Ronan bit out. "Living in that house is hell. How can I tolerate them for another three years?"

"You'll manage. I did. Once you turn eighteen, you can come and live with me. I'll have my own place by then, and the café will be established." If all went according to plan, he and Kyle could move in with her far sooner, but it would be cruel to give him false expectations.

He gave a bitter laugh. "You're deluding yourself. Aidan will never let that happen. You're stuck in that marriage until Mum and Dad repay their debt to him. We both know that'll be when hell freezes over."

His words were a slap. "Don't say that. I have to hope things will change."

"What will change?" Olivia whirled around at the sound of Aidan's voice.

"Ronan's grades in art," she improvised.

Aidan snorted. "He should concentrate on learning to read. You'd think he'd have mastered that simple skill by the age of fifteen."

"He's dyslexic, not stupid."

Ronan flushed and dug his thin hands into his coat pockets. "I'm going for a walk."

"You do that," Aidan sneered. "Just don't wander so far that you're reliant on street signs. We both know that won't end well."

"Leave him alone." Anger scorched her vocal chords. "Why do you always pick on him? He's a fifteen-year-old boy. Can't you find someone your own age to bully?"

She started to run after her brother, but Aidan grabbed her shoulder.

"Your duty is to stay here with me," he hissed into her ear. "We have a deal, remember?"

Olivia fixed him with a fulminating glare. "Go to hell and take your deal with you." She pulled her arm free and raced the street in the direction her brother had taken.

Ronan disappeared down the steps toward the beach. Her heart rate accelerated, but her pace didn't falter. Taking the slippery steps two at a time, she soon reached the sandy beach below.

The roar of the sea rang in her ears like a warning. "Ronan?"

Damn. She'd lost sight of him the moment he'd vanished between the boulders that led the way to Craggy Point. Pulling her thin jacket close, she shivered in the salty air. The beach gave her the creeps. She never ventured too near the water, not since the night Bry drowned. But she had to find her brother.

Why did Aidan have to goad the boy? Couldn't he confine his bullying to her? Why did her parents turn a blind eye– and a deaf ear– to Aidan's insults?

She'd passed the public toilets and reached the dunes when someone grabbed her by-now aching left arm. Her heart lurched in her chest when she smelled his cloying after shave. *Aidan.*

"Where do you think you're going?" He twisted her shoulder with vicious force.

"Get off me." She wrenched herself out of his grasp and took a step to the left.

He kept approaching.

Shit. She surveyed her surroundings, hoping to see someone, anyone. From what she could ascertain, they were alone in the dunes. If she screamed, her cry would be lost in the wind.

Her pulse pummeled in her wrist. Aidan had cornered her before in a rage, but she'd managed to wriggle her way out of the encounter. On this deserted area of the beach, there was no chance of escape. Why hadn't she taken the potential danger seriously? *Because he hasn't hit me in almost a year*. She'd grown lax in taking precautions to avoid these situations and arrogant in her assumption that she'd be out of his life within a couple of months.

She retreated a few steps, only to catch a heel on a stray rock and stumble in the sand. Her panic rose in time with her staccato breathing. Aidan continued his approach with clenched fists. The punch to her stomach was swift and brutal. The impact sucked the air from her lungs and the pain curled her into a comma. "You. Bastard."

His attention was fixed on her breasts, making her wish she'd chosen a loose top instead of this tight pullover. She drew her jacket across her chest. His lips curved into a leer. The pounding in her chest accelerated.

"You're still my wife, whatever lies you delude yourself with. Give up your plans to open that silly café. It'll never happen, and I'll never sign divorce papers." He squeezed her breast painfully.

She squirmed against him. "Stop it!"

Suddenly Aidan flew backward and Olivia was temporarily blinded by sand. When she registered what was happening, she saw Jonas on top of Aidan, punching him in the face. Aidan's head lolled, and blood spurted from his nose. Olivia was too shocked to emote.

Jonas got to his feet and offered her his hand. He was breathing heavily, and his dark hair was wild and disheveled. "Are you all right?"

"Now I am. Thanks for your help." She caught sight of little Luca standing outside the men's bathroom, staring with horror at the scene unfolding before him. "I'm sorry your son had to witness this."

"*You* have nothing to be sorry for." He didn't relinquish her hand, and his touch sent a tingling sensation down her arm. "Has he done this before?"

She glared at Aidan's prostrate form. "On occasion."

"Jesus, Olivia. You have to report him."

"You don't understand. He's my father's boss and my parents' creditor. Until I have the funding for my café secured, I can't afford to piss him off."

"So you'll let yourself be a punching bag for their sakes?"

"This town runs on cronyism, and Aidan's a solicitor. I don't stand a chance at making charges stick."

His features hardened. "Bollocks. Your parents' debt is not your responsibility. They need to cop on and grow up."

Olivia bristled at his words even though she knew he was right. He wasn't saying anything she hadn't thought a million times.

In the background, Aidan moaned, rising unsteadily from the sand and clutching his nose. "I'll get you for this, O'Mahony. I have influential friends in this town. You won't get served in any shop, pub, or restaurant within a twenty-kilometer radius." He sounded like a ham actor in a third-rate play. Hysterical laughter bubbled in Olivia's throat, but she had more sense than to indulge the impulse.

Jonas cast him a withering glare. "I'm not letting a wife-beating scumbag intimidate me. How would that information be received by your influential friends, not to mention the voters of Ballybeg? You're not our mayor yet."

"Fuck you," Aidan snarled. "I'll make you pay, see if I don't. Olivia, stop sniveling and come here."

Jonas's fingers hovered over her shoulder. "You don't have to go with him," he said gently. "Fiona and Gavin are at the parade. Why don't I give them a call?"

"I don't want to drag my friends into this mess. I haven't been entirely honest with them about...about how bad things are with Aidan."

He quirked an eyebrow. "Don't you think it's time to confide in them?"

She bit her lip. "Perhaps."

"And you *do* have somewhere to go. On a more permanent basis, that is." His steady gaze fixed her to the spot. "If you still want it, the lease for the cottage is yours."

CHAPTER TEN

It wasn't Jonas's first time in Ballybeg Garda Station. He'd interviewed countless Guards, or *Gardaí,* for the Detective Inspector Brady series, including several who worked here. In his relentless quest for accuracy, he'd visited morgues, law courts, and other places of relevance to a homicide detective. He'd shadowed policemen at work, observed an autopsy, and spent countless hours reading police training files. So he was familiar with the sounds, sights, and smells of a country police station.

What he was not used to was being the person interrogated. Hours had passed since Sergeant Seán Mackey showed up on his doorstep to "invite" him to answer a few questions regarding his "unprovoked attack" on Aidan Gant. Barely home from the after-hours doctor with Luca, he wasn't in the mood to deal with this crap. "I told you before. Gant was hurting Olivia, and I intervened. Would *you* stand by and let a guy abuse a woman?"

"I don't hold with domestic abuse." Sergeant Mackey's mouth was a tight line. "And I'm sure Garda Glenn here agrees with me."

Brian Glenn glanced up from his notebook and nodded. "Shame the man you're accusing happens to be Aidan Gant."

"Esteemed solicitor and member of the town council?" Jonas spat. "Bollocks. Brian, you've been stationed in Ballybeg long enough to have formed an impression of the man. And you don't strike me as a fool either, Mackey. You must know Aidan Gant is a sleaze."

Mackey shifted in his seat, a frown highlighting the fine lines etched around his mouth and eyes. Jonas had heard whisperings of some past scandal to do with the Ballybeg's new police sergeant, but he neither knew the particulars nor cared to ask. "I'll not comment on Gant," the sergeant said. "That's more than my job's worth. The problem is that the only adults who witnessed the fight are you, Gant, and Olivia, and you don't want your son questioned. At the moment, it's your word against Gant's. And there's no denying the man has a broken nose."

"And I'm not denying I broke it."

"No, you've been straight with us on that score. But that's where your and Gant's stories part ways." Mackey ran a hand through his closely cropped hair. "Gant claims it was an unprovoked attack. You say it was in defense of his wife." With a sigh, the man pushed back his cheap plastic chair. "Come on, Brian. Your notebook is needed elsewhere. We'll have to see what Olivia has to say for herself."

"She's here?" *Thank feck.* If she backed up his version of events, he might make it home to Luca before midnight.

"Yeah. It took us a while to track her down. She'd gone out for a meal with a friend, but she checked in a few minutes ago." Mackey paused in the doorway. "Can we get you a coffee?"

Jonas had drunk more than his fair share of station coffee on previous visits and knew better than to accept. "I'll pass, thanks."

"Suit yourself. You'll have a wait ahead of you, mind."

"I'm getting used to these four walls, Sergeant. The mustard color lends them a certain ambience. Maybe I'll put them in my next mystery novel."

A hint of a smile cracked through Mackey's stern expression. "You do that."

After the door shut behind the policemen, Jonas glanced at his watch. Just past ten o'clock. He drummed the wooden table in a restless rhythm.

A crack of thunder drew his attention to the tiny pane of glass that served for a window. Lightning zigzagged across the night sky and the wind roared. Luca hated storms. He hid under his bed until Jonas coaxed him out with the promise of hot cocoa and a story. The poor little guy would be extra sensitive tonight due to his earache. Gavin didn't know the cocoa trick.

A sour taste invaded Jonas's mouth. If it weren't for Aidan Gant, he'd be where he belonged– home with his son.

***

Seán Mackey's light blue eyes creased in concern. "Are you sure you don't want to press charges?"

Olivia dropped her gaze to her clenched fists and shook her head. "You know what Aidan's like. He'll lie his way out of this, just like he's done before. I only threatened him in the hope he'd drop the charges against Jonas. All *he* was doing was defending me."

Requiring rescuing was galling. Being rescued by Jonas O'Mahony was a new low in the humiliation stakes. Shame burned a path from her scalp to her toes. If she were taller and stronger, she could have defended herself.

"All right, Olivia," Seán said with a sigh. "We can't force you to press charges. Will you at least let us file a report?"

"All right. I don't want this to go to court."

"If he ever causes you grief again, give us a call, yeah?" Brian Glenn said. He was sitting beside Seán, pen and notebook in hand. So far, Olivia hadn't given him much info to write down.

"I will."

Seán's expression was speculative. "I take it this wasn't a one-off?"

She gave a noncommittal shrug. Seán and Brian were good guys, but they were still Guards– members of *An Garda Síochána*, Ireland's famously unarmed police force. She didn't trust cops, especially not the locals– the police commissioner was chummy with Aidan. "A cherub or two may have taken flight during past rows." A fist or two as well, but she preferred to focus on her excellent missile-launching skills. She'd always had good aim. Pity she wasn't handier with her punches.

"You shouldn't have to put up with this." There was an edge to Seán's voice. "No woman should."

Brian gestured to the arm she was cradling. "Can I get you more ice?"

"I'm good, thanks." A little white lie. The pain was worse than she'd anticipated. With a bit of luck, Aidan was writhing in agony. "Can I leave now, or do you two have more questions?"

Seán's brow furrowed. "We've no more questions at present, but where will you go? Surely you're not planning on heading home."

"No way." Her reply was emphatic. "I'm staying with my friend Fiona tonight. We were going to collect my stuff from Aidan's house when you called me."

Relief flooded the police sergeant's face. "That's for the best. Give us a minute to complete the paperwork, and you can leave."

"What about Jonas? Will you let him go?"

He gave her a measured look. "Your story tallies with his. I see no reason to keep him here."

The pressure weighing down her shoulders eased. She'd done her utmost to avoid involving anyone else in her marital difficulties. She could handle Aidan– most of the time– but he wasn't an enemy to underestimate. Jonas was now on his hit list.

A few minutes later, Olivia exited the interrogation room. She'd been in there less than an hour, but it had felt like more. A piping-hot shower to wash the day away was in order.

Fiona was waiting in the lobby, leafing through a glossy magazine. She recoiled at the sight of Olivia holding her arm at an awkward angle. "Oh, Liv. What did that bastard do to you? I knew you were in pain over dinner."

"It's nothing," Olivia assured her. "Believe me, Aidan looks much worse."

Fiona eyed her ice pack askance. "We should go to the hospital."

"Not necessary. Nothing's broken. If I keep it cool, the swelling shouldn't be too bad." No need to worry Fiona by mentioning the pain in her ribs.

Her friend tossed the magazine back on the pile. "You can't let Aidan get away with this. Café or no, you need out of that marriage. A few nights staying at our house isn't going to solve the problem. Why don't you move in with us until you find a place of your own?"

Olivia blinked back tears of gratitude. "I appreciate the offer, but I don't want to drag you into this mess any more than I already have. Besides, you and Gavin need your space."

Fiona rolled her eyes. "Stop being stubborn. If you're not keen on sharing with a couple, my aunt Bridie has a spare bedroom. She loathes Aidan, and she's always been fond of you."

"I still need to get my stuff from Aidan's house." God, facing him was the last thing she wanted to do.

"Not alone. And not tonight. You've been through enough for one day. Gavin and I will go with you tomorrow." Fiona cast a scathing look down the hallway. "He's here, you know."

"Seán told me." And even if the policeman hadn't tipped her off, Aidan's strident tones reverberated off the walls, alerting the entire building to his presence–and his displeasure.

Her friend's nostrils flared. "He's gone too far this time."

Olivia debated telling her about the other times Aidan had "gone too far" but rejected the idea. Fiona had a temper if riled. No point in giving her a reason to lose it when Aidan was in such close proximity. If she was going to be staying with Fiona, or next door in Bridie's cottage, there'd be plenty of time to tell her the unvarnished truth in a setting less likely to get the pair of them arrested.

"Come on." She slipped her good arm through her friend's. "Let's get going while Seán keeps Aidan occupied."

They'd almost reached the main door when Jonas entered the lobby.

Olivia froze and her stomach went into freefall. Here was another man she'd rather not face this evening. But the encounter was inevitable, so best get it over with. She touched Fiona's arm. "Give me a moment, will you?"

Her friend cast a wary glance down the hallway in the direction of Aidan's bellows. "Make it quick, Liv. I want to be out of here before Seán's finished with your toad of a husband. Otherwise, Aidan will have broken bollocks to match his nose."

A slow warmth suffused Olivia's body. She should have confided in Fiona months ago. "I'll meet you at the car in a couple of minutes."

Jonas stood silent and resolute at her approach, his dark orbs never leaving her face. She took a deep breath. "Thank you for defending me. I'm sorry for the consequences."

"No problem. Anyone would have done it."

His gruff voice sent tingles down her spine. "You have more faith in humanity than I do. How's your little boy feeling?"

"Not great. I ended up taking him to the doctor." He grimaced. "Ear infection."

"Poor kid. I hope his meds kick in soon."

Further down the corridor, a door slammed. Olivia whipped round in time to see Aidan stomp out of one of the interrogation rooms. His nose and left eye were red and swollen. The punch had been effective. On instinct, she took a step closer to Jonas.

Once he spotted them, Aidan's face turned puce. "You'll regret this, O'Mahony." His growl was low enough for his words to be inaudible to everyone but them. "And as for my wife..." He let the threat trail off in an ominous ellipsis.

Jonas's icy calm didn't break. "Watch your fists, Gant, especially around women. It wouldn't do for a man in your position to be charged with attacking a female."

"She's my wife." Spittle flew when he spoke.

"All the more reason for you to treat her with respect. If you want a sparring partner, take up boxing."

"All right, lads." Sergeant Seán Mackey entered the lobby at a run. "That's enough. Mr. Gant was leaving, I believe. I'll escort him to his car."

Aidan drew back his lips in a snarl but refrained from comment. Bestowing them with a parting glare, he let the station door slam in the police sergeant's face.

Seán shoved the door open and hovered on the top step. "Have a care, O'Mahony. Don't get too free with your punches again. Frankly, I prefer you interviewing me than the opposite way around. And if Aidan gives you any trouble, Olivia, give us a call."

"I will."

Seán rushed down the steps after Aidan.

Jonas escorted her in silence to Fiona's waiting car. They stopped beside the passenger door. "My offer still stands for the lease."

She felt a rush of relief mixed with dread. She'd been afraid he'd rescind the offer once he'd had time to think it over. She'd been equally afraid he'd follow through. "Then I accept."

He inclined his neck in a brusque nod. "Come by the cottage on Monday afternoon and we'll discuss the details. Say three o'clock?"

"Three o'clock it is."

He strode through the car park, his long legs covering more ground in one step than she did in three. Jonas O'Mahony her landlord...Was it a deal made in heaven or in hell?

CHAPTER ELEVEN

By Monday, Jonas's eyeballs felt as though they'd been sandpapered. With Luca sick and feverish all weekend, sleep was a commodity in short supply. He drained his coffee mug and shoved a plate of stale biscuits across the kitchen table toward his father. "Thanks for babysitting Luca. I'd rather not have to drag him next door while he's ill."

"No problem. Delighted to spend the bank holiday with my grandson. Shame he's too sick to enjoy it." The grooves on Liam's forehead deepened. "Your mother will be spitting mad about the rental contract."

"She'll have to deal with it." Jonas's voice held a hint of steel. "Gant was hurting Olivia. What would you have had me do in that circumstance? Ignore it and walk away? Hell, you raised me better than that."

"Aye, I know." Liam ran a hand through his dark hair, still as thick as it had been in his youth but now graying at the temples. "Unfortunately, Aidan Gant is connected."

"I don't give a toss about his connections. I doubt his sphere of influence extends to the publishing industry."

"Maybe not, but you never know what the future holds. Someday, you might need to get a prop– " Liam caught himself in time "– different job."

A proper job...right. Regardless of Jonas's level of success, his father would never regard writing as a suitable job for a man.

"I'm sorry, son," Liam said, red-faced. "I know you work hard at what you do. It's just..."

"Not what you'd expected one of your sons to do for a living?"

"No, but you're managing to support yourself and Luca."

Barely. He extracted the key to the neighboring cottage from his jeans pocket and pushed back his chair. "Olivia's due next door in a minute. Luca's medicine is in the fridge. He'll need the next dose in an hour."

"What time is the buyer due round to collect the motorcycle?" His father jerked a thumb out the front window to where Jonas's Harley stood on the front lawn.

"'Bout thirty minutes," he said gruffly. "Any problems, let me know."

When he stepped outside his cottage, Olivia was already waiting for him by the gate, hugging her coat in a vain effort to ward off the chill breeze. Her cheeks were paler than usual, making the smattering of freckles across her nose stand out. Shadows hung under eyes like bruises. Here was another person who hadn't spent a restful weekend.

She nodded at the Harley. "Nice bike."

"I'm selling it."

"Why?"

"You want a look inside the cottage or not?" He slid the key into the lock and ushered her inside the empty cottage. "Take a seat," he said, gesturing toward the old table in the center of the main room.

Olivia shrugged off her coat, revealing an emerald green dress. The material clung to her delicate curves, an all too vivid reminder of what lay beneath. Her long red hair was tied back with a green ribbon to match her dress. His fingers itched to untie it and watch her hair cascade down her back. He shifted position in his chair and cleared his throat. "I guess you haven't found anywhere else for the café?"

She arched a slim eyebrow. "Since Saturday? Hardly. Which is why I'm grateful you've agreed to give me the lease."

He grunted and stifled a yawn. "Sorry. I didn't get much sleep."

"I can imagine. How's Luca?"

"A little better, thanks. The antibiotics are beginning to work."

Olivia opened her handbag and extracted a colored box. "An Easter egg. For when he's feeling better."

Jonas blinked in surprise. "Thank you. He'll be thrilled."

"How's this going to work?" she asked with characteristic frankness. "Can you bear the idea of me living next door?"

"Living? I thought you intended to turn the cottage into a café."

"I do. However, I'll need somewhere to live, and I won't have an abundance of cash starting out. Mary was okay with me using the loft."

"Won't it be cramped?"

She shrugged, an almost imperceptible twitch of one elegant shoulder. "I can cope with cramped for a few months."

"In that case, I have no objection." Actually, he had several, but none were rational enough to voice. Instead he opened the spiral notebook before him and glanced at his notes. "If you're good with the financial agreement you had with Mary, let's stick with that."

Olivia's mouth twisted into a wry smile. "As you know, Mary and I never got far enough in our plans to have a written contract."

They looked at one another and, for a moment, time stood still. "I'll have my solicitor draw one up."

"Your solicitor?" She tugged on the beads of her necklace. "Not Aidan, I presume."

"God, no," he exclaimed, aghast. "I wouldn't willingly put business that man's way. I know someone in Dublin who's dealt with a few things for me. She'll take care of the contract."

Olivia nodded, her long fingers toying with the beaded necklace around her slender throat. "Won't the noise of the café bother your writing?"

"Unlikely. My father renovated this building for Mary a few years ago, back when the gift shop was in here. In order to get planning permission to run a business in a residential area, he had to ensure it was soundproofed. When Mary switched it back to a residential rental property, the soundproofing remained intact."

"Speaking of Liam, you said in your e-mail yesterday that you'd like him to get the contract to install the café?"

"Yes. He'll give you a fair deal, so no worries on that score."

"Won't he have a problem working for me?" she asked. "He and your mother aren't exactly my greatest fans."

"Work is money, and times are lean for the building trade. My dad won't let his personal opinion of you get in the way of doing a good job."

Olivia flinched, making him regret his choice of words. He hadn't been entirely honest, either. His mother would be furious over his rash promise to Olivia, but his father would work his calming magic over the telephone lines. At the end of the day, Mam was a financial realist. She and Dad needed the money, and work was work.

Olivia bit her lip, drawing his attention to their rosy hue and her straight pearly white teeth.

"No regrets?" he asked. Maybe he'd get lucky and she'd be the one to bail on their deal.

"No. This café is my ticket to freedom. I'd be a fool not to accept your offer."

"But...?" he prompted.

"But I'm aware you don't like me much. I'm wondering how this will pan out."

"I rather thought the not-liking part was mutual," Jonas countered.

"Touché," she said with a small smile.

"If I felt awkward, I wouldn't have offered you the premises," he lied.

She raised an eyebrow.

"Okay," he admitted. "It feels odd, but we'll get used to it. I need a tenant for this place, and you need space for your café. It's just business. We'll barely see one another."

Her tense shoulders relaxed perceptibly. "Thanks, Jonas. This means a lot to me." She leaned forward and squeezed his hand. Then, eyes widening, she whipped it away. They locked gazes for a beat.

"There is one other thing," he said. "A sort of caveat, if you like." *Hit her with it now and see if she runs.*

"Oh?"

"How do you feel about small children?"

She frowned. "That depends on the child."

"The thing is...," he began. Aw, hell. Best spit it out. "I'm looking for a babysitter for Luca. I need someone to collect him from his school in Cork twice a week and mind him for a couple of hours until I'm done writing for the evening."

Her forehead creased in perplexity. She folded her arms across her chest and fixed him with a bemused half smile. It was a gesture of "You must be desperate if you're asking me."

"Let's just say that offers have not been flooding in."

She considered for a moment before replying. "You'd entrust your son's welfare to me?"

"You're hardly a criminal, Olivia. And from what I hear, you pretty much raised your brothers. I'm assuming you know how to handle a little kid."

She inclined her head. "I still need to work my notice at Aidan's practice. I won't be free until May and then only until the café opens."

"That's fine. I can manage until May." It wasn't as if he had a choice.

"And afterward?"

"My mother will be back from her cruise by the start of June. I'm hoping to have found a regular babysitter beforehand."

"I'm aware Luca has special needs. Is there anything I need to watch out for?"

"No. He's on the autistic spectrum, but it seems to be a mild case. You'll notice oddities in his social interaction, and his speech can be repetitive at times. Other than that, he's a regular six-year-old boy."

"To be frank, apart from my brothers, I'm not exactly a kid person."

Jonas grinned. "Luca's not exactly a people person."

That elicited a small smile from her. "Then we'll get along fine." She reached for her bag. "If it's okay with you, I'd like to take some measurements while I'm here."

"Sure." He stood, almost knocking over his chair. "I'll get out of your way."

"No need. I don't mind if you want to stay."

His cheeks burned and he had that weird, fluttery sensation in his stomach. "I'd better get back to Luca," he said, running a hand through his hair. "He's playing Lego, but I don't like to leave him next door on his own for too long."

"I understand." Olivia hesitated as if she wanted to say something more, but the moment passed.

Jonas shuffled toward the exit. "Close the door when you're done. I'll lock up later."

"Thanks. Enjoy your evening."

"You too." He retreated with as much grace as a six-foot-two man could muster while walking backward. He needed to get a grip.

***

Olivia exhaled after Jonas left. He unsettled her. She needed to get over this strange sensitivity to his presence, especially if she was going to be seeing him on a regular basis. *Not to mention seeing his kid.* That he'd trust her to babysit was both weird and touching. She wasn't joking when she said she wasn't a kid person. Kyle and Ronan were family, but she wasn't the sort to coo over a baby. At least Luca was toilet trained. That counted for something, right?

Focus. The café. She visualized her café on its opening day. She knew where every piece of equipment would be placed. Her first menu was planned, as were the signature dishes for the first couple of months. After years of dreaming, the café would become a reality.

Aidan would pitch a fit once he realized she was serious about leaving, but here and now, she didn't give a feck. To hell with Aidan. To hell with Aidan's mother. To hell with her parents, for that matter. This was her dream, and she was making it come true.

She walked around the cottage with a swell of pride. In addition to the kitchen, it was divided into two rooms plus a loft upstairs. Until she could afford an alternative, she'd transform the loft into a makeshift apartment.

Downstairs she'd take out the doors separating the two rooms to make it one large area. The café would have a simple, but cozy, ambience. The décor should reflect the mood she wanted to create. She'd chosen cream paint for the walls and vintage floral stencils to decorate the rim. Her brother Kyle had promised to help her. When she'd first mentioned opening a café years ago, her mother and a few of her artist friends had promised paintings of local landscapes. Given the circumstances, Victoria wouldn't follow through. Time to search for an alternative.

She'd leave windows at the front of the café unadorned. The tables and chairs were wood and wicker pieces she'd found several years ago at a closing-down sale for a restaurant in Cork. Her grandfather had helped her to restore them, and he was keeping them in his garage until she needed them.

She ran a fingernail down her menu plan. Her food wasn't exotic. She used fresh ingredients to create simple meals that tasted great. She had a twist on traditional Irish dishes such as Irish stew and a variety of sweets and desserts. She'd have fresh bread twice a day and fresh dishes every day. At first, she'd have a minimal staff. She and Jill would manage on their own with Jill's sister helping on Saturdays and over the lunchtime rush.

Working her way around the room with the measuring tape, she planned where to position each table. She didn't want her customers to feel cramped, but neither did she have the luxury of space to place the tables too far away from one another. She corrected her floor plan and made random notes in the margins.

The shrill ring of her phone made her heart leap. *Not Aidan, pretty please.* She wasn't in the mood to deal with him. He'd been out when she and Fiona had collected her stuff earlier, but she couldn't avoid him forever.

She inhaled deeply and checked the display. She frowned. What did Dad want?

"Olivia?" Her father sounded tentative.

"Hi, Dad. What's up?"

"Where are you? The reception is patchy."

"The cottage on Curzon Street." *Damn.* In her relief at the call not being from Aidan, she'd spoken without thinking. Curse her for a fool.

"Eh?" said her father in confusion. "But you lost the bid on the lease."

"I did," Olivia admitted, "but Jonas O'Mahony offered to rent the rooms to me after all. The café is happening."

"That's good," he said in a dubious tone. "If it's what you want."

"It is. Very much. But please don't tell Mum until everything is signed and official."

"I don't like keeping secrets from Victoria, but she's already furious over you leaving Aidan. I don't think she could cope with the idea it's permanent."

Dear old Mum, always thinking of herself. The temptation to make a scathing comment was overwhelming, but Olivia bit her tongue. "I mean it, Dad. This is important. I don't want her blabbing it around town before my loan is confirmed."

"In that case, I'll keep mum." He chuckled at his lame joke.

"Do you promise?"

"Yeah."

Olivia wished she believed him. He hadn't betrayed her yet when she'd asked him to keep a secret, but she didn't underestimate her mother's wield over him. Still, if she were foolish enough to blurt it out, she'd have to live with the consequences.

"Are you still staying with Fiona?"

"No. I moved into Bridie Byrne's spare room yesterday. I'll be there until the cottage is habitable."

"Rather you than me. Bridie always looks at me like I'm something the cat dragged in." He paused and gave a faux hearty laugh: "Say, love, I need to ask you a favor."

And now we come to the real reason for the phone call, she thought with a sigh. *Money.*

"You couldn't lend me a few quid? Just to tide me over until the end of the week."

"How much do you need? I'm not exactly flush with cash myself at the moment."

"Fifty. I can pay you back on Friday. Aidan wants me to stuff envelopes for his campaign, so I'll have some money owed to me."

"Okay, but I'll need it back. I'll give it to you tomorrow at the office."

"You're coming into work?" he asked in surprise.

"Of course. I have to work my notice. You know it'll take at least four years for the divorce to go through, right? I'll have enough legal dealings with Aidan over the coming years without handing him ammunition on a platter."

She rang off. If the gods were smiling down on her tomorrow morning, Aidan would give her the silent treatment.

CHAPTER TWELVE

The gods were not benevolently inclined. Olivia started her Tuesday morning floating on a cloud of optimism. She'd left her letter of resignation on Aidan's nightstand on Sunday afternoon when she and Fiona had collected her stuff plus a registered copy of that letter would arrive in tomorrow's post. In four weeks, she'd be out of this place.

"Olivia," Aidan snapped, jarring her out of her delightful reverie. He hurled a bunch of papers onto her desk. "Get your head out of your arse and get to work. I need these typed up and sent to clients."

He went back into his office, slamming the door behind him. Her soon-to-be ex-husband was furious she'd quit but powerless to stop her. He was equally powerless to prevent her taking the first steps toward getting a divorce. Her heart swelled. For once, *she* had the upper hand.

Dad was at his desk, pretending to work. He'd barely acknowledged her presence, bar the reminder of the money she'd promised him. Though unsurprising, his rejection stung. Even if he was concerned about losing the bits of work Aidan threw his way, she wished he'd show a bit of backbone. She gritted her teeth and opened up her mail client. Time to get to work.

When her mother sauntered in the door shortly after her ten o'clock coffee break, Olivia's fluffy cloud of optimism took on a decidedly gray tinge. Victoria wore a floral maxi dress and wafted lilac perfume. Olivia's nostrils itched.

"Hello, darling," she said breezily and treated her husband to a passionate kiss.

Olivia gave an internal eye roll. Her parents loved public displays of affection. They were the sort of feckless, reckless couple so caught up in one another that they failed to acknowledge the rest of the world, their children included.

The moment Victoria made a beeline for Aidan's office, Olivia's sense of foreboding turned to full-blown panic. Her mother knocked, and Aidan bade her enter.

"Dad?" she asked once the door shut behind Victoria.

"Hmm?" He was finding his stack of campaign brochures fascinating.

A wave of nausea hit her like a tsunami. "You told Mum, didn't you?"

He hunched his shoulders and he muttered a response. Her stomach sank. No wonder he hadn't been able to look her in the eye this morning. She shouldn't be surprised, but she'd hoped he'd have enough paternal feeling toward her not to betray her secret to her mother. She was an eejit for letting it slip in the first place. Why was he such a wimp?

"You swore to me you wouldn't tell her." She choked back tears. "Now she's going to tell Aidan, and he'll do something to sabotage the café."

"Don't exaggerate, Olivia." Her father's laugh was hollow. "Even if she does tell him, he can't stop you now that you have the lease."

If only she were so sanguine. The next half hour dragged. Her father had errands to run for Aidan and escaped the office with indecent haste. Olivia tried to focus on work, but her attention wandered to the low rumble of voices from Aidan's office. Feck Victoria. If she had an ounce of maternal feeling, she'd want her daughter to be happy. While she'd never been deliberately cruel, her offhand comments and blatant disregard for anyone's comfort apart from her own and her husband's made Olivia wary of her motives.

When her mobile phone began to ring, one glance at caller display told her the game was up. She swallowed hard. Maybe, just maybe, there was still a chance.

"Olivia?" An anxious voice was rarely the bearer of good news. "This is Mairéad from the bank. I'm sorry to tell you this, but your loan has been denied."

"What?" Olivia gasped. "But I have an appointment with Paddy this afternoon."

"I'm calling to cancel it," said Mairéad with obvious regret. "I'm sorry. I know how much the café meant to you."

Olivia's fingers went rigid. "Don't I get an explanation? Paddy told me I had until after Easter to get a lease, and I have one. Can I speak with him?"

"I'm afraid he's busy at the moment..." Mairéad's voice trailed off. "Olivia, it's hopeless. My advice to you would be to try another bank, preferably outside Ballybeg. But that's strictly between us."

Her gaze darted to the door of Aidan's office. The bastard. He'd set this up. If she'd had any sense– at least one of foreboding– she should have foreseen that Aidan would scheme to put a stop to her plans. "Thanks, Mairéad. I know you're only the messenger."

She hung up and glared at Aidan's door. Her entire body quivered with ill-suppressed fury. The absolute prick. She shoved back her desk chair and made to stand. At that moment, her mother emerged from Aidan's lair. Her demeanor was furtive and shifty.

Olivia's breath turned to ice. "My loan application was rejected."

Victoria flinched but betrayed no flicker of surprise.

"Did you tell Aidan about Jonas's offer?"

A muscle in her mother's cheek twitched. "He had a right to know, Olivia. He is your husband."

"How could you? You knew he'd do his utmost to stop it from happening."

"It's for the best, believe me." Victoria's gaze didn't leave the carpet.

The cloying perfume hung in the air like a shroud. "For you or for me?"

"Don't be self-centered. You know we depend on Aidan."

"No, *you* depend on Aidan, Mother," snapped Olivia. "I'm sick of being the sacrificial lamb on the altar of your financial irresponsibility."

Victoria's emerald green eyes rose. "He's your husband. Your duty is to be with him."

"My duty? And what about his duty toward me?" Olivia's chest swelled in outrage. "He sleeps with any tart he can get his slimy way with and treats me like dirt. You're my mother. Don't you want me to be happy?"

"Of course I do, darling. But I think you need to try harder. Relationships take a lot of work, you know."

"You selfish bitch. You only ever think of yourself, don't you?"

Victoria's mouth turned down, displaying hurt. "Of course not. I'm thinking of what's best for our family. You don't want the boys to be homeless, do you?"

"If you and Dad lose the house, it'll be your own fault. Stop shoving responsibility for your mistakes off on me."

"How dare you judge me?" Her mother's lower lip quivered. "You know nothing of the sacrifices I've made for your sake."

"Deciding to have me and marry Dad was your decision."

A tear slid down Victoria's cheek. "I had to drop out of art school."

Olivia rolled her eyes. Any moment now, the violins would start playing. "If you'd been motivated, you could have gone back any time these past twenty-nine years."

"It's not that simple."

"Perhaps not. But don't blame me, Dad, or the boys for your life decisions."

"I am an artist, Olivia. Have you any idea what it's like to have your creativity crushed?"

No. She was more familiar with having her self-esteem trampled.

"By domesticity?" she asked. Oh, the irony. Her mother wouldn't know how to operate a washing machine if her life depended on it.

Victoria sniffed. "Among other things. I know I haven't been the perfect mother, but I've tried my best."

"If manipulating me into staying in a crappy marriage is an example of you 'trying your best,' you've got a lot to learn." Olivia stood. She was four centimeters taller than Victoria, but her mother's towering heels gave her the advantage. "I want you to leave."

Victoria didn't move.

Olivia strode toward the door and yanked it open. "Leave," she repeated, her voice ice cold.

Victoria tossed her auburn curls over her shoulder. "Very well. I hope you'll reflect on your behavior and apologize to me. You're behaving like a spoiled child."

That was rich coming from her. Olivia was close to exploding. She let the door slam behind her so-called mother and stomped back to her desk.

She needed to contemplate her next move. There *had* to be a bank willing to give her a start-up loan, especially given the reasonable terms of the lease. The local enterprise board had already approved her start-up grant, meaning she had to raise fifty percent of the capital. With thirty percent in savings, she needed a bank willing to loan her the last twenty percent.

She dragged air into her lungs. So near, yet so far. She eyed the paperweight on her desk and resisted the urge to hurl it at Aidan's door. Knowing her luck, the bastard would choose that moment to walk through it, and she'd have given him a real reason to haul her into court.

If she had the materials to hand, she'd be tempted to make a voodoo doll of her mother. *Ah, hell.* These negative thoughts were getting her no nearer to finding a solution. Feck Aidan and his rules about not making personal calls during working hours. Olivia wrenched open her desk drawer and extracted her copy of the yellow pages. Time to start calling banks.

CHAPTER THIRTEEN

"So Jacinta." Jonas examined the creased resumé. "What sort of childcare experience do you have? I don't see any mentioned here."

Jacinta stared at him through large vacant eyes and chewed gum. "What do you mean childcare experience? Like a daycare center or something?"

"Precisely."

"Nah. But I pet-sat for my neighbor a few years ago."

"Pet-sat?" A vision of Wiggly Poo, Gavin's dog, sprang to mind.

"Yeah." She shifted the gum from one plump cheek to the other. "An aquarium."

"Did the fish survive?" asked Luca, regarding his would-be babysitter with suspicion.

Jacinta shrugged. "Most of them. There were a couple of floaters by the end of the week, but what can you do?"

Luca exchanged a significant look with his father. "I don't want to be a floater."

"Right." Jonas thrust a determined hand at his guest. "Thanks for coming by Jacinta. I'll see you out."

Jacinta was startled out of her bovine placidity. "What? That's it? Did I get the job?"

"I'm afraid not. I'm looking for someone with childcare experience, preferably with kids on the autism spectrum. That's what I said on the phone."

"Yeah, but I didn't know what you meant. What spectrum?" Blinking, Jacinta allowed herself to be led to the front door, bundled into her raincoat, and politely-but-firmly shoved off the premises.

"Bye, now. Watch the step."

"I never," the woman huffed, her confusion turning to annoyance as comprehension dawned. "Shortest interview I've had in my life." She stomped out the gate and careened into Olivia, who was getting out of her car.

If Olivia was surprised to be stampeded by an irate stranger, she rallied. "Good morning. Glad to see I'm not the only person in Ballybeg who puts a frown on your face."

Jonas laughed. "A potential babysitter."

An amused half-smile lurked on Olivia's face. "Won't do?"

Luca peeked out from behind his father's legs. "She's a fish killer."

"Good lord." Olivia approached the door and shook out her umbrella. "How were the other candidates?"

"Equally uninspiring." Jonas gestured for her to enter. "We had a militant smoker who refused point-blank to respect our home as a no-smoking zone."

"Then there was the chakras lady," Luca piped up. "She was going to chakra autism out of me."

Olivia's slim shoulders heaved with laughter. The narrow entry way seemed to shrink with her in it. Which, given her size, was ridiculous. He felt a stirring in his groin and exhaled sharply. Now was not the time for his libido to make its presence known.

"I promise not to smoke, kill fish, or chakra anything when I babysit for you, Luca. Sound good?"

The boy nodded. "Thanks for my Easter egg. It was yummy."

Her warm smile was infectious. "You're welcome. Are you feeling better?"

"Yes. But I'm done talking. I need to finish building my spaceship."

"Go on," Jonas patted him on the shoulder, and the boy scampered off in the direction of the living room.

Olivia slipped off her blue raincoat, sending rivulets of water dripping onto the thread-worn mat. "Sorry to barge in without calling first."

"No problem. For once, our living room is looking respectable. Come on through."

"Yeah," Luca called over his shoulder. "Dad cleared the sofa. Now we can sit on it."

Jonas's cheeks grew warm. "We're still settling into the new house."

When she registered the moving boxes stacked in a haphazard fashion throughout the cottage, Olivia's eyes danced with merriment. "So I see."

"What can I do for you?" Jonas asked, settling into an overstuffed armchair. "Do you need the key to the cottage?"

"No, not at the moment." Her every thought flickered across her face in the jerky motion of an old film reel.

Her total inability to suppress emotions was one of the reasons he'd fallen in love with her all those years ago.

"What's up?"

Her lower jaw flexed and she averted her gaze. "I have a favor to ask."

"Is this about the lease?" *Feck.* If she backed out of the deal now, the time he'd spent placating his mother on the phone last night would have been for nothing. That phone call had more than filled this week's hassle quota.

"Yes, it's about the lease." Her tone was tentative. "My loan application was rejected on Tuesday. I need to find a bank willing to loan me money, and I haven't found one yet."

Jonas frowned. "I thought the loan was a done deal once you had the lease."

"So did I."

He shifted in his seat. "Where does that leave our arrangement?"

"As it stood before, if you're willing. I can cover the rent for a few months, plus your father's fee. My start-up grant was approved on the condition I raise the rest of the capital. I do have some savings, and they will cover most of the set-up costs. I need a bank willing to loan me the difference or I'll have very little to live on while I establish the business."

Jonas leaned forward. "Did Aidan wreck your chance of getting the loan approved?"

She fiddled with her fingers. "I can't prove anything – and he admits nothing– but I suspect he exerted influence over Paddy O'Neill."

"The vindictive bastard." He should have expected Aidan would do something to jeopardize the café.

"My sentiments exactly, but it doesn't do me any good to dwell on it."

"Don't stress it. I'm not going to back out of our deal." As long as she had the first few months of rent, he could afford to be magnanimous.

"Thanks, Jonas." She paused and then laughed. "I seem to be saying that a lot these days, don't I? Who'd have thought?"

Jonas shifted, a prickling warmth creeping up his neck. "No need to thank me. We both benefit from the arrangement. You get a place for your café. I get a babysitter for the month of May."

"Speaking of which, when would you like me to start looking after Luca? I still have to work my notice at Aidan's practice, but I have some holidays saved up."

He stared at her, trying to make his mouth form words. Few people on the planet possessed the ability to rob him of speech. Olivia was one. "You don't mind using your holidays?"

"Of course not. We have a deal."

"How does next Monday sound? We can start off by you having him for an hour or two and work it up from there."

Her fingers flew over her phone's display, bringing up her calendar. "Yeah, Monday afternoon should work. The new oven is being installed in the morning, and I want to try it out. Are you interested in helping me bake, Luca?"

The boy didn't glance up from his Lego. "What? Yummy stuff?"

"I hope so. I'm trying a few scone recipes in the new oven. You can be my taste tester."

Luca fixed Olivia with an unblinking stare. "Okay. But I'll tell you if they're gross. If that'll upset you, I'm the wrong kid for the job."

Olivia choked back laughter. "Honesty is what I'm looking for. I think you'll be ideal."

Her eyes met Jonas's for the briefest of moments, and the smile on her face faded. "I'd better get going. I'm on my lunch break, and I don't want to push my luck with Aidan."

Jonas leaped to his feet and accompanied her to the front door.

She touched his motorcycle helmet, still in its usual spot. A pang of regret squeezed his insides. "Did you buy a new bike?"

"No. I might someday, when Luca is past his ph– "

"His what?"

"Phase. He was getting panic attacks whenever I went out on my bike. Worried I'd have an accident." He focused on the smooth surface of the helmet. "The attacks stopped the day I sold the Harley."

"Wow. You loved that bike. I remember– " she stopped and their eyes locked, shared memories reflected.

Olivia cleared her throat. "I'd better go."

"Best of luck with the loan."

"Thanks. I'll need it. See you next week."

After she stepped out into the rain, he stared at her retreating back through the colored glass.

"Dad?"

"Hmm?"

"Olivia is pretty."

Yes, she was. More than pretty. Beautiful enough to rob him of speech and sanity.

"She's a lot prettier than Jacinta. And she smells better too."

Jonas let out a bark of laughter and ruffled his son's hair. "Come on, mate. Let's finish putting together your spaceship."

CHAPTER FOURTEEN

She was humming again. Jonas shoved his desk chair back from the computer screen. More than two weeks had passed since he'd lost his mind and offered Olivia the lease for the cottage. In that time, rainy April had changed to warm May. The cottages were soundproofed, but the heat had driven him to open his office window.

His new neighbor was proving to be a damned nuisance. If she wasn't humming, she was singing, and if she wasn't humming or singing, she was chattering to her friend Jill or to his father's workmen. The irritatingly cheerful noises next door, combined with the delicious baking smells, were tormenting his senses. They were making it impossible to concentrate on the task at hand: namely, killing his next victim in the most gruesome manner imaginable.

Jonas massaged his throbbing forehead. After a brief reprieve when the earache cleared up, Luca was back to not sleeping. And if Luca didn't sleep, his father didn't, either. To add to the pressure, Jonas was due to meet his agent in Dublin in a few weeks. He'd promised her polished proposals for his next two novels plus two scripts for a potential new TV series. For the first time in his career, he was facing a deadline he doubted he could meet. And for the first time in months, he craved a cigarette. But it had taken him so long to kick the habit there was no way he was going to succumb.

He needed air. Yeah, a walk along the beach would do him good. Jonas locked the door of the cottage and headed down the short garden path. Christ, not even the garden was safe. The flowers reminded him of Olivia's perfume– something fresh and floral.

"Dad." Luca stood on the threshold of the café, a cream bun in one hand and his dinosaur encyclopedia in the other. "Where are you going?"

"For a walk. Want to join me?"

The boy shook his head. "We're busy baking. Wanna come in? I have to pick fresh flowers from the garden. I'm helping with the window display."

Jonas hesitated. He should keep walking. Melodious humming and the scent of fresh scones wafted through the door. "Maybe for a minute."

Inside the cottage, the café was taking shape. The kitchen was already in place, and the newly painted white walls gleamed. Olivia was alone in the kitchen, wrestling a tray from the oven.

"Hey," he said. "Hope I'm not interrupting."

***

She jumped at the sound of his voice and her hand brushed against the oven door, sending heat searing through the soft flesh. "What are you doing here?" In the few days since she'd taken possession of the cottage, he'd never once ventured inside, confining their contact to curt business e-mails and text messages.

"The smell wafting in my windows lured me round." An amused half-smile broadened. "Among other things."

A jolt of electricity coursed through her veins. "Other things?" she asked, tilting her nose in the air. She channeled bored indifference. At least, that was the aim.

"Luca asked me in. Do you know you have berry juice all over your cheek?"

Drat. Her right hand flew to her face on instinct, the stinging pain reminding her it was the one she'd just burned. She emitted an involuntary hiss.

"We need to get that hand under cold water." He moved toward her with the stealth and grace of a panther. "Sorry for startling you. I knocked, but I guess you didn't hear me with your humming."

She cradled her sore hand protectively. "It's fine," she lied. Actually, it hurt like the devil.

Jonas raised an eyebrow. What cruel gods had blessed that man with such long eyelashes and bestowed short, stubby ones on her? "Do you want a blister?" he demanded.

"No," she muttered.

"Put it under running water."

He turned on the kitchen tap and let the water run a moment. When he was satisfied with the temperature, he reached for her arm. As if in a trance, she let him guide her hand toward the cool flow. The rush of adrenalin this time had little to do with the relief of ice-cold water cascading over her burn.

"Is that better?"

"Yes," she murmured. There was something perverse about getting turned on while treating a burn injury. She hadn't been this close to Jonas in years. Not since... before Bry drowned. She swallowed hard, and her heart beat an uneven rhythm in her chest. When was the last time she'd felt sexually aroused? Six months? A year? So long ago, she'd all but forgotten the sensation.

His strong fingers skimmed the sore spot on her hand. "You need ointment and a bandage."

"There's no need." She made to pull her hand free and winced from the pain.

The sensual lips formed a sardonic half smile. "There's every need. Do you have a first aid kit? If not, I have one next door."

"There's one in the cupboard over the stove."

He pulled away, causing an odd yearning in her for his return. "This it?" He held up a small green pouch for her inspection.

She nodded and watched him wash his hands before removing ointment and gauze from the kit. Her intake of breath when he spread gel on her hand was as much a reaction to his touch as it was to the pain from her wound. His big hands were surprisingly gentle. The sensation of his fingertips moving across wounded skin was part bliss, part torture. He was close enough for her to catch a whiff of his aftershave– something spicy paired with something inescapably male. Her breath caught somewhere between her lungs and throat.

"Did your father tell you about the sink? He said I should ask you to fix it, but I didn't want to interrupt your writing time." Now she was babbling. *Fantastic.*

His dark eyes rose. "What's wrong with the sink?"

"The part underneath the sink is leaking."

"I'm no plumbing expert, but I'll check it out. Did Dad leave any tools here?"

"Yeah." She pointed to a small tool kit on the kitchen counter. "You sure this isn't dragging you away from your writing?"

"Nah," he replied, investigating the contents of the box. "I need a break. Sometimes focusing on something practical helps clear my mind." He knelt down before the sink, fiddled around, and poked his head out. "This needs tightening. Won't take me a minute."

The denim of his jeans molded his buttocks to perfection. Warmth coursed through her body. She should look away but couldn't drag her attention from him. She fanned herself. The heat was unbearable– and it wasn't all down to the warm weather. "Thanks. I was worried I'd have a flood in here before evening."

"It's not that serious," he said in amusement.

He removed a few tools from the kit, the names of which eluded Olivia. She'd imagined having Liam O'Mahony and his crew underfoot would be awkward, but it was nothing compared to being in close proximity with his son. Actually, she and Liam had formed a working arrangement that suited both of them: They ignored one another unless communication was necessary, and Liam got on with his job. Olivia looked around the café in appreciation. There was no denying he'd done excellent work in record time. Although there were still a few minor things to be done, she was on schedule to open on the first of June.

"Not bad, eh?" Jonas's deep rumble interrupted her thoughts. He clambered to his feet and cast his gaze around the kitchen.

"The café? Yeah, your dad and his team are doing themselves proud."

"You and Luca are practicing using the equipment?" he asked, nodding toward the cooling tray of berry scones.

"I want to become familiar with the oven before we open. Getting the timing wrong for a recipe when we're in a rush would be disastrous."

"I'm sure you'll have everything under control. You're the type."

"Are you disparaging my Type A personality?"

He chuckled. "Your words, Olivia, not mine."

For an instant, their gazes held and time stood still. He took a step closer, his eyes warm with– was that desire?– and his gaze riveted on her mouth. Her breath caught. Was he about to...

"Dad? Olivia?"

They froze millimeters apart.

Luca stood in the center of the café, bearing a basket of flowers. "What do you think? They're pretty, aren't they? I picked ten of each color."

"Uh, yeah." Olivia took an awkward step back and shoved a stray strand of hair behind her ear. "They're gorgeous. Thanks for picking them."

The little boy smiled but didn't meet her eyes. They were making progress, she and Luca. More frequent eye contact would come with time.

In the distance, the church bells chimed.

Jonas cleared his throat. "Is it that time already? I'd better get back to work. Send Luca over for his dinner in an hour or so."

On instinct, she caught his arm. His warm brown eyes burned into her. "Speaking of Luca...I'm to collect him tomorrow at three o'clock, is that right?" she asked in a faltering voice. It would be her first time looking after Luca outside the café, and she was dreading the occasion. Baking with him for an hour was one thing. What would she do to entertain him all afternoon?

"Yeah, if you can swing it."

"Of course I can. Babysitting was part of our arrangement. What time should I bring him home?"

Jonas disengaged himself from her grasp and packed his father's tools back into their box. "I finish writing at around seven."

"Okay. We'll be back by then. I'll give him something to eat before I drop him home."

He shook his head. "No need to go to any trouble."

"It's not a bother," she insisted. "I eat dinner at around five. Does he have any food allergies?"

“No food allergies. Pollen and dust set off his asthma. You got my e-mail with details on his asthma meds?”

“Yeah. My youngest brother has it, so I know what to do.”

“Excellent.” He gave a brief nod, his gaze darting away. “If there’s any problem, give me a ring.”

“There shouldn’t be,” she assured him with more confidence than she felt. “I’ll be round after lunch to collect his car seat.”

“Okay.” He placed the tool kit back on the counter. “See you tomorrow.”

He flashed her a bone-melting smile and exited the café, leaving Olivia with the tantalizing scent of his aftershave and the unwelcome notion she was finding him far too attractive for comfort.

CHAPTER FIFTEEN

Luca's program was held in the center of Cork City. Olivia arrived early, found a parking space near Mercy University Hospital, and availed herself of the opportunity to window-shop while she killed some time. The summer fashions were out in force. She gazed wistfully in the window of a tiny boutique on Oliver Plunkett Street. If only the price tags weren't way beyond her tight budget.

The main shopping area was a short walk down the quays from the building in which Luca's therapy program was housed. She found the modern red brick building with ease and took the elevator to the third floor.

The instant she stepped out of the lift, she was greeted by the sound of kids yelling. *Oh, boy.*

Luca's teacher-therapist, Ms. O'Brien, was expecting her and waved through the glass door in greeting. Ms. O'Brien proved to be young, blond, and exuberant.

"It's lovely to meet you," she gushed, pumping Olivia's hand as if she were a visiting celebrity. "Jonas said you were coming today. I will warn you Luca is a bit out of sorts. He likes routine, and he's used to his dad or his gran collecting him. I reminded him throughout the morning that you're coming. Hopefully, that will make the transition smoother." The teacher pivoted on her fuchsia slippers and trilled: "Luca! Olivia's here."

Luca emerged from the mass of children. He looked unimpressed to see her. "Where's my dad?"

"I told you, pet." Ms. O'Brien beamed at him, unperturbed by his surly attitude. "Your dad can't collect you today. Olivia will babysit you for the next few hours."

Luca's gaze was trained on a point past Olivia's shoulder.

"Eye contact," whispered Miss O'Brien.

The boy ignored her. "What will we do all afternoon? I don't want to bake again. It's getting boring."

Olivia gave him an ineffectual pat on the shoulder. "We'll figure something out. Do you have your coat?"

His eyes never leaving the mysterious point past her left shoulder, Luca fetched his jacket from a low peg in the cloakroom. Olivia helped him to do up the zip while Ms. O'Brien located his shoes. Hopefully his wariness would ease off over the course of the afternoon.

Ms. O'Brien handed her the little boy's school bag. "I'll see you tomorrow, Luca. Have fun with Olivia."

Luca and Olivia slid one another dubious glances, his eyes skimming past hers for a second. *Fun...for four hours?* The drive back to Ballybeg would take thirty minutes, give or take, leaving a good couple of hours before it was time to bring him home. It had been a long time since she'd babysat a small child. When her brothers were young, she'd followed their lead and figured it out as she went along.

But this kid was different. He came fully formed with a preprogrammed agenda and set ideas but wasn't always the best at communicating his expectations. Olivia swallowed a sigh. She'd agreed to look after the child, and she'd follow through.

They exited the building and paused on the pavement. Drops of rain had started to fall. "So...what would you like to do today, Luca? Play a game? Read a story? Eat a snack?" Her mouth stretched into a rictus of a smile. The options she'd reeled off sounded lame even to her ears. Judging by the expression on his face, Luca found them equally uninspired.

"Are we going back to Ballybeg?" he demanded.

It hadn't occurred to her to do otherwise. But come to think of it, it might be easier to keep him entertained in the city than in Bridie's ornament-crammed house. Until Liam O'Mahony and his crew had a chance to convert the cottage's loft into a temporary apartment, she was still availing herself of Bridie's hospitality.

Olivia scanned her surroundings. A brightly colored plastic sign caught her attention. *Playland: A Paradise for Children of All Ages.* Perfect. With a bit of luck, it was also a sanctuary for desperate babysitters. "Have you been to Playland before?"

Luca eyed the colorful sign warily and shook his head.

"Come on. Let's give it a go." She took his hand in hers. It felt small, warm, and suspiciously sticky. They crossed the street and pushed open the bright green door.

Inside, Playland was more reminiscent of purgatory than paradise. Oppressive heat, clashing colors, and the cacophony of a hundred squealing children. And if the stench was anything to go by, there was a plumbing problem in the bathrooms. *Well, feck.* To think she'd forked over twenty-five euros for this hellhole...

She exhaled through clenched teeth and attempted to let go of Luca's hand. "Let's take off your jacket and shoes. Why don't you try out that climbing frame? The winding slide at the top looks cool."

Luca clung to her hand with a vise-like grip. This did not bode well.

She tried again. "The sliding tube might be fun. Or the bouncy castle?"

The little boy shook his head.

"Come on, Luca. You have to try something." She tugged down the zip of his jacket and hung it by the entrance. His shoes came next. He placed them neatly underneath the coat. "See?" she said with determined cheer. "You're all set to play."

"I wanna go home," he said. "It's too loud."

"We've already paid. Let's try to have fun. There's got to be something here you like."

The kid scanned the room. "I guess that climbing wall looks okay."

"Fantastic. You go on up, and I'll take a photo with my phone to send your dad. Sound good?"

Luca shrugged. "I suppose." Looking like a convicted man on the way to meet his executioner, he took a cautious step toward the climbing wall. Bracing himself, he began his ascent, careful and deliberate.

"You're doing great," she called, standing back to get a good shot. "Your dad will be so proud."

Everything was fine until he reached the second to last rung. He froze, hanging there suspended, neither moving up nor down. *Aw, feck.* She shoved her phone into her pocket and battled her way through hordes of children.

"What's wrong with him?" demanded a pug-faced girl of around seven. "Why isn't he moving?"

"I don't know," Olivia said. "Maybe he's afraid."

Pug-Face wrinkled her flat nose. "He's a scaredy cat."

"We're all scared of something, kid. Now move your ar– bum and let me get through." She reached the bottom of the climbing wall. Her charge hadn't moved a millimeter. "Come on, Luca," she shouted in what she hoped was an encouraging tone. "Climb down a bit, and I'll lift you down the rest of the way."

The boy didn't so much as twitch a muscle, never mind move. He was chanting something under his breath, half moan, half prayer. Sweat beaded beneath the collar of her blouse and underneath her arms. Desperation and central heating were doing a number on her. She stretched up, but he was too high to reach.

Being short was wretched. Not even her four-inch heels added sufficient height.

"Luca, you can't stay up there all afternoon. There's a queue of kids behind you waiting to use the slide. You need to either climb up to the platform and slide down or reverse."

No response, not even a flicker of movement. The chanting grew louder. *Drat.* What was she to do?

"He's a right thicko," Pug-Face said with sufficient volume to reach Luca and half the Playland clientele. "We've got one in my class. He goes to special ed."

"He's not thick," Olivia said through gritted teeth. "He's scared."

Pug-Face was unimpressed. "He's bloody thick. Why's he moaning like that?"

"Piss off and play," snapped Olivia. "You're not helping the situation."

More and more children began complaining about the blocked access to the slide, the sea of disgruntled little faces growing ever wider. The noise was driving her to the edge. How many kids did they squeeze into this joint, anyway? There had to be a hundred brats clamoring for Luca to move. Okay, maybe a hundred was an exaggeration, but there were enough to make her vow to get her tubes tied at the earliest opportunity.

At the top of the ladder, Luca remained resolutely still.

"Right. Guess I'll have to join him." She kicked off her heels and yanked her pencil skirt up her thighs. Had she known scaling a kid's climbing wall would be on today's agenda, she'd have worn jeans. The last of the queuing children reluctantly cleared a path for her.

The first part was easy. But the higher she climbed, the clearer it became that the grips in the wall were designed for hands and feet far smaller than hers. After a few embarrassing missteps, she overtook Luca and pulled herself up onto the small platform separating the climbing wall from the slide.

"Give me one of your hands," she said, panting.

Luca hesitated, then slowly reached a tentative arm up.

"Good boy. And now the other."

She hauled the child up beside her. He sat rigid on the wooden platform, hands over ears, his incessant chanting a monotonous mantra. "Luca, we're going to have to go down the slide. You know that, don't you? We can't sit up here all day. There are kids waiting."

"Get down, you moron," Pug-Face shouted, pudgy arms folded over her fluorescent pink T-shirt. "I want a turn."

"Yeah," yelled another kid. "Stop making that stupid noise and slide down."

"Why does he have his hands over his ears?" a small girl asked in confusion. "If his singing's too loud for him, why doesn't he stop?"

"Because he's a thicko," Pug-Face repeated smugly. "Even if he doesn't have a flat face like the one in my class."

"Jaysus, girl," Olivia snapped. "You're one to talk. Take a look in the mirror before criticizing another kid."

Pug-Face's lower lip quivered. "Mammy, did you hear what she said to me?"

A woman with electrocuted bleach-blond hair and an orange spray tan materialized by the girl's side. She gawked up at Olivia. "Did you just insult my Patsy?"

Olivia met her glare for glare. "Yes, I did. I've been trying to coax Luca down, and your Patsy's constant taunting is *not* helping the situation."

The woman crossed her arms over her leopard print chest in a pose to match her daughter's. "I've raised her to speak her mind. If she doesn't like someone, she should say so."

"That's all well and good, but not when she's using it to make ableist comments."

"What are you on about?" Leopard-Print stared at her. "You're as thick as your kid. Shut him up and get him down. Patsy wants a turn."

"He's a thicko," whined Pug-Face aka Patsy. "He needs to go to a home for spastics."

"Did you hear what she said?" Olivia took Luca's small hand in hers and glared at the girl's mother. "Is this what you mean about Patsy being entitled to speak her mind?"

The woman's Oompa Loompa face twisted in disgust. "He is a spastic, isn't he? He's not normal."

Luca stiffened beside her, his small body going even more rigid than it had been before.

Olivia squeezed his hand. "Do you even know what spastic means, you daft woman? Because if you did, you'd know what you're saying makes no damn sense."

"Whatever he is, he belongs in a home."

The taut thread of what was left of Olivia's frayed patience snapped. "Patsy can bloody well wait. Luca and I are going to sit up here for as long as it takes. We'll come down when we're good and ready."

With that, she put her hands over her ears and began to chant, mimicking Luca's tone. The louder she got, the quieter the boy became. Finally he stopped altogether, his dark orbs meeting hers. It was the first time he'd initiated and maintained eye contact. The dark shade and almond shape of his eyes were identical to his father's.

She gave him a smile. "You ready to slide down? You can sit on my lap."

He dropped his hands from his ears and nodded.

At the bottom of the slide, a crowd of irate parents and children awaited. A beefy man wearing a bright yellow Playland T-shirt loomed over them. The embroidered label on his chest proclaimed him to be the manager of the establishment. "I'm going to have to ask you to leave. We can't have one child disrupting everyone else's fun."

"Luca got scared," she snapped, glaring up at the big man. "He didn't set out to sabotage other people's fun."

"She insulted my Patsy," whined the leopard print woman.

"Your Patsy needs to learn manners and tolerance. Calling people names isn't a desirable character trait."

"Ladies, please." The Playland manager wore an exasperated expression. "You're setting a terrible example for the children."

"What crap," Olivia said. "Most of them are behaving like feral beasts. I doubt we can set them a worse example."

The manager's face turned beet red. "It's time you left."

"I've been chucked out of classier places than this joint. Your clientele stinks and so do your bathrooms." Olivia struggled to her feet and grabbed Luca's hand. "Come on, kid. Let's exit this hellhole."

CHAPTER SIXTEEN

Jonas stood in the hallway of his cottage, doubled up with laughter. "Playland?" he exclaimed between heaves. "Were you out of your mind? That place is a cesspit."

Olivia wrinkled her gorgeous little nose. "It certainly smelled like one."

His hand skimmed her shoulder when he took her coat and hung it on the makeshift coat stand next to Luca's little jacket. Her sweet, musky scent teased his erogenous zones when she moved past him toward the living room.

"I'm going to bed," Luca said, tearing off in the direction of his room and his beloved dino encyclopedia.

"Hey, wait a minute. Don't I get a good night kiss?"

The boy jerked to a halt, hesitated, then turned back to plant a reluctant kiss on his father's cheek.

"I'll be in later to tuck you in, okay?"

Luca nodded. "Night, Dad. Night Olivia."

"Sleep well, Luca," Olivia said, but the boy was already disappearing into the sanctuary of his bedroom.

Jonas exchanged an amused glance with her. "He needs a bit of down time before sleep. A place like Playland isn't ideal for a kid like him. Sensory overload."

"His senses weren't the only ones done in by that place and its clientele," she said dryly. "It's an interactive ad for contraception."

He laughed and ushered her over to the sofa– tidy for once, thank feck. "I can't believe you got yourselves thrown out of a children's play center."

Her dark blue eyes twinkled with merriment. "Laugh away, O'Mahony. I seem to recall you had quite a talent for getting us barred from places in our misspent youth."

He grinned at the memory. "Just the once. And that was because the manager harassed you. Bry was as much to blame."

They froze at the mention of his little brother's name, the humor of the past few minutes evaporating in a millisecond.

"He was a good guy," she said quietly, "and a good friend. I'm sorry for my part in what happened."

"I..." He paused, grappling for the right words. "You know I don't blame you. It was an accident."

A flashback to that awful night hit him like a blow to the solar plexus. The memory of a wet, bedraggled, and terrified Olivia running toward him on the beach. The knowledge that he'd have been at the beach party earlier had it not been for his train from Dublin being delayed. The nagging doubt about whether or not his presence would have made any damn difference to the tragic outcome.

Her mouth trembled, and she pressed her hands to her lips. "I can't remember which of us suggested swimming out to the rock that night. I think he did. He was so keen to impress me, still convinced I'd change my mind and date him instead of you. The warning flag was up on the beach, but we were too drunk to care. We'd raced one another to the rock so many times over the years. It never occurred to me that anything could go wrong." She broke off on a sob and buried her face into her lap.

Jonas sank onto the sofa beside her and stroked her back. "We can play the *what if?* game for the rest of our lives. What if I'd taken an earlier connection? What if you and I had never hooked up the previous weekend in Tipperary and triggered Bry's jealousy and competitiveness? What if the beach party had taken place the previous night when the water was calm? We can go over and over the possibilities until we drive ourselves mad. But there's no point. Nothing can erase what happened."

She raised her head and dabbed at her eyes with her sleeve. "Bry drowned and I didn't. It makes no sense. He was always the strongest swimmer of the three of us."

"A case of shit happens, Olivia. For whatever reason, his time was up and yours wasn't." He routed in his pockets and produced a small packet of disposable children's tissues. One trick he'd learned to master since Mam left on her cruise was to carry spare tissues at all times. He dabbed her face with it like he would for Luca, realizing his mistake when he observed her bemused expression. "Sorry. Force of habit."

She reached for the tissue, her hand closing over his. "Thank you."

He stared into her eyes, mesmerized by the swirls of emotion reflected. "Do you want to join me for a glass of wine?"

Her hesitation lasted a heartbeat. "Why not?"

Jonas located two white wine glasses in the back of a kitchen cupboard and checked they were clean. He uncorked the bottle, poured, and brought the glasses back into the living room. "Here you are. *Sláinte.*"

He took a sip of his wine, watching how her pink lips touched the rim of her glass. Whatever lipstick she'd been wearing earlier had worn off, exposing their natural rosy hue. The urge to nibble them sent a surge of heat to his groin. He took a hasty gulp of wine, spluttering when it went down the wrong way.

"You okay?" Her brow creased in concern.

"I'm fine," he gasped and took another sip.

"This wine is delicious." She licked her luscious lips in appreciation. If she'd deliberately set out to torture him, she couldn't have done a more effective job. "I like my wine crisp and dry but with a hint of fruit. I'm guessing wine experts would have a more eloquent way of describing it."

He was more than willing to follow her lead and change the topic of conversation. "I'm no wine expert. But I know what I like when I taste it. Luca's mother gave me a few tips. She's a qualified sommelier."

Olivia ran a fingertip around the rim of her glass. "I didn't know that."

He shrugged. "No reason you should."

"Do you have much contact with her?"

"At the moment, none." He swirled the rich golden liquid. "She just got married."

"Ah," she said with a grimace. "Awkward. How do you feel about it?"

"Indifference, but I feel bad for Luca. She didn't even invite him."

Her eyes widened in horror. "You're not serious?"

"Alas, yes," he said with a tinge of bitterness. "Some people aren't cut out for parenthood."

"No, some people aren't. Something with which I'm all too familiar." Her eyelashes fluttered down, and her cheeks were a most becoming tinge of pink.

Jonas didn't know Olivia's parents well, but they'd never made a good impression. They'd always been genial enough when he'd visited their house as a teenager, but distracted and self-absorbed. Olivia had rarely invited him and Bry round to her house, preferring to meet at theirs or on neutral territory. Funny how that realization had never occurred to him at the time.

"Do you miss living in Dublin?" she asked, still toying with her glass. "I'd imagine Ballybeg seems rather tame after the bustle of a big city."

He considered a moment. "I miss certain aspects of city life, but I prefer raising a child down here. I still go up to Dublin every three to four months to see my agent, attend book signings, give interviews, and so on."

"Where did you inherit your creative streak?"

He smiled. "I have no idea. It's a mystery to my parents– no pun intended. They're not big readers. My dad can't understand how I can make money from writing."

"But you do."

"Yes. Not as much as some people seem to think, but enough to provide for Luca. The Irish market is a small one. I've been lucky to have success in the UK too. My main source of income at the moment is from the Detective Inspector Brady TV series. Because I contributed to the scripts, I get royalties from international distribution, DVDs, and so on."

She took another sip of her wine. There was something erotic about the movement of her throat when she swallowed.

"Are you published in America?" she asked.

"Not in print but in e-book format. Kate– my agent– is in negotiations with a New York publisher, but there's no guarantee it'll pan out. It's hard for foreign writers to break into the crime fiction market. There are a lot of talented homegrown authors."

"Making a living wage is hard for everyone these days, regardless of industry. Poor Jill's not even getting invited to interviews, never mind getting job offers."

"At least she has a job at your café once you open."

"Temporarily. She needs the money, and I need someone to help out. I know she'll move on once she finds a job in her field, but at least this is something to tide her over."

Jonas fingered the stem of his glass. "How are things with Aidan?" he asked, keen to shift the focus away from him. "Have you set the divorce process in motion?"

"This is Ireland, Jonas. I can't even *file* for a divorce until I've been living apart from Aidan for at least four years. Depending on the backlog of cases when I am allowed to file, it could take five years in total.

"Wow. That's a long time to be stuck with a spouse you don't want."

"True. I won't be allowed to remarry for the next few years– not that I'm planning to. In the meantime, I've filed for a legal separation. If Aidan and I agree on a financial settlement soon, it should be through within a few weeks."

He raised an eyebrow. "That's pretty quick."

"Not quick enough. I filed the week after I moved out. We have no children, and I'm not looking for a huge financial settlement. That speeds things up considerably."

"Seriously, why did you marry Aidan in the first place? I've never understood your motivation."

She quirked an eyebrow. "Come on, Jonas. You and everyone else in Ballybeg guessed correctly– I married Aidan for his money."

"I don't believe you're that mercenary."

"Don't you?" She smiled. "Perhaps not in the way people think. I grew up with very little money. Getting our electricity cut off was a regular occurrence. I didn't want that for my future. After..." She hesitated, her brow furrowing. "After Bry died and we split up, I was lost for a time. Couldn't concentrate on my uni course and failed my exams. Couldn't motivate myself to organize my future. And into that depressive haze stepped Aidan. He was a friend of my parents. I'd known him all my life. He was handsome, suave, and sophisticated. I fell for the idea of the man, not the man himself, but I didn't realize it at the time. Does that make sense?"

"In a weird way, yes." He reached for the bottle and topped up their glasses. "Go on."

She took a sip of her wine and toyed with the stem. "During our engagement, Aidan was charm personified. He encouraged me to pursue my dream of becoming a qualified chef and paid my cookery school fees. For the first couple of years of our marriage, everything was okay.

The cracks started to show around year three. I'd passed my exams and applied for jobs at local restaurants. Aidan freaked when I said I wanted to work outside the home. He had envisaged my cookery school course as a hobby and preferred me in the permanent role of wealthy housewife– a sort of status symbol to prove to the world that he had so much money his wife didn't need to work."

"How did you end up working for him at his practice?"

She sighed. "When the property market collapsed, my parents defaulted on their mortgage and almost lost their home. Aidan bailed them out at the last second and has made significant financial contributions to them ever since. He made it crystal clear that his generosity came with a hefty price tag. Part of that price tag was me agreeing to work as his secretary. In Aidan's mind, the secretarial job gave me something to do outside the home but still enabled him to keep a close eye on me."

"He wanted to control you."

"Of course. And it worked. Fast forward a few years, and I was well and truly trapped. I had hardly any savings of my own and a husband who vacillated between indifference and bullying. My parents were beholden to him financially, and because of that, my brothers' welfare depended on my continuing to play my role."

"Where did the plan for the café fit into all this?"

"Last year, Aidan and I ended our marriage in all but name. I moved into the guest room, and he was willing to consider a formal separation after the mayoral elections were over. What he didn't anticipate was me seeking to establish my own business. I'd managed to squirrel away a bit of money over the years. Aidan paid my salary into his own bank account, but I saved whatever cash I got my hands on."

"He paid your salary into *his* account?" Jonas said, appalled. "Why didn't you leave? You'd have found some sort of job."

"Desperation. Fear. Guilt." She shrugged. "I don't know. My parents' debt to Aidan played a role. I don't give a damn what happens to my parents. Don't mistake my reluctance to piss off Aidan for filial devotion. But I *do* care what happens to my brothers. If my parents lose their home, so do the boys. Until they finish school, they need to have some semblance of stability."

"But at what price?" He leaned forward and took one of her hands in his. "I know it's none of my business, but I've done quite a bit of research on spousal abuse for my books. I don't believe the day of the parade was the first time he hit you."

She bit her lip. "It wasn't."

He stroked the soft skin of her wrist. "Why in the name of goodness didn't you call the police?"

"For all the reasons I've already listed. Besides, Aidan is respected in this town– goodness knows why, but there you have it. In contrast, my parents are Ballybeg's token bohemians. Most people around here believe the apple doesn't fall far from the tree. How many would take my word over Aidan's?"

"I would," he said, stroking her hair.

"You're one of a very few," she whispered, close enough that her breath tickled his cheek.

He cupped her chin and lowered his mouth to hers. She smelled flowery and fresh, like clean sheets on a summer day. This woman had defended his son against harassers. The thought made his heart swell and his already turned-on body even harder.

Their mouths clashed and meshed. He tugged on her hair, pulling her closer. His hands found her hair ribbon, and her hair cascaded down her back in silky waves. She broke the contact.

"What did you do that for?" Her voice was low and husky.

"Kiss you, or take down your hair?"

"Both."

"Because I wanted to." He ran his fingers through silky strands. "Do you want me to, Olivia?"

"Yes...No...Yes."

"Not sure? Perhaps this will persuade you." He teased one of her ears with his tongue, nipping the lobe playfully.

She gasped. "You remembered?"

"Of course. I remember everything about you. You were my first..." He checked himself. "First woman I loved."

Olivia's laugh reverberated against his chest. "Nice save, O'Mahony. I *knew* you were a virgin when we first had sex. Why didn't you tell me?"

"You knew? Damn. Was I that bad?"

"Not at all. I guessed because you didn't seem to know what you were doing any more than I did."

He spanked her behind. "We figured it out soon enough."

"So we did." She gazed up at him, her eyes cloudy with longing. He bent to kiss her.

"Dad! My curtains are all wrong."

Jonas drew back. "On my way," he called. "Sorry, Olivia. Luca is particular about his curtains. They need to hang perfectly straight or he can't sleep."

"It's okay." She shoved a lock of red hair back from her forehead. "I'd better go before this goes any further."

"I don't think it *can* go any further," he said with a low laugh. "I have no idea where my condoms are."

She quirked an eyebrow. "Somewhere in an unpacked moving box, perhaps?"

He grinned. "More than likely. I've promised Luca I'll unpack the last of them this weekend."

"Besides, I think it's too..." She broke off, uncertainty flickering across her beautiful face.

He stroked her cheek. "Too soon?"

"Maybe. I know it sounds daft after everything I've said about Aidan, but it doesn't feel right to sleep with another man until the legal separation comes through, even if we have been living separate lives for over a year."

He grinned. "Not waiting five years until the divorce is final?"

She swatted him playfully. "I'm not *that* much of a martyr."

"That gives me hope that I might aid and assist in your future nonmartyrdom." He retrieved her ribbon from the living room floor and handed it to her. "Thank you for standing up for Luca today. It means a lot to me."

"No problem. He's a good kid, and no one deserves little shits making snide remarks about them." She hovered on the doorstep. "Good night, Jonas."

"Daaaad! My curtains!"

"Duty calls." He dropped a kiss onto her forehead. "Sweet dreams, Olivia."

CHAPTER SEVENTEEN

If Olivia's week had been on fast forward, it couldn't have gone by any quicker. Just as well. Keeping busy kept her from dwelling on The Kiss. Her life was complicated enough without adding her conflicted feelings about Jonas into the mix.

On Tuesday, a bank in Cork City approved a small business loan, and she was able to order the last few items she needed for the café. Liam O'Mahony and his crew finished their work on Friday afternoon, including installing a trap door for the cottage's loft bedroom to give her privacy from the café below.

Friday also marked Olivia's last day working for Aidan. After all the years dreaming about escape, it was almost anticlimactic. Aidan was out on campaign business for most of the day, but Brona, the solicitor who worked part-time, and Martin, Aidan's paralegal, bought her flowers to mark the occasion.

By Friday evening, exhausted but exhilarated, she prepared a sherry trifle at the café and packed it into her little car. She'd arranged to have dinner with her grandfather and Bridie Byrne, her host for the past few weeks, and dessert was to be her contribution to the meal.

The lights were on when she pulled up at her grandfather's house. He lived in a two-bedroom new-build on the outskirts of Ballybeg. When he spotted Olivia climbing out of her car, Jasper, her grandfather's Cavalier King Charles spaniel, yipped in unbridled delight.

"Come in, my dear," said her grandfather from the open doorway. He wore tweeds but had replaced his smart walking shoes for comfortable slippers. "Down, Jasper boy," he ordered. Jasper paid him no heed. "Daft dog," he snapped. "Go to your corner."

Jasper wagged his tail and regarded his master with cheerful indifference.

Olivia laughed and reached down to stroke Jasper's silky fur. "Is Bridie already here?"

"Indeed I am," a booming voice said from the hallway. "I don't want to miss your sherry trifle." Bridie Byrne was a broad-hipped and broad-minded woman in her sixties who never had an opinion she didn't express. She was also Olivia's grandfather's good friend. Whether Bridie and the Major were more than friends was a subject of much speculation in Ballybeg.

Olivia slipped off her coat and handed it to her grandfather. His house was cozy and crammed full of ornaments. They were out of place when contrasted with the modern architecture. The predominant colors were rusty orange and brown. Granddad had bucked the trend for polished wood floors in favor of thick carpets. Olivia's feet sank into them when she followed him and Bridie down the hallway toward the kitchen, Jasper close at her heels. The tempting aroma of roast chicken made her mouth water. "That smells good."

"I hope so," he said with a chuckle. "It's the one semi-fancy dish I know how to make."

Olivia inhaled and moaned in appreciation. "It's been ages since I had roast chicken. Aidan's not into poultry."

"And you're not into red meat. I can guess who won that argument," her grandfather said in an arch tone. Although he'd never cared for Aidan, he'd rarely said anything negative in the years Olivia was living under the same roof as her husband.

She laughed. "Put it this way, I've prepared more roasts of beef than I care to remember."

Bridie took china plates out of a cupboard. "I made chestnut stuffing to go with the chicken. It's the recipe you gave me years ago, when you attended that cookery school."

"Yes, that's a good one." She peered into the oven. "Ooh...roast potatoes too."

"And gravy." Her grandfather laughed. "Can't have a proper roast without gravy."

"Thanks for going to so much effort."

"Entertaining you is no effort at all, my dear." He dished generous portions onto three plates, and they carried them to the dining room.

The food was even more delicious than it smelled. They washed it down with wine and laughter. When the meal was finished, Bridie helped Olivia to clear the plates. "Are you looking forward to moving into the cottage?"

"Yes. It'll be strange, though," Olivia mused. "I've never lived on my own before."

"It can be lonely at times, but you'll get used to it." Bridie squeezed her arm. "I've enjoyed having you to stay. I got used to having someone around when Fiona lived with me last year."

"I'm grateful to you for taking me in. Fiona offered to have me stay with her and Gavin, but I think they need their space."

Bridie let out a cackle of laughter. "Go on with you, missy. You didn't fancy living with a shoe-eating dog."

Olivia grinned. "Wiggly Poo's wild behavior *was* a consideration."

"Jokes aside, I have a business proposition for you," the older woman said. "Did I tell you I'm on the organizing committee for this year's Ballybeg Sports Day?"

"You mentioned being asked to join."

"One of my responsibilities is booking catering for the event. I told the committee that you helped Fiona with scones and sweet treats for the Book Mark last year and that I've asked you to be our regular supplier once you open for business. And I told them I'd like you to supply the desserts for this year's event."

"Seriously? That would be fantastic. Thank you so much."

"Thank *you*. It's self-preservation, believe me. Last year, Nora Fitzgerald's fool of a husband persuaded the committee to let him do the baking with predictably disastrous results."

When Olivia and Bridie returned to the tiny dining room, the Major had produced a bottle of sherry. "Can I tempt you, ladies?"

"None for me, thanks," Bridie said. "I'm going to take Jasper for a walk."

Olivia blinked. "What about dessert? I thought you were looking forward to the trifle."

Bridie's eyes twinkled. "I am. That's why I need to work off a few calories before I indulge. I've arranged to meet Fiona and Wiggly Poo out by Craggy Point."

"How will Wiggly Poo cope with Jasper?"

Bridie gave a bark of laughter. "They get on fine. Jasper is one of the few dogs Wiggly Poo doesn't regard as dinner."

"In that case, enjoy your walk."

"I intend to." Bridie dropped a kiss onto the Major's bald pate. "Save some dessert for me."

After Bridie left, Olivia served the trifle. "Bridie was about as subtle as a boulder. I assume you want to talk to me about something."

"Actually, yes." Granddad swirled his sherry, and she waited for him to begin. "You know, of course, that my father's family once owned land in Ballybeg."

That was an understatement. Until they were driven out during the Irish War of Independence, his family had owned most of Ballybeg.

"Anyway," he continued, "my grandfather was more perceptive than many Protestant landlords of that time. He'd seen the way things were going long before the rebels took his land and had a contingency plan."

"Careful, Granddad," Olivia said with a grin. "Long before *the Irish* reclaimed *their* land."

His white mustache bobbed. "Right. At any rate, my grandfather managed to hang onto Clonmore House right through my childhood. Even though I grew up in England and served in the British army, I've always had an affection for Ballybeg and intended to retire here once my army days were done."

"And you did. Was it strange coming back here with the big house gone?"

"No. My father sold it when I was in my twenties. That he'd held on that long was something of a miracle. I had no expectation of inheriting the estate intact, if at all. Times had changed, and the house has changed owners several times since then."

"I hear it does a roaring business in its current incarnation," she remarked between spoonfuls of trifle. "It's an excellent location for a golf hotel."

"That brings me to my point. I'm not rambling about my family's past for no reason. When I retired, I used part of my savings to build this house. I also invested in the new hotel in my family's former home."

Olivia's jaw dropped. "You own Clonmore Castle Hotel?"

"Only a percentage, and a small percentage at that. However, it adds to my yearly income and has enabled me to build up my savings."

"I had no idea."

"No. I've deliberately not told your mother about my share in the hotel. Your aunt Elisabeth knows, but she's financially independent. Your mother, on the other hand – "

"– would bleed you dry."

"Yes." He sighed. "When your parents almost lost their home, I couldn't afford to pay off their mortgage. At the point Aidan stepped in, I was considering offering them enough money to rent a house for a few months on the condition that they both made an effort to find work."

Olivia grimaced. "They wouldn't have, you know. They'd have taken your money and blown it."

"Yes. Yet I still regret letting Aidan step in and take over."

"You couldn't have foreseen the consequences."

"No, but perhaps I can help mitigate the damage." He topped up her sherry glass. "With that in mind, I have a proposition for you."

Olivia raised an eyebrow. "A proposition?"

"Yes. I know you've poured all your savings into the café. I'd like to offer you a little money to put toward your living costs for the next few months. Between the business and the cost of setting your divorce in motion, I figure you need it."

"Granddad, are you sure you can afford it? It might take me a couple of years to pay you back."

"I wouldn't offer if I couldn't manage without the money," he said firmly. "I'm glad to help at least one of my grandchildren. I feel bad enough that I can't offer your brothers a home. I've tried, but your mother won't hear of it."

"Would you want to take on two teenage boys at your age?"

He sighed. "Frankly, no, but your parents' chaotic lifestyle isn't creating a healthy home environment. I don't think Kyle cares, but Ronan needs stability."

"I know. Once I have the café up and running and can afford to rent a house, I'm going to offer to have them live with me until they finish school."

Her grandfather patted her hand. "All the more reason to offer you a loan. However, there is one condition."

"I'm not to tell Mum?"

He looked her square in the eye. "Precisely. Victoria will inherit money from me when I'm dead, but at least I won't be around to see her waste it."

"Thanks for the offer, Grandad. I appreciate it. Now that my bank loan has come through, my start-up grant will be paid out within the next few weeks. I'll need to be careful until the café starts turning a profit. Your money will help me breathe a little easier."

"If it reduces your stress level, I'm pleased." The grooves on his lined forehead deepened. "You deserve more from life than constantly being forced to cope with situations that aren't ideal."

"Isn't that most people's lot in life?" she said with a smile, but there was no denying that having the financing of the café sorted out was a huge relief. Now the main obstacle to the café running smoothly was her attraction to her sinfully handsome landlord.

CHAPTER EIGHTEEN

The champagne cork popped. If Olivia's grin was half as wide as Jill's, she was pretty sure she bore a striking resemblance to the Cheshire cat. The past few weeks had been hectic. They'd worked from dawn until dusk planning menus, sewing tablecloths, and decorating the café. But it had been worth the effort. Today, the Cottage Café was open for business.

"Get that down you." Jill handed Olivia one of the elegant champagne flutes Granddad had loaned them from his Waterford Crystal collection.

"Cheers," yelled Kyle, waving a cup of apple punch. To their sister's amazement, he and Ronan had hauled their teenage arses out of bed early to help set up the café for its opening day. Apart from a thwarted attempt to spike the punch, they'd been on their best behavior. To no one's surprise, she hadn't invited her parents. Since the argument with her mother, they weren't on speaking terms.

Olivia raised her glass and addressed the crowd. "Thanks for coming, everyone. I appreciate all you've done to get the café ready. I owe special thanks to Kyle for the beautiful stencil work on the walls; to Ronan for helping arrange and decorate the tables; to Granddad for everything he's done to support me in following my dream; to Bridie for coming to my rescue when I needed a roof over my head; to Jonas and Luca, my landlord and chief taste-tester respectively; and last but definitely not least, to Jill and Fiona for being the best friends a woman could ask for. Now all that remains to be said is eat, drink, and be merry."

Everyone cheered.

"Not a bad speech, sis." Ronan slapped her on the back. "Even if you'll never win any debating contests."

She laughed. "That's your role, little brother. Just don't get into any more fights at school."

Taking a sip of champagne, she surveyed the café with a swell of pride. It looked just as she'd imagined. The wicker chairs and tables were perfectly aligned and decorated. The display case was filled with freshly baked goods to tempt customers to order a little something to eat with their tea or coffee. The gift stand was small but well stocked with Olivia's hand-knitted scarves, bath products created by a local beautician, and beautiful beaded necklaces.

She was relishing the taste of champagne bubbles on her tongue when Jonas and Luca squeezed through the revelers. Jonas had made an effort for the occasion– his black shirt was wrinkle-free, and his dark jeans less scruffy than his usual attire. He glanced around with obvious approval. "Place looks great, Olivia."

A ready smile sprang to her mouth. "Your father and his team did a great job."

"Yeah, they did, but I was referring to how well you've set it up for the opening. The display window is bound to entice customers through the door, and the smell will keep them here."

"Fingers crossed." The only smell she was aware of at this moment was his subtle male scent teasing her senses. Since the night of that crazy, sexy kiss, her thoughts strayed in his direction with alarming frequency. *Focus, Olivia.* She beckoned to Luca. "Why don't you sample the butterfly cakes? I'd like your opinion before customers start arriving."

Luca examined the tray of cakes and pointed to one on the left. "The sprinkles are out of alignment."

Olivia stifled a grin. To her eye, the cake was identical to its companions. "Why don't you eat it and tell me if it tastes good in spite of the sprinkle situation?"

Luca took a delicate bite out of the sugary treat.

"By the expression of ecstasy on his face, I suspect it's a hit," his father said dryly. "Is it a thumbs-up, Luca?"

The boy inclined his head and gave them a cream-covered thumbs-up. "I'd better taste test the raspberry muffins too."

"You do that," Olivia said. "Ask Ronan to pour you a glass of apple punch."

Luca made a beeline for the muffins.

"Out of alignment," Olivia said with a laugh. "Do you teach him these phrases?"

Jonas grinned. "God, no. He picks them up. Precision is important to him. Kids with Asperger's like order, and they find it difficult to filter information in the way the rest of us do, so something that isn't quite right stands out."

"Do you notice a difference since he started the therapy in Cork?"

"I think so. His eye contact is improving, but I'm less aware of that than a stranger would be. He's always been pretty good at making and maintaining eye contact with people he knows well."

"Does the health insurance cover his therapies?"

"To an extent. I pay out of pocket for the program in Cork."

"I'm going to miss babysitting the little guy. He's welcome to pop into the café whenever he wants."

Jonas's smile warmed her from the inside out. "Thank you. I know he'll appreciate that."

"When does his new sitter start?"

"Next week," he said, reaching for a fairy cake. "She's a childcare student who did work experience with Luca's class. Miss O'Brien, his teacher, recommended her."

"I hope it works out." Her gaze was drawn to his mouth, watching him take a bite of fairy cake.

He favored her with one of his crinkly-eyed smiles. "This tastes divine."

Jill's sister Naomi appeared before them, a slight flush on her cheeks. "Jonas…would you mind autographing one of my Detective Inspector Brady books for me? Only if it's not too much trouble."

"No trouble at all," he replied smoothly. "I didn't realize you were a fan."

Neither had Olivia. She'd made a point of avoiding Jonas's novels for years, tuning out conversation if they were mentioned. Petty, true, but reflective of her feelings for the man. But that was then. What she thought of him now was too confusing to process.

Naomi whipped out a well-worn paperback and handed it to Jonas. "This is my favorite one in the series."

Olivia agreed with her assessment. After devouring the first Brady novel in one night, she went out and bought the rest of the series, reading them in quick succession. Jonas's clever insights into his characters' personalities impressed her as did his focus on everyday people driven to murder. There were no omniscient serial killers in his books.

Jonas smiled and took the book from Naomi. "I have a particular affection for that one too. It was the first time I tried writing two stories parallel, and I was convinced it would be a disaster. No one was more surprised than I when it actually worked."

He withdrew a fountain pen from his shirt pocket and wrote his signature with a flourish. His handwriting was neater than Olivia expected. It was difficult to imagine those big hands tapping away at a keyboard, but they'd proven adept at undoing her hair ribbon, among other things...

"Olivia," called her grandfather, drawing her attention away from Jonas and the gushing Naomi. "What do you think of the window decorations?"

They'd strewn rose petals from his garden to create a fairytale effect. It was cute without venturing into kitsch territory.

"They're gorgeous, Granddad," she assured him. "Thank you so much for your help."

"You're welcome, my dear. I have one granddaughter, and I'm entitled to spoil her."

An influx of customers heralded an hour that passed by in a whirl. The new coffee machine was a great hit, as were the bread and cakes. Naomi was a little awkward with the customers at first, but unstiffened as she gained confidence. Jill was a natural. Fingers crossed these were good omens for the café's future.

Olivia was chatting with a few of her grandfather's bridge-playing companions when a hushed silence fell over the café. The chill that slithered down her spine alerted her to his presence before her eyes confirmed it.

Aidan.

He strode into the café, dapper in a three-piece suit and handmade Italian loafers. Olivia's mood descended from elated to deflated.

Jutting her jaw, she marched toward him. "I'd like you to leave."

"What?" He sneered. "You're evicting a potential customer on your opening day? If you have no more business sense than that, you'll be crawling back to me in weeks."

She gritted her teeth. "Don't hold your breath. Now get out."

"Nonsense." He pushed past her, advancing on the punch bowl where little Luca was standing. "There's a new café in town. An excellent opportunity for me to mingle with my constituents."

"You're on the town council, Aidan," she snapped, moving briskly to keep pace. "You're not mayor yet."

The sneer stiffened into a rictus. "If all goes to plan, I will be next month."

God forbid. She knew the sort of politics Aidan endorsed, and they were enough to make any emancipated woman weep. "Leave now, or I'll call the police. I'm serious."

He ignored her and poured himself a generous helping of punch. He'd be distraught when he discovered it was of the alcohol-free variety.

"Is there a problem?" Jonas's expression was grimmer than the reaper.

"Ah, O'Mahony." Aidan flashed him an insincere smile around his punch cup. "I should have known you'd show your carcass at this shindig."

"I do live next door."

"How cozy," Aidan drawled. "All the better to steal my wife away from me. I wonder what Olivia's solicitor would have to say about this arrangement."

"I wonder what yours would have to say about Moira Keating," she snapped, "or are you being foolish enough to represent yourself?"

"A man is entitled to seek his pleasure elsewhere if his wife fails to satisfy him in the bedroom."

A muscle in Jonas's jaw flexed. "Planning on putting that little morsel in your campaign brochure?"

Aidan laughed and drained his punch. Immediately his face turned an interesting shade of puce and he began to gag. "What. The. Fuck?"

"Don't you like the punch?" Luca asked, his expression deadpan.

Olivia seized a bowl of chips, dumped its contents onto a table, and shoved the bowl under Aidan's chin. "If you must retch, use this."

"Are you trying to poison me?" he gasped and let out a loud fart. "Jesus Christ. What was in that stuff?"

She folded her arms across her chest and stared her estranged husband down. "No one else seems to have found the punch objectionable."

Aidan made a retching noise, followed by another explosive fart.

Jonas placed a palm between Aidan's shoulder blades and propelled him toward the door. The older man took mincing steps, clenching his buttocks. "Take this to be a sign," Jonas said, "that the Cottage Café isn't destined to become your regular hangout."

"Fuck. You. O'Mahony."

"You say that a lot. One for the campaign posters, perhaps?" With a final shove, Jonas catapulted Aidan out into the street and shut the café door.

A moment of stunned silence reigned.

"Someone," said Bridie Byrne, her strident tones slicing through the silence, "should give that child a medal. Whatever did you put in the punch?"

All eyes focused on Luca. The little boy shrugged and produced an empty bottle from his pocket.

"Finbar's Farting Fluid," Jonas read aloud. "Jaysus, I remember this stuff. You can buy it from the joke shop on Patrick Street. It's lethal. Aidan will be glued to the toilet until Christmas."

Olivia, struggling to maintain her composure, addressed the miscreant. "You just happened to have a bottle in your pocket?"

Luca's gaze was steady and unperturbed. "Doesn't everyone?"

CHAPTER NINETEEN

By the middle of June, Luca was on his summer holidays and was thoroughly bored. And if Luca was bored, everyone around him knew about it. His new babysitter was a good sport, but it would take a while for her to build up a rapport with the boy. Meanwhile, her charge made it his mission to sneak into his father's office as frequently as possible.

One evening shortly before seven o'clock, Jonas pushed his chair back from his computer. "Okay, Mister Ants-in-his-Pants. I'm all yours. What do you want to do before bedtime?"

"Visit Granny and Granddad."

"No can do, kiddo. Granny and Aunt Mary won't get home from the airport for another couple of hours. I said we'd call round for breakfast tomorrow."

"Do you think Granny brought me back a present from her cruise?" Luca asked, making his father smile at his deceptively disinterested tone.

"I believe she might have mentioned having a surprise for you in her suitcase." Jonas ruffled the little boy's hair. "If visiting your grandparents is off the cards, what would you like to do between now and bedtime?"

Luca answered without hesitation. "Call into the café. Then walk on the beach."

Jonas glanced at his watch. "It's nearly closing time."

"We'd better hurry up." The boy tugged at his sleeve. "Come on, Dad. We can buy scones to eat on the beach."

"All right. Don't forget your jacket. It gets chilly down by the water."

By the time Jonas had locked the cottage, Luca had already scampered next door. As he'd predicted, Olivia was ringing up the bill for the last customers of the day. She looked tired but cheerful. He found himself grinning like a loon when she spotted him. Her answering smile made his heart swell.

"Luca wants scones to take with us on our evening walk."

"Are berry ones acceptable?" Olivia directed the question at the little boy, who'd marched behind the counter with a predatory air. "We're sold out of every other flavor."

"The berry scones are my favorites."

She winked at Jonas. "In that case, I'll pop two into a bag with a couple of paper napkins. You can have a proper picnic."

"Business good?" He indicated the almost empty display cabinet.

"Too good." She beamed with pride. "We're struggling to keep up with the demand."

"You were smart to open at the start of the tourist season."

"I'd hoped the timing would kick-start trade, but I didn't expect the café to take off like it has."

"I'm glad for you, Olivia. You deserve your success." He rolled the question on his tongue before he posed it. "I was wondering if...well..."

"Yes?" she prompted, a knowing glint in her eyes.

"...if you'd like to go out to dinner sometime?"

The smile widened. "I'd love to. When did you have in mind?"

"I'll be away for a couple of days as of this Thursday, so how about the following week? Maybe Wednesday?"

"Next Wednesday sounds good. Where are you off to this weekend?"

"I have meetings in Belfast and Dublin with my agent and a few TV execs."

"Ah," she said, brightening. "Is this about your TV series?"

"Yes." It was his turn to smile. "There'll definitely be more Detective Inspector Brady episodes next winter, and I'm hoping my new miniseries will get the green light too."

"Excellent news. Congratulations."

"Daaad." Luca appeared at his side, clutching the bag of scones. "Are we going for our walk?"

"When I pay Olivia." He slipped the money onto the counter, his fingers brushing against hers for a delicious instant. "Enjoy your evening."

***

Through the café window, Olivia watched Jonas and Luca cross the street and walk in the direction of the beach. Was she mad to accept his dinner invitation? And if so, did she care? If the past few weeks had taught her anything, it was to let go of the past and live life on her own terms.

In the two weeks since the café opened, she'd seen little of Jonas. She was backachingly busy from morning until night, and he had a looming deadline. She'd seen more of his pint-sized mirror image. Luca had wasted no time in dragging his new babysitter over to the café for Olivia's inspection.

The beeper on the oven went off, calling her back to the kitchen. She removed a tray of fruitcakes. *Mmm*...she sniffed the tray in appreciation. The aroma of baking never failed to lift her mood. Actually, her mood had been great since she'd signed the lease for the café. She might not be completely shot of Aidan, but she was well on her way to achieving financial independence.

The jangle of the door indicated the arrival of another late customer. "Hang on a sec," she shouted.

The kitchen door slid open. "It's only me."

The familiar sound of his voice sent shivers skittering through her body.

The visitor was Aidan.

CHAPTER TWENTY

Olivia's former husband slunk into the kitchen. He seemed calm, and he seemed sober. Definite pluses, but she'd known Aidan too long to trust appearances. She groped in her apron pocket for her phone. "Leave now, or I'm calling the cops." A treacherous trickle of sweat snaked down her back.

"Don't be ridiculous, Olivia. I don't want to hurt you. I'm here to talk."

He moved a step closer. She took a step back, deftly maneuvering herself behind the work counter. From the corner of her eye, she could see the door leading from the kitchen to the small lane behind the cottage. A quick sprint and she'd be free.

Her finger hovered over the number for emergency services. "Do we have anything left to talk about, Aidan?" Her voice dripped ice. "Apart from stuff our solicitors can deal with?"

"I think we do, yes." He was dressed in a pressed suit, his hair gelled back in his preferred style. He was a handsome man– if your taste ran to Ken doll lookalikes. His only facial flaw was a small scar on his cheek, courtesy of an attack by two Chihuahuas at last year's Christmas bazaar.

"I trust you're recovered from your ailment?" she asked in a silky voice.

His forced composure wavered. "Unfortunately for you, yes. You won't be a wealthy widow just yet."

He leaned against the kitchen counter, making his intention to stay clear. Her fight-or-flight response was at the ready. Trust him to corner her in the kitchen, where they weren't visible from the street. She'd lay bets he'd waited until Jonas and Luca left. What Aidan didn't know was that Fiona and Jill were expecting to meet her in MacCarthy's pub in fifteen minutes. If she was late, they'd come looking for her. But in certain circumstances, fifteen minutes was an eternity.

"There's no need to be frightened." Aidan gave a hollow laugh. "I don't bite."

No, he'd never done that. He confined himself to well-placed punches.

She cast him a look that would have made Medusa proud. "What's this about?"

He loosened his tie. "I'm not going to contest the divorce."

Her breath left her lungs in a whoosh. "Why the change of heart?"

"You're moving on with your life. It's time I did the same."

"Yes," she said, instantly wary. "Moving on would be best for both of us."

He gave an exaggerated sigh. "I did love you, you know."

Her ears pricked up. What bullshit line was he about to spin this time?

"When we were first together," he clarified, seeing her expression of incredulity. "Oh, I was aware it wasn't mutual. I'm not a fool. You married me for my money. But I hoped in time you'd come to have feelings for me."

She had developed feelings for him, but not the way he meant– she was pretty sure "loathing" wasn't the emotion to which he was referring. "You married me because I reminded you of my mother."

He shrugged, not bothering to deny it. "I was in love with Victoria for years, but she married your father. There were certain aspects to your personality and appearance that reminded me of her, although you're not much alike."

"As you reminded me on a daily basis."

"Don't hate your mother. She's had a hard life."

Olivia snorted. "If she has, it's been of her own making."

"Perhaps. But I didn't come here to talk about Victoria. I came to apologize for what happened on the beach."

"What about all the other times? Are you sorry for them, too?"

A muscle in his cheek spasmed. "I don't know what comes over me. We seem to bring out the worst in each other."

If she hadn't already suspected Aidan had an ulterior motive for this visit, his insincere apology confirmed her suspicions. What was he playing at? "I agree we bring out each other's bad sides, but that's no excuse for hurting me."

"I know. Can't we forget it and move on?" he asked in a beseeching tone. "I've said I won't contest the divorce proceedings, and I mean it. I'll provide you with a settlement. It won't be massive, but it'll be more than is currently reflected in my bank accounts. Mother's agreed to help out."

Olivia's bullshit radar was at full alert. "Hmm...sounds tempting. What's the catch?"

His insincere politician's smile slid back into place. "You don't discuss our marriage with anyone."

She rolled her eyes. "Who would I discuss it with, apart from the people I've already confided in?"

"I don't know, Olivia," he said with a touch of impatience. "I simply don't want our dirty laundry aired in public."

She sniffed in disgust. "You don't want me trash talking you in the run up to the mayoral elections."

"Precisely. I need to exercise some damage control."

"And a vindictive ex-wife who claims you were abusive toward her wouldn't go over well with the voters?"

Aidan's mouth hardened. "Your words, not mine."

"Yes, they are my words. And accurate ones at that." She stared him down. "What about my parents' debt?"

"That's got nothing to do with you."

"No, nor do I care what happens to them. I'm concerned about the boys."

"The debt still stands." His expression hardened. "They borrowed money from me, and I expect them to continue paying it back. Their financial obligation to me is not your problem. I don't know why you've always insisted on making it so."

Ah, the irony of hearing sound advice from her crazy ex. "Aidan, let me get this straight– you don't contest the divorce, and I get a settlement. In return, I keep my trap shut."

"Exactly. Do we have a deal?"

"I'm not committing myself to anything yet. Not before I've had time to think it over. I also expect you to show evidence of this settlement to my solicitor before I sign your gagging agreement."

"Olivia," he protested, "I'd hardly call it gagging."

"How else would you define it?" She arched an eyebrow. He opened his mouth to argue the point but she silenced him with a warning finger. "No, Aidan. Don't spout legalese. I'm not in the mood. I've said I'll consider your proposition. You know my lawyer's address. Once I've discussed the matter with him, we can talk further."

"Fair enough," he said. "And I did mean it about loving you."

"Perhaps you did, but whatever you felt for me died a long time ago. Let's not pretend otherwise." In his own warped way, perhaps Aidan *had* loved her, but not in a manner destined to bring either of them joy.

He nodded grimly. "I'll see myself out."

When the café door closed behind him, she slid the lock into place and sagged against the frame. If she signed a gag order, she was a hypocrite, but one with the financial independence she'd always craved. Could she stand by and watch Aidan shake voters' hands and promote traditional family values? And what did it matter if she did? Weren't all politicians crooks?

She glanced at her watch. She had three minutes to make it to MacCarthy's before her friends called out the cavalry. An evening out would do her good. She had a lot to think about. After all, it wasn't every day she was asked to sacrifice her principles for a wad of cash.

***

Fiona's jaw dropped. "He made you an indecent proposal?"

"Shh," admonished Olivia. "Keep your voice down." They were attracting far too much interest from the people at the next table. "And it wasn't *that* sort of indecent proposal."

"The slimy fecker," Fiona said in disgust. "It's bad enough having him on the town council. If he goes into proper politics, he might end up in parliament."

Olivia gave an exaggerated shudder. "Perish the thought."

They were sitting at their preferred table in the snug of MacCarthy's pub. While she'd formed friendships with Fiona and Jill at separate times in her life– Jill at cookery school and Fiona at secondary school– she was pleased to see how well they got along with one another.

"I never liked that man," said Fiona dourly.

"Thanks for mentioning that little tidbit *before* I married him," Olivia said sardonically.

Fiona toyed with her lip ring. "Would it have made a difference?"

Olivia sighed. "Probably not."

Jill fiddled with a ragged beer mat. "Are you seriously considering agreeing to his terms?"

"It's tempting. It would give me enough money to rent a house large enough for my brothers to move in." Olivia wrinkled her brow. "Kyle was in trouble with the police again last week for underage drinking and rowdiness. It wouldn't happen if he lived with me."

"Jaysus, Olivia," Jill said. "I wouldn't sign a piece of paper to benefit Aidan, no matter what sort of money he was offering."

"If Aidan had any sense, he'd realize I'd never sell my story to a newspaper. I hate people knowing my business. I'm hardly going to reveal all to the media." Olivia squeezed her lemon slice and watched the yellow droplets disperse in her gin and tonic. "As for whether or not I accept the deal, I'm going to sleep on it."

"Always the money, Liv," Fiona admonished. "Any money Aidan offers is tainted. It might bring you financial security, for what that's worth these days, but it'll never make you happy."

"Perhaps you're right." She met Fiona's sardonic gaze. "Okay, I *know* you're right, but I'm not making a decision until I've had time to think it over."

Jill had reached the beermat-ripping stage, a clear sign she was stressed or irritated. "I'm with Fiona on this one. If you accept the money, you'll live to regret it."

"Okay," she said with a small laugh, "you've both made your point. I'll sleep on it and call my solicitor tomorrow. By the way, Jill, you were paying particular attention to the post this morning. Expecting anything special?"

Jill grimaced. "Yeah. And it showed up. Which means I'm now a nervous wreck."

"Is it a job interview?" Fiona asked curiously. "You said you were only going to be working at the café on a temporary basis."

Jill nodded. "I've been invited to interview for a position at a multinational drinks company on Friday. They even sent me a train ticket to Dublin. Because my interview is scheduled at the end of the day, they'll put me up in a hotel for the night."

"Hey, that's wonderful news." Olivia squeezed her friend's arm. While she'd be disappointed to lose Jill from the café, she'd known it was a short-term arrangement.

"It is, but I'm trying not to get too excited. They're interviewing several candidates before me. The competition's bound to be fierce. Plus...there's a catch."

"Isn't there always," Olivia said dryly. "Come on. Spill."

"Richard works for the company."

"Ah." Olivia drew the syllable out with emphasis.

Fiona raised an eyebrow in question. "Who's Richard?"

"My ex," Jill said. "Olivia calls him Ratfink, if that tips you off."

Fiona grinned. "She may have mentioned a Ratfink at some point."

Olivia smiled over the rim of her gin glass. "Ratfink doesn't *quite* reach Aidan's low standards, but what man does?"

"If Ratfink– Richard– works for this company, would you turn down a job with them on his account?" Fiona asked.

"Given that this is the first interview I've gotten in months, I don't think I'm in a position to be picky."

"Cross that bridge when you come to it," Olivia said. "At the very least, you'll get a free trip to the Big Smoke."

"True," Jill mused. "It's been ages since I was last in Dublin."

"Same here. Must be two years since I visited you, Fiona."

"More like three," Fiona said.

"That long?" asked Jill in surprise. "Why don't you two join me? We could meet Friday evening after my interview, then go shopping on Saturday."

The idea was tantalizingly tempting. If the timing were different, Olivia would seize the opportunity. "I'm nervous leaving the café so soon after opening."

"I get that. Why don't I ask my sister to come in on Friday afternoon, and you can join me in the evening? She works at the café on Saturdays anyway, so you can leave her any last-minute instructions. Come on, it'll be a laugh. When was the last time we had a night out anyplace but Ballybeg?"

"So long ago I can't remember." Olivia's tone was wistful.

Fiona took a sip of her drink. "I'm game if Olivia is. My new teaching job doesn't start until after the summer holidays, so I can be flexible."

"All right. You've convinced me." Olivia turned to Jill. "I'll talk to Naomi and come up with a solution for the café. If I'm confident I can leave it without incurring disaster, I'll go."

Jill beamed. "Excellent. The train journey is between two and a half and three hours, depending on the connection. Why don't we meet at the hotel at around seven? My interview should be well over by then."

"Which hotel are you staying at?"

"The Ashbourne."

Olivia whistled. "Swanky. I've always wanted to stay there."

"One of my aunts is assistant manager. She's already given me a room upgrade. As long as you and Fiona don't mind sharing a bed, we'll have loads of space."

"Leaving you two with more cash for shopping on Saturday." Fiona said with a laugh.

Visions of the latest fashions danced in Olivia's head. She couldn't afford to go wild, but her budget would extend to a couple of inexpensive items. "Will our evening involve cocktails?"

"We'll make sure of it." Jill laughed. "I haven't had a mai tai in years."

"Nor I." Ballybeg might sport more pubs than grocers, but none of them catered to a cocktail-drinking clientele.

"I know a few good cocktail bars in Dublin," Fiona said. "Come to think of it, the hotel bar serves a mean cocktail, if I recall correctly."

Jill raised her beer glass. "Here's to fun, frolics, and friendship in the Big Smoke."

"I'll drink to that," Olivia said. "*Sláinte.*"

CHAPTER TWENTY-ONE

Jonas slung his carrier bag on the hotel room bed and collapsed into a plush armchair. After two days of meetings in Belfast and Dublin, he was bone tired and hoarse from talking. The good news was that he'd signed a deal for a new miniseries due to start filming the following year. He'd also received interest in a TV script based on *Trial by Blood*, the book his agent had failed to sell a couple of months previously. Tomorrow morning, he was scheduled to attend a book signing at a large Dublin library. Once that was over, he was free to return to Ballybeg and Luca.

Speaking of whom...He hit speed dial on his phone. "Hey, kiddo. Are you behaving yourself for Nana and Granddad?"

"Most of the time," his son replied with his customary directness. "They weren't too thrilled when I cut the living room curtains."

"What did you do that for?"

"One side was uneven. I took a scissors to it and Nana had a fit."

"Oh, dear. Not good, Luca. We've talked about this before. It doesn't matter if something doesn't fit or is uneven. You're not allowed to cut someone else's property without checking with them first."

"I know. I helped Nana in the garden to show I was sorry."

"I'll bring her a large box of chocolates from Dublin." Maybe he'd throw in a bottle of whiskey. It sounded as though his parents would need it after three days looking after their grandson.

"Will you be home soon? Granddad tries but he's crap at reading bedtime stories. His character voices are all wrong."

The image of his gruff father attempting to do voices brought a smile to Jonas's lips. "I'll be home tomorrow evening and back on story-reading duty. Can you keep out of mischief until then?"

"I can try."

"That's good enough for me. Night, mate. Sleep well."

"Night, Dad. See you soon."

Jonas rang off and checked his watch. Seven o'clock. He yawned, stretched his aching back, and forced himself to his feet. He'd arranged to meet a friend from his journalism days for a drink down in the hotel bar. Back in the day, the cocktail bar at the Ashbourne Hotel had been one of his pickup joints of choice. The memories made him smile. Those days were long gone. This evening, all he wanted was a quick drink with an old pal followed by bed– alone.

***

"Wow. Nice place."

It was an understatement. The opulence of the Ashbourne Hotel took Olivia's breath away. Although she preferred modern, minimalist decor, she had to admit that that the Ashbourne was splendid. It was situated in a beautiful old building dating from the nineteenth century that had been carefully restored at the start of the millennium. It combined old-world elegance with modern convenience. The spacious lobby was resplendent with polished wood, plush carpet, gilt-edged mirrors, and a magnificent chandelier. A sweeping staircase led up to the three floors above.

"I've never been here before." Jill looked down at the luxurious white carpet beneath her feet as they ascended the stairs. "At least, not inside. I'm almost afraid to walk on this thing in case I get it dirty."

When they reached their room, Fiona set her bag on the floor while Jill fiddled with the key card. She, alone of the three, had refused the porter's help with her luggage, but then Fiona tended to travel light. "I've been to the hotel cocktail bar several times but I've never stayed overnight. A bit out of my budget. If it weren't for Jill's aunt's discount, I wouldn't be staying here tonight."

"Nor I," Olivia said, "but seeing as we are here, let's start the weekend in style. Why don't we get changed and head down to the bar for cocktails?"

Jill opened the door and led the way inside their spacious double room. "Cocktails are definitely on my agenda, but you two can to go down first and nab us a table. I'll join you later. I have a few e-mails to send after my interview and some follow-up documents."

"Fair enough, but don't work all night. We're here to have fun." Olivia retrieved her luggage from the porter's trolley. She tossed the bags onto one of the two large double beds and then strode to the window. The room overlooked O'Connell Street, one of the main thoroughfares in Dublin's city center. Bright lights and bustle beckoned.

She and Fiona took turns in the bathroom. When Fiona emerged from the shower, her curls wet and wild, Olivia had finished drying and styling her hair. "Have you decided what you want to wear this evening?"

The expression on Fiona's face was comical. "Nooo...I squashed a few outfits into my bag and figured you'd help me pick."

Olivia laughed. "Let me have a root through what you brought."

Fiona unzipped her bag and threw it open for her friend's inspection.

"Hmm." Olivia held up a particularly unflattering garment. "I suppose we can jazz this up with one of my scarves."

"I take it my wardrobe's been rejected," said Fiona with a wry grin.

"Put it this way– I'd like to add a touch of color to your outfit."

"Black, black, and black not cutting it?"

"Not quite." Olivia reached over to her suitcase and unlocked the clasp. "I think I have something that will do the trick." Extracting a bright red silk scarf, she held it up against Fiona. "See? The shade suits your coloring. Even if you wear a black outfit, this scarf and slash of matching lipstick will turn boring to classy."

"It is pretty," said Fiona, fingering the material dubiously, "but I'm not an accessories person. Just as well. Wiggly Poo considers them to be snack food."

Olivia laughed. "Are he and Gavin pining for you?"

"Put it this way: I've received several dog and master selfies in the few hours since I last saw them, but they can survive without me for a day."

While Fiona was getting dressed, Olivia applied makeup. When she was satisfied with her artfully arranged red curls, she slipped into the clingy cocktail dress she'd bought months ago but had never had an occasion to wear. She turned to check her reflection in the full-length mirror. Stunning, even if she did say so herself. Shame it wasn't suitable attire for the restaurant Jonas had invited her to for their date next week. She'd have enjoyed the sensation of him unzipping her...Now where had that naughty thought sprung from?

"What do you think?" Fiona had wrapped the scarf around her neck.

As Olivia had suspected, the color suited her. "Gorgeous."

"I feel odd wearing this, but I must admit it's pretty." Fiona fingered the scarf and stared at their reflections in the mirror. "Your dress is stunning. The blue is fabulous with your pale skin and red hair."

"Thanks," Olivia said. "I might as well wear it this evening, seeing as I was reckless enough to buy it in a sale a few months ago. It's not like I have the opportunity to wear a dress like this on a night out in Ballybeg."

"Hmm...," Fiona said with grin, "I'll have to give Jonas a hint."

"Fee," she said in warning tone. "My separation's not through yet."

"So?" Fiona raised an eyebrow. "Aidan was a crap husband, and you've been separated in all but name for over a year. Time to live again."

"My friendship with Jonas is...progressing."

Fiona howled with laughter. "We need to give him a prod to make it *progress* a little faster."

"I'd like to, Fee, but my history with Jonas isn't exactly a happy one."

Her friend's smile was sly. "All the more reason to make your present with him *very* satisfactory."

"Okay, enough with the matchmaking. Come here and let me finish doing your makeup." She sat Fiona at the dressing table. After a light application of foundation, she blended a subtle shade of eye shadow and a lashing of mascara, finishing with a lick of red lipstick the precise shade of the scarf. "Not bad," she said, regarding their reflections in the mirror. "Not bad at all. We're going to have to send a photo to Gavin. Now let's hit the bar."

Jill was seated at the room's small desk, typing furiously on her laptop. "Have fun. Save a place for me. I'll join you in fifteen, okay?"

Olivia wagged a finger at her friend. "If you don't, we'll storm the room and drag you down."

Jill gave her a mock salute. "Message received and understood. Will you order a mai tai for me?"

"Will do." Olivia grabbed her handbag, and she and Fiona exited the room.

When they reached the hotel bar, it was already filling up with Friday night revelers. They squeezed through the crowd and nabbed the last unoccupied table.

Olivia perused the cocktail menu. "I think a frozen strawberry daiquiri would be just the thing to get our weekend celebrations off to a suitably decadent start."

"I think I'll have the same."

The waiter was unloading their drinks when Jill arrived. "Hey, girls." She twirled a beaded dreadlock around her index finger and glanced over her shoulder in a distracted manner. "Richard's here. You don't mind if I go over to say hi? I'll only be a moment."

Olivia choked on her drink. "Ratfink?" she spluttered. "Why the hell would you want to say hello to that creep? That dead relationship should never be resuscitated."

"Come on," Jill said pleadingly. "He's not *that* bad, surely?"

"Sorry, but the man is a snake."

"Well, he's seen me now." Jill's almond eyes widened in a pleading fashion. "I can't ignore him, especially with him working for the company I've just interviewed with."

"Oh, go on," Olivia said with a sigh. "If you want to hook up with that slimeball, you're old enough to know what you're doing."

"I'm not going to hook up with him," Jill protested. "Merely make peace. I don't want to be on bad terms with him if I get the job and he ends up being my team leader."

Olivia raised an eyebrow. "Just be sure that 'peace' is all you're making with him."

"Direct as always, Liv." Jill squeezed her shoulder. "Enjoy yourselves. I'll be back in a bit." She melted into the crowd, dreadlocks bobbing.

Olivia shuddered and took a generous gulp of strawberry daiquiri. "What on earth does she see in that creep?"

"You were your tactful self." Fiona grinned over her cocktail glass.

"Put it this way– I might be shite at picking partners for myself, but I have an instinct when it comes to my friends. I knew you and Gavin were perfect for one another, and I'm equally positive that Ratfink will bring Jill nothing but grief."

Fiona laughed. "Gavin and I were a train wreck that somehow worked out. I doubt you could have predicted that outcome."

"What?" she teased. "Drunk Elvis impersonator marries two mad Irish tourists in Las Vegas, and it turns out to be legally binding?"

"Not to mention the crashed wedding part." Fiona made a faux grimace.

"Speaking of jilted brides, how is your dear cousin Muireann?"

"Very pregnant. She's due to pop any day now."

"Wow." Olivia shuddered. "Rather her than me in this heat. Actually, rather her than me in any weather. Are her parents still not speaking to her?"

"Uncle Bernard is adamant she's never darkening his door again, but given that he's still holed up in their holiday home in Marbella until the furor of the shopping center debacle blows over, his blustering is hardly relevant. As for Aunt Deirdre, her resilience crumbled the moment she saw the first ultrasound pics. She's staying with Muireann in Clare until the baby is born."

Olivia shook her head. "How quickly things change. This time last year, you were planning your Australian trip, and Muireann was planning her wedding to Gavin."

"Crazy sauce. But I think it worked out for the best. Was Aidan badly affected by the collapse of the shopping center development scheme?"

"He took a financial hit, no question. How bad, I can't say. He never confided in me. I will say that he's been on edge for months, but that might be stress over the upcoming elections." She gestured to her friend's empty glass. "Do you want another drink? It's my round."

"Definitely." Fiona flashed a wicked smile. "While you're getting the drinks, I'm going to mosey over to Jill and her on-off dude. I know curiosity is alleged to have killed the cat, but I'm more of a dog person, ya know? I admit to unabashed curiosity over a guy you call Ratfink."

"Go for it. If you can manage to distract her from his dubious charms, I'll be forever grateful. Believe it or not, Jill's taste in men is even worse than my choice in husbands."

Fiona laughed and disappeared into the throng. Clutching an empty cocktail glass in each hand, Olivia wove her way through the masses and made a beeline for the bar.

And stopped dead.

Leaning on the counter stood Jonas O'Mahony, looking as suave and lethal as James Bond.

CHAPTER TWENTY-TWO

"Jonas?" The familiar voice jolted his attention away from his pint. His friend Joe had just left the bar, and Jonas was contemplating sleep. Like a mirage, Olivia glided toward him, her elegant dress swishing with every step she took on her sexy high heels. "What the…" He blinked. "What are you doing in Dublin?"

"Of all the gin joints in all the world. You mentioned having meetings in Belfast and Dublin but I didn't expect to run into you here." She tilted her head to the side and examined his suit and tie. "I wouldn't have thought it, but you wear a suit well."

His gaze was riveted on her pink lips. "The suit is a leftover from my meetings this afternoon. Remember the TV script I mentioned? It's a goer. RTE have commissioned a six-episode series."

Her eyes widened. "Hey, that's fantastic news. Congratulations." She placed a hand on his arm as she spoke.

"Thank you. I'm relieved. Luca's fees for next quarter are looming." He leaned closer, drawn by her sweet scent and the sight of that luscious, kissable mouth. "What brings you to the Big Smoke?"

Her hip brushed his thigh, sending a shot of pure lust to his groin. "Jill had a job interview today," she murmured into his ear. "Fiona and I came up to join her for the night."

"Sounds like fun." He was finding it hard to breathe, let alone talk. If she kept this up, he'd kiss her right here in the middle of the bar, and to hell with what anyone thought.

"Yeah. Jill's aunt got us a good deal on the room"– Was it his over-imaginative libido, or did she add special emphasis to the word *room*?– "so we're celebrating the weekend in style." The slight slur to her voice indicated that the bright red cocktail in her hand wasn't her first.

"You're certainly stylish." He raked her clingy blue dress.

She tugged at his tie and pressed her body against his. Yeah, she was tipsy. "You were wearing a tie at Gavin and Muireann's nonwedding too. I noticed. You wear them well."

"I wear them with reluctance." He untangled her fingers from the knot of his tie but didn't let them go. "Purely for the TV execs' benefit."

She tugged at the tie, her glossy lips curving into a seductive smile. "I'm more than happy to help you remove it."

"Olivia, are you sure– "

"Shh," she whispered, and laid a finger over his lips. "My legal separation should be through next week. It's time to move forward with the rest of my life, don't you think?"

Memories of those heady days of their brief teenage love affair performed a Technicolor dance in his mind. They'd been besotted with one another– mind, body, and soul. *Until that awful night.* He ran his fingers over her bare shoulder, toying with the spaghetti straps of her dress. If Olivia was ready to move on from Aidan, it was time for him to let go of the past. "Do you want to dance? There's a dance floor downstairs."

"Fiona and Jill– "

"– have seen us together and are giving you the thumbs-up."

Olivia whipped round and laughed when she spied her friends on the other side of the bar. "I'm no better at dancing than I was ten years ago."

He flashed her a wicked smile. "I have fond memories of you trampling my feet. I'll take my chances."

"Cheeky sod." She gave him a playful swat. "As I recall, you were no better than I was."

His grin widened. "But we were very compatible when it came to other things."

The memories came back in all their pixelated glory. They stared at one another for a beat until she blushed and averted her gaze. Jonas grabbed her hand and carved a path through the throng.

Downstairs the dance floor was packed with revelers at various stages of inebriation. The very worst chart music blasted from the speakers, much to their amusement.

"I can't picture you dancing to this song."

Jonas grinned. "I can't picture me dancing at all. Which is why I'm damn glad there are no mirrors down here."

He grabbed her waist and, in one fluid movement, twirled her onto the dance floor. A fellow dancer careened into them, crushed her against his chest. Her breasts pressed against his torso, and she ran a playful finger over his biceps. This close, he could taste her perfume on his tongue.

When his lips met hers, the world went still. She met him tongue for tongue in a passionate dance, pulling him closer, devouring him. Jonas craved more. He skidded his mouth along her cheek, stopping to tease her earlobe. "Do you want to go upstairs?" he whispered, nibbling the lobe and making her gasp.

"Yes," she replied breathlessly.

He grabbed her hand and maneuvered her back through the crowd. In the lobby, he pressed a button to summon the lift, never taking his attention off Olivia. When the lift arrived, they stumbled in. Jonas pressed her against the plush red velvet hangings and plundered her mouth. She slipped a hand underneath his shirt, making him growl.

When the lift shuddered to a halt, they broke their embrace and stepped into the bright lights of the corridor. They stopped in front of a door. "This is my room." Jonas fumbled with the key card and the door sprang open. He pulled her inside the room milliseconds before his mouth claimed hers once more. "Strip," he murmured against her throat, unzipping the back of her cocktail dress in one fluid movement. "I want to see you naked."

Biting her lip, she stood back and let the blue silk slip off her shoulders, cascade down her body, and pool at her feet.

Next she turned her attention to her bra. She unfastened it slowly, easing it down her breasts, revealing one bare nipple at a time before flinging the garment to the floor. He whistled his appreciation, making her laugh. "You like what you see?"

"You're beautiful." The pulse in his neck throbbed as he perused her half-naked body. She was even sexier than she'd been twelve years ago. Long red hair hung loose over her shoulders, brushing against her breasts that were high and fuller than he remembered. The rich hue of her hair complemented her ivory skin. While slim, she was no longer a skinny eighteen. Her rib cage tapered to a small waist before flaring out to form perfectly proportioned hips. "Now your knickers."

She licked her lips and his cock strained against his trousers. Giving him a knowing smile, she hooked her thumbs into the edges of her lacy thong. She tugged the garment over her hips, thighs, and legs before kicking it off with more enthusiasm than grace. Hands on hips, she stood before him, naked save for her strappy high-heeled shoes.

He let his gaze meander to her belly and between her thighs. And sucked in a breath as his cock became even harder. She'd shaved her public hair– or waxed, or done whatever it was that women did to achieve a silky smooth expanse of skin. "Jaysus. I am a lucky man."

"Now it's your turn." Her husky voice held a hint of a challenge.

He required no further invitation. Getting himself out of the unfamiliar tie took some fumbling, but once achieved, he had his shirt off so fast he lost a button or two in the process. The belt and trousers were discarded with speed, followed by his socks and underwear. He stood before her naked, hard, ready.

Her mouth formed a come-hither smile to match her beckoning finger. He closed the space between them and ran his hands through her hair, wondering at the color, inhaling the scent of her fruity shampoo. Beginning with the barest of angel kisses on her temple, he progressed to nibbling her earlobes. He heard her sharp intake of breath, felt her sag against his chest.

She trailed her fingers over his stomach. "Nice abs."

"Gav's to blame. He has me out running in preparation for the Ballybeg Sports Day."

Olivia gave a husky laugh, then slid her arms up his bare back and pulled him closer. Her bare breasts pressed against his naked chest. He bit his lip when her hand slipped down to stroke his shaft. Her free hand skimmed his spine before coming to rest on his left buttock. She traced the outline of his tattoo. "So you *do* still have it."

He returned the favor, teasing her buttock and pinching her adorable little leprechaun tattoo, a twin of his own. "I do indeed. I'm rather fond of it, as it happens."

"I was sure you'd have it removed."

"*You* didn't."

She blushed. "Despite everything that happened afterward, that night was one of the best of my life." Vivid memories of her eighteenth birthday danced before her eyes. Jonas had been studying in Dublin, and they'd arranged to meet in Cashel, a small town in Tipperary, halfway between Dublin and Ballybeg. Like a homing pigeon, Jonas had honed in on the lone bar in the town that served cocktails. "I drank my first and last tequila sunrise."

"What about your second and third?" he teased. "We were pretty drunk by the time we passed the tattoo parlor."

"I thought I was hallucinating. I didn't expect to find one in a town that small."

"What possessed us to pick the leprechaun design?"

She laughed. "I can't remember. All I know is that it seemed like a great idea at the time. Do you remember the grimy bed-and-breakfast with damp running down the wallpaper?"

He broke into a wicked grin. "Nope, but I remember what happened in the bed."

She poked her tongue out at him. "So do I."

"That's why I didn't want to get rid of the tattoo," he said, suddenly serious. "Whatever happened after, whatever's happened since, that weekend in Tipperary was magic."

Her eyes met his. "Yeah, it was."

He cupped her chin. "Want to recreate some of that magic?"

"Yes," she whispered, melting the moment he captured her lips in a scorching kiss.

He broke away, his breathing heavy. Then he rolled her onto her stomach. She giggled when he blew a raspberry on her tattoo. "Do you have condoms this time?" she teased. "Not stuck in an unpacked moving box in Ballybeg?"

He threw back his head and laughed. "All the boxes are now unpacked. As it happens, I have a couple of condoms in my wallet. Bought specially for you."

"Is that so?" she murmured, pulling his head to hers. "It would be a shame to let them go to waste..."

With a low growl, he kissed her, cupping her gorgeous tattooed arse. He pulled her up onto the dresser, sweeping his toiletries to the side to make space. His fingers slid over her inner thighs, making her gasp. When he found her clitoris, he stroked it gently, teasing the nub, hearing her moan at his touch.

She wrapped her legs around his waist and pulled him closer. "You. Inside me. Now."

He continued stroking her clitoris, felt it harden. "Don't you want more foreplay?"

"We've had months of foreplay, Jonas," she gasped. "I want sex."

"Far be it from me to disappoint a lady." Rummaging through his discarded wallet, he struck gold. She laughed into his neck while he fumbled with the foil package.

And then he was inside her. She was slick, wet, warm. He waited a moment to let her adjust to his size, but she pulled him closer and ground against him. "Impatient puss."

"Impatient? I've waited years for this."

"Ye–?"

She smothered his response with a kiss, maneuvering her hips to drive him deeper inside her.

Abandoning his attempt to take it slow and sensual, Jonas thrust fast and hard, the momentum building until the only thing penetrating his consciousness was her, him, them, this. When she cried out, he had a millisecond to register her orgasm before his own hit, blasting them into the stratosphere of mutual bliss.

***

Olivia woke to sunlight streaming through the sheer curtains. At first, she was disorientated. Then the relaxed state of her body and the vague ache between her legs reminded her of the events of the previous night. She'd had sex with Jonas. She'd had sex with Jonas three times. *Holy hell.*

He stirred beside her, turning over on his pillow. It had been so long since she'd woken up next to a naked man. She'd forgotten how much she relished the sensation of bare skin against skin. It was so much more than physical or sexual pleasure.

"Hello, beautiful lady."

He looked delectable, the mussed hair and rough stubble adding to his sex appeal. Deep brown eyes stared into hers, and his lips curved into a smile. Olivia sensed the now-familiar stirrings of sexual desire and reached for him.

Their lips met in a kiss, distracting her from any morning-after regrets she might or might not have entertained. He was gentle at first but quickly became more insistent. He nibbled her shoulder, then burned a path to her left breast. When he sucked her nipple, she moaned in pleasure.

"I'm regretting ordering room service," he murmured against her breast. "I woke up famished and ordered a full Irish for both of us. Now my mind is on you, not food."

She laughed. "I'm starving. I certainly won't say no."

He flashed her a wolfish grin, his eyes running appreciatively over her naked body. "So am I," he said, giving a wealth of meaning to the words. "Do you think we'd have time for a quickie before our breakfast arrives?"

She felt a stab of lust between her legs. "I could be persuaded."

When a hard knock sounded on the hotel room door, Jonas was on the verge of coaxing yet another orgasm out of her. "Damn. Room service was fast."

"Too fast," he groaned.

Olivia was still searching for her underwear when there was a second knock on the door– harder this time, more insistent.

"Put this on." Jonas tossed her a hotel bathrobe. "I've found my trousers, so at least half of me will be covered."

Olivia donned the voluminous robe and tied it at the waist. "I'll deal with breakfast if you round up our underwear."

"Deal." He blew her a kiss. "You're one hell of a sexy woman, do you know that?"

"And you're one hell of a sexy man."

With a smile on her face, Olivia opened the door. When she registered Sergeant Seán Mackey's familiar features, her smile evaporated. He was in uniform, his expression grim. "Seán...what on earth are you doing here?"

"Fiona told me which room you were in." He removed his hat. "I have bad news, I'm afraid."

Her heart lurched. *Please not Ronan or Kyle.*

Seán's hard blue eyes met hers. "Aidan Gant was murdered last night."

CHAPTER TWENTY-THREE

The room swam out of focus. An icy chill spread from her core, paralyzing each limb in turn. "Aidan's dead?" *As if death wasn't the logical outcome of a murder*...A dull roar echoed in her ears.

"Yes." The policeman's voice sounded distant, indistinct.

The floor beneath her feet shifted, tipping her forward. A hand steadied her before her brain registered she was falling. The warm weight of Jonas's palm on her shoulder was reassuring. "Come," he said, guiding her to the bed. "Sit."

She obeyed. Her body was wracked by shivers, and she hugged herself to stop the shaking. Jonas put a glass to her lips. "Get this down you. You're in shock."

When she drank, the shivers morphed into shudders. "Ugh. Whiskey is vile."

"It did the trick, though." Jonas stroked stray strands of hair from her face.

"I'm sorry, Olivia, but I need to ask you a few questions." Seán pulled out the dressing table chair and sat. "Then I'll drive you back to Ballybeg."

Her head jerked up. "Am I under arrest?"

"No, not at this stage." The police sergeant slipped a notebook and pen from his shirt pocket. "Have you been at the hotel all night?"

"Fiona and I met Jill at the hotel at just after seven o'clock." She darted a look at Jonas. "I haven't left since."

"That's Fiona Byrne and Jill Bekele?" Seán scribbled the names without waiting for confirmation. "Know anyone with a particular grudge against Aidan?"

"No one with a grudge great enough to kill him." Olivia swallowed past the lump in her throat. "How did he die?"

A brief look of amusement flickered across Seán's handsome features, quickly replaced by studied sobriety. "He was hit over the head with a garden gnome."

"One of his prize-winning gnomes? Was it the Chucky lookalike? That one always gave me the creeps." The words tumbled out, unfiltered.

The policeman's mouth twitched but he maintained his composure. "Here's a friendly tip: no jokes about the murder weapon when you're grilled by the NBCI team."

"Who?"

"The National Bureau of Criminal Investigation," Jonas explained. "My fictional detective works for them."

"Officially, they're supposed to assist local police with a murder enquiry." Seán's jaw flexed. "In reality, they run the show, especially if the locals have little experience with investigating serious crimes. If you find my questions uncomfortable, you'd better brace yourself for the NBCI's."

"Why didn't they send Dublin police officers to inform Olivia?" Jonas asked. "Surely you didn't drive all the way from Ballybeg in the middle of a murder investigation."

The police sergeant shook his head. "I was already in Dublin. It's my weekend off and I still have my old apartment on the Northside. When the superintendent phoned to say my leave was canceled, I volunteered to break the news to Olivia and drive her home."

"How very considerate of you." There was a hard edge to Jonas's tone.

The police sergeant's gaze roamed over Olivia's bathrobe and bare feet. "I don't agree with the crazy divorce laws in this country. You're entitled to move on with your life, but you'll have to be prepared for a grilling about your relationship with Jonas. There's no way round it. As far as the law is concerned, you were still Aidan's wife at the time of his death."

Which made her his widow today. A widow wearing an oversized hotel bathrobe with nothing underneath, sitting next to her new lover. Even in her shocked state, she knew it made a lousy impression. She tightened her belt and ignored the cold fear seeping into her bones. "What happens now?"

"You get dressed, and we'll head to Ballybeg."

A horrible thought struck her. "Will I have to identify the body?"

"Patricia Gant has already done that. She was the one who found him and notified the police."

Olivia shuddered. "Poor Patricia. She must be distraught."

"Are you two close?"

"No, but we're not on bad terms, either. We've developed an understanding over the years."

The policeman capped his pen and returned it to his shirt pocket. "We'll need to talk to you later, too, O'Mahony."

"Why?" Olivia demanded. "Jonas had nothing to do with Aidan's death."

"For both your sakes, I hope that's true, but it's widely known that he and Aidan fought recently."

Her mind was foggy, but the full implications of Aidan's murder were starting to penetrate. "Jonas is your number one suspect? For defending me on the beach?"

"He's not *my* number one anything. Once the NBCI guys show up, it won't even be my case. As I said before, you'll have to be prepared to answer uncomfortable questions. Speaking of which"– Seán checked his watch and got to his feet– "we'd better get a move on."

Olivia looked around her vaguely, at a loss. "Okay. I need to get dressed and pack my things."

"One of your friends is already on it. Reception sent me to the room you were sharing. I didn't tell Fiona why I was here, but I did ask her to pack your bag."

"Should I come, too?" Jonas asked, frowning. "Seeing as you want to talk to me."

"Best not." The police sergeant's tone brooked no argument. "But we will want to talk to you today, if possible."

"Fair enough. I'll be back in Ballybeg by late afternoon. When should I come by the station?"

"Say five o'clock? The detective leading the case will be there by then." Seán turned toward Olivia. "I'll meet you in the lobby in fifteen minutes. Will that be enough time for you to get ready?"

"Yes. I'll see you then."

When the door closed behind the policeman, Olivia locked eyes with Jonas. "I loathed Aidan but...murder?"

The truth of her situation was slowly trickling into her consciousness. Aidan was dead. There would be no divorce. She was a widow. And most likely a murder suspect. Disjointed thoughts tumbled through her mind. The ringing in her ears grew louder, and she struggled to breath.

Jonas placed a hand between her shoulder blades. "Slow down. Take nice, deep breaths."

She nodded, trying to focus on getting enough oxygen.

He sat on the bed beside her and rubbed her back in a circular motion. "What's your room number? I can ring Fiona and arrange to collect your bags."

"204." The rapid rate of her breathing was easing off, but speech was a challenge.

Jonas continued to rub her back. "Shall I tell her what's happened, or would you prefer to do that yourself?"

"No, go ahead. She and Jill will be wondering what's going on."

"Okay." He picked up the phone on the bedside table. At that moment, room service arrived. Olivia staggered to her feet and dealt with the porter. Before Seán had arrived, she was ravenous. Now the very thought of food turned her stomach.

Jonas hung up the phone. "I've arranged to meet Fiona and collect your stuff." He moved to the breakfast tray, poured a cup of piping hot tea, and added a generous heap of sugar. "Drink this. It'll do you good."

Her hand fluttered to her throat. "I'll be late to meet Seán."

"Feck Seán. Five extra minutes won't make a difference. You've had a shock. Get some sugar into you and then go downstairs. Fiona's got an outfit organized for you to wear."

While Jonas was gone to get her luggage, Olivia sipped sweet tea and stared into space. *For better or worse...* She'd married Aidan and spent the past eight years with him. *For richer or poorer...*For the first time in her life, she didn't give a toss about her financial situation. *In sickness and in health...*If Aidan died, she'd expect it to be from an illness. Despite his fit appearance, he was a functional alcoholic and was careless with his health. *Till death do us part...*

A few minutes later, Jonas returned. Fiona had placed a mismatched outfit for her at the top of her case, alongside her cosmetic bag. Good old Fee. Practical to the last with zero fashion sense. After a lightning quick shower, she threw her clothes on in silence, not bothering with makeup. Grabbing her handbag from the nightstand, she walked to the door, pausing to give Jonas a kiss on the cheek. "Thanks," she said softly. "For last night. I'm sorry it ended like this."

Jonas drew her to his chest, and her tears began to flow in earnest. "All thanks should be on my part," he said in a hoarse voice. "And I was rather hoping it wouldn't be just last night."

"But you can see things are different now." She reached for a tissue from the box on the dressing table. The same dressing table on which they'd had hot sex the night before...how long ago that seemed now.

"I don't see that things between us are different, but we don't need to have this conversation right now." He dropped a kiss on her forehead. "I'll give you a call later, okay?"

"All right." Today would be unspeakably awful. She'd never seen a dead body before, let alone a victim of murder. She'd attended a few wakes in her time, dragged by her ultra-Catholic Grandmother Dunne, but she'd always looked away from the corpse. This time she wouldn't have that luxury.

Taking a deep breath, she stepped through the hotel room door, ready if not prepared to face the inevitable unpleasantness of the day ahead.

CHAPTER TWENTY-FOUR

The drive to Ballybeg was a blur of gray motorways, green fields, and cloud-speckled blue sky. Olivia barely registered the passing landmarks. Her thoughts were consumed by death. She hadn't loved Aidan. Hell, for the past few years, she hadn't even liked him. But murder? Even he didn't deserve such a fate.

It wasn't as if she mourned him. She was no hypocrite. But death was so…final. Only yesterday, she couldn't wait to be free of him. Today, she regretted all the things left unsaid that might have given her a sense of closure.

A vision of the gnome danced before her, and a treacherous hysterical laugh bubbled up her throat. Once the laughter began, she was powerless to stop it until it morphed into guttural sobs.

Seán reached across from the driver's seat and handed her a fresh tissue. "I know it's tough, but you're going to have to pull yourself together before you meet Connelly, the guy heading the NBCI team. Trust me when I say the man's an arse. If you show any sign of weakness, he'll go for the jugular."

She dabbed at her eyes, relieved she hadn't bothered with makeup. "Thanks for the tip. How do you know Connelly?"

"I worked with him in Dublin." A brief silence. "He used to be my boss."

She stared at him, slack-jawed. "*You* worked for the National Bureau of Criminal Investigation? How did you end up stationed in Ballybeg?"

"Long story. Definitely one for another day."

"Did it have something to do with this Connelly guy?"

"Just mind your step around the man, okay?" A muscle in his jaw flexed. "Look, I don't know what happened to Gant. My instinct tells me you didn't kill him, but my instinct won't convince a judge or jury."

No, unfortunately, it would not.

The remaining half hour of the drive passed in silence. By the time Seán drove through the gate of Olivia's former home, the clawing dread she'd felt since that morning had turned into a vicious headache. She massaged her temples in a futile attempt to alleviate the pain, averting her gaze from the army of gnomes that flanked each side of the driveway. She'd never liked them, had poked fun at Aidan for being proud of his collection, but never in a million years had she imagined one would be used to kill him.

They were met at the door by two NBCI officers, both grim-faced men in suits who glared at her with open hostility. Brian Glenn hovered in the background, assisting the forensics team. He didn't meet her eye. And so it had begun– the suspicions, the assumptions, the judgments.

Had it not been for the several pairs of eyes boring holes in her back, nothing in the entrance foyer would have seemed out of the ordinary. "Is he..." Her voice broke. "Is he still here?"

"No," Seán said gently. "The body has been taken to the pathologist. Your mother-in-law identified him. What we need you to do is look at the crime scene and tell us if you notice anything missing from the room."

"Where did it happen?"

"In his office. From what Patricia Gant indicated, the murder weapon– "

"The gnome?"

"Yes. It was in Aidan's office because he needed to repair it." She fingered the spot at the base of her throat where a beaded necklace usually hung. In her haste to dress, she'd forgotten it. "Aidan did all that stuff himself. Also touching up their paint. He'd spend hours in there, tinkering with his gnomes. I think it was the only time he was truly content."

She was babbling, not to mention delaying the inevitable. She propelled herself forward, each leaden step bringing her closer to the office. A white-suited forensics worker backed out of the room, carrying a box filled with small plastic bags and test tubes.

*Another few steps...*She came to an abrupt halt outside the office. The door was wide open, giving her a full view of the carnage within. A thin trickle of red stained the wall, but the Persian carpet was thick with blood.

Bile surged up her throat. She took a step back, exhaling sharply. Her ears rang with a strange, clanging noise. This couldn't be happening. Any moment, she'd wake up and it would all have been a horrible nightmare.

"You must be the wife."

At the sound of the nasal Dublin accent, she spun round. The man standing before her was fiftyish. Heavyset with coarse features and raisin orbs spaced too close together. Although he was barely a few centimeters taller than she was, his presence dominated.

"You must be Detective Connelly."

The nostrils of his crooked nose flared. "Detective *Inspector* Connelly."

Fabulous. Why hadn't she thought to ask Seán his rank? The man didn't offer his hand in greeting.

"Is anything missing?" Connelly demanded. "Anything out of place?"

She raised an eyebrow. "Apart from the blood?"

The man's closely spaced eyes grew even narrower. "Smart aleck, aren't you? Just answer the question."

Hesitantly, she took a step closer to the office entrance. It was like wading through water. Her limbs were heavy, as if the entire force of gravity was upon them. And the smell...she'd never smelt death before, yet she was in no doubt that she was smelling it now beneath the acrid smell of blood. She stuffed her knuckles into her mouth to stop the gagging.

Despite her revulsion, she forced herself to scan the room. A forensics photographer was hard at work, snapping photos of every surface. There was no sign of the murderous gnome.

She stepped back and shook her head. "Everything looks to be where Aidan usually kept it. But you have to understand that his office was his sanctuary. I rarely came in here, and I haven't lived in this house for months."

Connelly stabbed her with his dark-eyed stare. "So I understand. Where were you last night, Mrs. Gant?"

"Olivia, please. Mrs. Gant makes me think of my mother-in-law."

"Mrs. Gant." The detective emphasized every syllable. "Answer the question."

A cold trickle of dread snaked down her spine. Apart from being an obvious dickhead, this man already had her pegged as guilty. "I was at the Ashbourne Hotel in Dublin."

"Alone?"

"No. I went up to Dublin with two friends. Fiona Byrne and Jill Bekele."

"You were with them all night?"

"Well..." She hesitated for a beat. "Not all night."

"Where were you if not with your friends?"

"I..." She took a gulp of air, trying to stem the dizziness. "I spent the night with a guy I know."

"Does this guy have a name?"

"Jonas O'Mahony."

Connelly's hard stare bore into her. "Would that be the same Jonas O'Mahony who punched the deceased a few months ago?"

She gave a stiff-necked nod.

Seán materialized at her side. "O'Mahony is due at the station at five o'clock this evening. I can also verify that both he and Olivia were at the Ashbourne when I went there this morning." He gave Olivia a side glance. "They didn't look like they'd left the room all night."

"If I wanted your opinion, Mackey, I'd have asked for it." Connelly's expression had turned from hostile to thunderous. "Take your partner over there and go give out traffic tickets or herd sheep. Whatever it is police usually do in Ballybeg."

Disgust flickered over Seán's face. Giving Olivia a brief nod, he turned to leave the house with Brian.

Another scribbled note in his notebook. She wondered if Connelly was keeping a running tally of all the incriminating evidence against her. The way he looked at her made her skin crawl. She'd had nothing to do with Aidan's death and had no reason to feel responsible. Damn the man for making her feel guilty for a crime she didn't commit.

She scanned the room. The Murano glass vase she'd bought Aidan on their honeymoon was lying on its side on the floor. Miraculously, it was still intact. She reached for it. The man grabbed her wrist. She blinked back tears from the crushing pressure.

"Don't touch anything, Mrs. Gant," he said severely. "This is a crime scene. Everything needs to stay exactly as it is."

She wrenched her arm out of his grasp and massaged her wrist. She resented his tone, resented his insistence at using a name she didn't acknowledge. She debated arguing the point with him once more but didn't want to give him the satisfaction of getting a rise out of her. He was there to investigate Aidan's murder. Although the inquest wouldn't be held until Tuesday, it was clear to everyone that they were dealing with a homicide. As the victim's estranged wife, she was the prime suspect. *Feck them all.*

"I can't tell if anything's missing," she said in a flat tone. "Everything's all over the place. It's usually so... orderly."

The man scribbled another note in his notebook. His gaze collided with hers. "Any idea who could have done this?"

Olivia shook her head. "Sergeant Mackey already asked me that. Aidan was a solicitor, a member of the town council, and running for mayor. Of course there were people he'd pissed off over the years, but murder? I can't see it."

"Yet someone did murder him."

"Yes," she said, "someone did."

The smell of blood assailed her nostrils. She tasted bile. Covering her mouth with a hand, she lurched out the door, nearly colliding with a uniformed policeman on the steps.

Two more meters...She vomited into the fountain, narrowly missing a gnome. So much for showing no sign of weakness in front of the police. Their accusatory stares bore into her back. Wiping her mouth with a tissue, she addressed the young man guarding the door. "I think I'll go home," she told him.

"Where would home be, Mrs. Gant?" asked the homicide detective, looming at her back.

"My cottage," she snapped, finally at the end of her tether. "Where else? You know perfectly well that Aidan and I are...were...separated. I no longer live here. Ask my mother-in-law if you don't believe me."

"Quite the temper, haven't we?" the man drawled. His self-satisfied smirk made her blood boil. "I will talk to Mrs. Gant Senior again. You can be assured of that. She had a few choice words to say about you when I met her this morning."

Olivia was sure Patricia had had plenty to say about her, probably at ear-shattering decibels. Despite developing a cordial relationship over the years, they'd never been friends, and Patricia was the sort of person who always sought someone else to blame for her woes. Aidan's death would have devastated her, and Olivia was an easy target for her grief-fuelled rage. "Is Patricia here now?"

He smirked. "Luckily for you, no."

Olivia nodded dully. A dizzy sensation overtook her. In her mind's eye, she saw Aidan's body lying face down on the office floor, the back of his head bashed in. Her morbid imagination was in overdrive.

The detective inclined his head, the hardness of his stare never slackening in intensity. "We'll be in touch, Mrs. Gant. Don't stray too far from Ballybeg."

CHAPTER TWENTY-FIVE

Olivia was down the drive and out the gate before she remembered that she was without a vehicle. *Feck*. She sagged against the wall and ran through her options. Aidan's house was located on the outskirts of Ballybeg, less than a thirty-minute walk from the town center and her cottage. She could call someone to collect her, but it might take them longer to get here than it would for her to go home on foot. Mustering her remaining strength, she started to walk.

The road into town meandered past tumble-down farmhouses and luxurious new-builds. The former were owned by people whose families had farmed the land around Ballybeg for generations. The latter were divided into two categories: deluxe holiday rentals, and mansions belonging to Cork City's newly rich (the extra living space more than compensated the short commute to their jobs in the city). For a local boy to afford a house as grand as the Gant residence, Aidan's father had done extremely well for himself. Aidan, had he lived longer, was poised to do even better.

Olivia's brisk pace didn't falter until she reached a partially dug-up tract of land. If Fiona's uncle, Bernard Byrne, hadn't fiddled the books, this would have been the site of the controversial new shopping center. Aidan had been one of the investors, and one of the people to lose money when Bernard did a runner. Could that have had something to do with the murder? But how? Using a gnome as the weapon seemed personal, impulsive.

She continued walking, only veering from the main road when she reached the small woods near Ballybeg Primary School. There was a clearing in the woods with a makeshift playground. She'd played here with Fiona as a child and had taken Luca a couple of times recently.

Thankfully, the playground was deserted. Olivia claimed her favorite bench and pulled out her phone to send a quick text message to Fiona and Jill. They'd be out of their minds with worry. She should call them instead of texting, but she didn't feel up to dealing with the inevitable questions. She needed a moment to think, a minute to breathe.

Once the text was sent, she contemplated her next move. Where could she go? The café was out of the question. Every gossip in Ballybeg would be there, feigning a desire for one of her buttered scones but in truth looking for the latest salacious detail of the investigation. *Gawd.* She put her face in her hands and groaned.

A familiar child's voice drifted over the breeze. For a moment, she thought her mind was playing tricks on her.

"Olivia!"

She looked up to see Luca bounding toward her. His dark hair was in need of a cut, the fringe almost covering his eyes.

"Hey, there." Her gaze strayed beyond the little boy to his father.

Jonas was wearing more clothing than the last time she'd seen him. The thought brought heat to her cheeks and a pain to her breast. They stared at one another for a long moment. Part of her wanted to leap up and throw herself into his arms. The other part was cemented to the bench. Would he reject her now that Aidan had been murdered? He'd said he didn't want their night together to be a one-off, but he'd had the whole day to come to his senses, not to mention the specter of a police interview looming over him.

"Olivia."

"Jonas." She was reminded of their awkward greeting that day in the dental surgery. It seemed ages ago, yet it had only been a few months. "Did you just get home from Dublin?"

"Yeah. Luca and I are here for a quick play before I drop him back to my parents' house. I'm due at the station in an hour." His dark eyes searched her face. "How are you?"

"Okay. I'm going to have to call Patricia." Her voice wobbled. "I'm not looking forward to that conversation."

He knelt beside her and took her hands in his. "How was it at the house?"

"As you might expect. It was a murder scene."

He nodded, slowly and deliberately, as if weighing his words. "Have the police formally questioned you yet?"

"I don't think so. I...don't know. They asked questions. I answered them." She stared at the dry leaves beneath her feet. "Seán was right. The NBCI guy is a right arse."

"Do the smart thing and get yourself a lawyer. Don't answer any more questions without one."

"Problem is, who? The only lawyers I know are in Aidan's circle of contacts."

"Karen McCormack? I've interviewed her a few times for my detective series. She has a practice in Cork City."

"The name doesn't ring a bell, which is probably a good sign. Yeah, give me her number and I'll call her. Thank you." She bit her lip. "I'm sorry you've been dragged into this."

He kissed her on the cheek. "Don't worry about me. Once you call Karen, don't worry about anything. Neither you nor I killed Aidan. The police will have a devil of a time proving we did."

CHAPTER TWENTY-SIX

On the Monday after the murder, Jonas pulled into a parking space outside the turquoise façade of the Book Mark. He glanced at his reflection in the rearview mirror. It wasn't a pleasant sight. Dark hollows under his eyes and a persistent headache were his reward for two sleepless nights. The grilling by Detective Inspector Connelly and his team had been unpleasant, but it paled in comparison to the prospect of telling his mother he'd slept with Olivia. That was going to be one hell of a conversation.

Tossing this morning's edition of one of the national newspapers onto the passenger seat, he rubbed his aching temples. Joe, the journalist pal he'd met at the hotel bar Friday evening, had already called to find out if he had any inside info on the Ballybeg murder. The media hadn't yet picked up on his link to Olivia, but it was only a matter of time. He'd have to tell Mam today or risk her hearing about it on the news. *What a bloody nightmare.* Grabbing a box from the backseat, he got out of the car.

Inside the Book Mark, Bridie Byrne was totting up numbers in a ledger while Fiona and Gavin drank coffee at a table in the bookshop's small café.

They all looked up when he entered.

"Hey there, stranger." Gavin stood and clapped him on the back. "Come join us for a coffee. You look like you need one."

"No amount of caffeine could jolt me into functional consciousness today, but I wouldn't say no to an espresso." Jonas deposited the box on an unoccupied table and slumped into a chair. "I brought the mystery books for your window display, Bridie. All the crime fiction authors at the reading in Belfast signed a few copies for you."

The older woman beamed. "You're a sweetheart. My customers will be delighted."

Fiona placed an espresso cup under the spout of the coffee machine and hit a button. She was fiddling with her lip ring and appeared agitated. "Have you seen Olivia? I'm worried about her. She's not answering her phone."

"I got a text from her yesterday, but she hasn't been back to her cottage since Friday." Jonas rubbed his jaw, noting this morning's lousy attempt at a shave. "I called into the café before I came here. Jill said she was expecting Olivia to arrive at any moment."

Bridie raised her head from the account book. "Olivia is staying with the Major for a few days. Jill and Naomi are running the café and doing the baking, hence our well-stocked scone basket."

Fiona put her hands on her hips. "You didn't think to mention this to me?"

Bridie peered at her niece over half-moon spectacles. "*You* didn't think to ask."

"Have you seen her?" Fiona demanded. "How is she?"

"Apart from her estranged husband being clobbered to death with a garden gnome?" Bridie raised a sardonic eyebrow. "Hard to tell. I'm no psychologist, but I'd guess she didn't respond to your calls because she knew that whatever hold she had over her emotions would crumble the moment she heard a friend's voice. Old codgers like me and the Major don't count. We serve cups of tea, talk about the weather, and pretend we don't know she's having sex with Jonas."

That jolted him out of his exhausted haze. "What? How the hell did you know that?"

"How the hell did I *not* know that?" Gavin waggled a finger at his wife. "Have you been holding out on me?"

Fiona gave an insouciant shrug. "I was being discreet."

"You, discreet?" her husband guffawed. "That'll be the day."

Fiona placed a double espresso on Jonas's table and shivered. "I hated Aidan, but even he didn't deserve to be murdered. I wonder who did it."

"*Death by Gnome...*" Gavin mused over his coffee cup. "Now there's a title for Jonas's next book."

Jonas choked back a laugh. "Don't start. I'm trying to ignore all the plot ideas this has generated and focus on reality."

"Who do you have pegged as the murderer?"

"I haven't pegged anyone for anything"– Three pairs of eyes waited expectantly– "but if I were compiling a list of potential suspects, I doubt it would include anyone the police haven't already thought of: members of the town council, Aidan's opponents in the mayoral race, and his girlfriends– current and former."

"A lot of people were upset when the shopping center project fell through," said Bridie, "but my brother was to blame for that. Thank goodness Fiona and I got our inheritance money out of the rat before he absconded. Did you hear Muireann had her baby? A little boy named James."

"Gavin mentioned it, yes." Dismissing newborns from his mind, Jonas considered the shopping center angle. "I can see your point about people being upset when the plan fell apart, but the development was controversial. Many locals were delighted it never got built. From what I understand, Aidan lost money on the deal. There doesn't seem to be any reason to suspect he benefitted from Bernard's embezzlement."

Bridie shrugged. "It's a puzzle, isn't it?"

Jonas drained his cup and got to his feet. "Thanks for the coffee, Fiona. I'd better get to work. I'll stop by the café on my way and tell Olivia to give you a call."

"Please do."

"Thanks again for the signed books," Bridie called. "If you see Olivia, tell her I'll be by the Cottage Café this afternoon to discuss the catering for Ballybeg Sports Day."

"In which you and I are participating, remember?" Gavin cast him a wicked grin.

Jonas groaned. "I think I blocked it from my memory. I know I tried."

"No chance. I'll ring your doorbell at six tomorrow evening. Luca knows to be ready."

"Will he be running with Wiggly Poo again?"

"That's the plan. Let's wear out our kid and dog, eh?"

"Always the optimist, Gav," Jonas said with a grin. "Judging by past experience, they'll outrun and outwear us."

CHAPTER TWENTY-SEVEN

The police might have a devil of a time proving their guilt, but the people of Ballybeg wasted no time in passing judgment. As Olivia had suspected, the café was packed all day Monday. In addition to the Cottage Café's many regulars, a steady turnover of new customers came to stare and dig for gossip.

"A terrible thing to have happened," Nora Fitzgerald said with relish over her morning tea and buttered scone. "A fine figure of a man cut down in his prime. And with a garden gnome of all things."

Olivia gritted her teeth and concentrated on loading plates onto a tray. Mrs. Fitzgerald was one of the café's most loyal customers. As much as it pained her, she'd have to tolerate the comments or risk losing Nora's custom.

"Ah, give over, Nora." Bridie Byrne shut the café door behind her and glared at her friend. "Have you no other topic of conversation? You've been making the same trite remarks all weekend."

"We've a murderer in our midst." Nora's shrill voice rose to a crescendo. "Aren't you concerned?"

"Not in the least." Bridie sank her considerable weight into a chair and helped herself to a berry scone. "Aidan Gant would've driven a saint to murder. The only surprise is that someone didn't clobber him to death before now."

Bridie caught Olivia's eye and winked, eliciting a small smile. Bridie was nosy and bossy, but she was a good sort. She wouldn't forget the older woman's willingness to offer up her spare room for the couple of weeks following the beach incident.

Nora Fitzgerald wasn't a bad sort, either. Having known Olivia all her life, she breezed in and out of the café with a sense of entitlement, determined to ferret out whatever nuggets of gossip she could discover. She was a nice woman in her way, but Olivia was fed up being the focus of speculation. First it was her separation from Aidan. Now it was her possible involvement in his murder. Much as she loved living in Ballybeg, there were times she longed for the anonymity of a big city. This week definitely qualified as one of those times.

Wiping sweat from her brow, she carried a tray of hot buttered scones, clotted cream, and freshly brewed coffee to a table of curious customers. Their inquisitive stares made her cringe. She longed to hide in the kitchen and shut out the world. Sleep eluded her these days, and her panic attacks were back in full force. If it weren't for the tablets her doctor had prescribed, she wouldn't be functioning in any capacity. But function she must. She had a business to run.

Plastering a smile on her face, she faked warm hospitality. "Can I get you anything else?"

The customers shook their heads, the tempting aromas proving a momentary distraction from goggling at Olivia. After refilling the sugar dispenser, she retreated to the kitchen, leaving Jill in charge out front. Thank goodness for the sliding door between the café and the kitchen. She usually left it open, but today she was grateful for the option to shut out the noise.

She sniffed the air in distaste. Baking was a form of solace, a refuge in times of stress. Unfortunately, its therapeutic wonders were on strike. She poked the latest batch of scones. Dry and overdone would be a compliment; they were burnt to a crisp. *Feck.* She'd have to start from scratch. She squeezed her eyes shut. This was not like her. With a sigh, she reached for the flour and went to work. She'd popped a fresh batch into the oven when the door slid open. Jonas stepped into the kitchen. A knot formed in her stomach.

"I called in a couple of times this morning to see if you were here." He appeared ill at ease, his Adam's apple working overtime. "How are you doing?"

Olivia focused on the dough she was kneading for soda bread. "Thanks, but there's no need to check up on me. I'm fine."

Tentatively, his hand touched her back. The warmth sent a shock of sensation through her thin blouse. "Don't shut me out, Olivia. I realize you've had a shock. I'm not going to push you to make a decision on whether or not to keep seeing me. Take your time. I think we've made enough progress over the past few months to consider ourselves friends."

All of a sudden, the room was stiflingly warm and he was too close. "How can we continue to see each other after what's happened?"

"How can we not?" His voice broke as he slid his arms around her waist. "Our night together wasn't some random fling, Olivia. It meant something. You mean something to me. I threw it away once before. I won't make the same mistake a second time."

She buried her face into his chest, inhaling his now-familiar scent. "I don't want to throw it away, either. If only the timing wasn't lousy. Everyone thinks we killed Aidan. If they don't think *we* did it, they definitely think *I* did. Did you see the looks those ladies gave you in the café?"

"How did you know about that?" he asked with a small laugh. "You were in here when I walked through."

"Because I can guess," she said bitterly. "I've had to deal with them all morning. Thanks to the local rag, everyone knows I was in your hotel room when Seán came to tell me about Aidan's murder."

"The local rag got that story? Damn. I was hoping to break it to my mother before the media did." He ran a hand through his hair and groaned. "Damn them out there in the café. Let them think what they want. You and Gant were separated for months before anything happened between us. He was hardly a faithful husband when you were together."

Olivia rubbed her bone-dry eyes. "Everyone knows that, and no one cared until Aidan was killed. As for the NBCI crowd, are they even looking for anyone else? The looks Connelly gives me make me feel like I'm already in handcuffs."

Jonas pulled her close and kissed the top of her head. "We've done nothing wrong, Olivia. There's not a shred of physical evidence to link you to the crime."

"You're more optimistic than I am," she said, pulling away from his embrace. "Why couldn't they have kept the investigation local? The only one of them with a scrap of sense is Seán Mackey."

"Bringing in outside help is standard procedure for a murder. Detective Inspector Connelly and his team have a reputation for getting results. The Ballybeg police haven't dealt with a murder in more than twenty years, and that was a straightforward case of murder-suicide."

Calmed by his soothing voice and common sense, her breathing eased into a normal pattern. "How can you stay calm? I'm a nervous wreck."

"Panicking is counterproductive. The police will want straight answers, and that's what we'll give them." He cupped her face gently in his hands, his finger tickling her nose playfully. "All this worrying isn't healthy. Come on. Sit down and have a cup of tea."

Her mouth curved in a reluctant half smile. "You sound like my grandfather."

Jonas laughed. "I sound like my mother. That's even worse."

She bit her lip. "I'm sorry you've been dragged into all this."

"Stop apologizing. It's not your fault. I don't regret punching Aidan, and I definitely don't regret sleeping with you."

She slipped out of his arms and went to stand by the small window over the sink. A cool breeze meandered its way inside. She shivered and hugged herself. "I can't believe he's dead," she whispered. "And to die in such a way. I couldn't stand him, but I wouldn't wish this on anyone."

"Nor I. It does, however, eliminate the need for a divorce."

She spun round. "Jonas," she exclaimed. "How can you be so callous?"

"I don't mean to be callous. I'm saying what the police are thinking, not to mention the entire population. Speculation is rife on how much you stand to inherit."

Her laugh was bitter. "I doubt I'll get much. As I've said before, Aidan was careful to keep as much as he could in his mother's name. The grim irony is that I'd have done better financially had he lived. He'd just suggested a golden handcuffs deal, whereby I'd get a substantial payment in return for keeping my trap shut about his affairs and domestic violence."

Jonas's eyes widened, and he took a step back. "Do the police know about this?"

She nodded. "The conversation took place the last time I saw Aidan. So, yeah, I mentioned I saw him in the café. I told them what we'd discussed, but they didn't seem to believe me. Apparently, they could find no record of the settlement details."

Jonas frowned. "Who handled Aidan's affairs?"

"Most of it he did himself, but he was using a solicitor from Cork to handle our divorce. As far as I know, he was going to handle the settlement."

"You have to contact Aidan's solicitor. Don't you realize it lessens your motive for killing Aidan? If you were going to get more money out of him through the divorce, why murder him first?"

"Yes, it occurred to me." Her voice rose a notch. "I'm not a fool. I told Connelly about it, but he was dismissive."

"What about Karen McCormack, the solicitor I recommended? Did you tell her?"

"Of course I did," she snapped. "I might not write detective fiction, but I'm not a complete imbecile."

"I'm not implying that you are," he said gently. "I'm trying to help."

She swallowed past the lump in her throat. "I'm sorry for losing my temper. My emotions are all over the place at the moment."

"No worries." Jonas stroked the back of her neck. "Can anyone verify what was said when you and Aidan discussed the settlement?"

She sighed. "Unfortunately not. There was no one to overhear our conversation, but I did tell Fiona and Jill about it right after."

He considered for a moment. "Not ideal, but at least they can verify you told them about it before Aidan was killed."

"Aidan said he was going to send his solicitor a copy of the proposed settlement. Let's hope he followed through."

"For your sake, I hope so too." He bent down and gave her a brief kiss on the forehead. "Listen, I'd better pay my mother a visit. If I don't hear from you within the next couple of days, I'll come looking for you."

She gave him a warm smile. "I'll call you as soon as I've spoken to Aidan's solicitor. How's that?"

"Okay." He released her hand slowly. "Talk then."

After Jonas left, she squared her shoulders and got back to work. They needed loaves of soda bread for the evening crowd, and the bread was not about to bake itself. She was up to her elbows in dough when Jill burst into the kitchen.

"There's a riot out there, Olivia. Come quick!" She had never seen Jill's placid face flustered.

She wiped her hands on her apron. "I'll come right away."

With the sliding door open, raised voices were audible.

"What on earth?" She hurried into the café and surveyed the scene. Bridie Byrne and her friends wore belligerent expressions. Newly arrived were Julie Jobson and a couple of her pals. *Blast.* This was not going to be pretty.

When Julie caught sight of Olivia, her face adopted an expression of sheer hatred. "Murderer! First, your brothers attack James. Now you've killed Aidan. Violence must run in your family."

Olivia's world spun on its axis. The lingering suspicion she'd had that Julie had been among Aidan's many conquests crystallized. Somehow, the idea of Aidan with Julie hurt more than all the others. He knew Julie had bullied Olivia in school.

"I didn't kill Aidan." Her voice shook, but she wouldn't let herself cry. Not in public, and certainly not in front of Julie Jobson.

"Well, if you didn't kill Aidan, he must have done it." Julie pointed a purple talon at the wall, presumably indicating Jonas's cottage.

"Don't be daft. Just because Jonas writes murder mysteries doesn't mean he has firsthand experience."

Julie curled her lips in distaste. "Bridie was gloating she can't keep his books in stock. Crime author suspected of murder? You couldn't buy publicity that good."

As perverse as it sounded, Julie was right: the notoriety would likely increase his book sales. A murder mystery author suspected of a brutal crime? *Cha-ching*. Not that he'd have chosen this route to gain extra sales, but that was the way the world worked.

"You're sick, you know that?" snarled Julie.

"And you're a fool," said Bridie. "How dare you come in here accusing Olivia and Jonas of murder? Have you any proof?"

"I'm sure the police will take care of that," Julie said with a sniff.

Olivia lifted her chin in defiance. "I'm sure they won't. They can't prove what didn't happen."

"Julie's only saying what the whole town is thinking," said an elderly man with a cane. Olivia recognized him as one of Aidan's fellow town councilors. As far as she was aware, he hadn't darkened the door of the café once before today.

She froze him with an icy glare. "Are you in the habit of spreading slander, Councilor Evans? Hardly fitting for a man in your position."

"It won't be slander when the police arrest you and your boyfriend."

"Leave Jonas out of this." Olivia folded her arms across her chest. "He's not here to defend himself."

"And Aidan is?" countered Councilor Evans. "Poor Patricia was bereft when he married you. You're no better than your mother, and everyone knows what she's like."

Her already frayed temper ripped. "Are you quite finished?" Her voice trembled, but she stood her ground. "If so, I'd like you to leave. You can take Julie and her pals with you."

Councilor Evans bestowed her with a parting look of loathing and made his unsteady way to the café door. Julie and company followed suit.

Ignoring the stares of the café patrons– some gleeful, others sympathetic– she hurried in the direction of the kitchen.

She wouldn't cry. Hot tears stung her eyes, but she wouldn't let them fall. She didn't want to give the vultures the satisfaction of seeing they'd gotten to her. And they had. Far more than she cared to admit. She grasped the kitchen counter to stop from shaking. She'd opened a new business in Ballybeg. It wasn't as if she could up and leave, but she didn't know how much more of the stares and the jibes she could take before she'd crack."

CHAPTER TWENTY-EIGHT

"How could you?" Nuala O'Mahony's hands trembled with such force that when she set her cup on the table, tea sloshed onto the stained wood. "I told you not to get mixed up with that girl. She brought you nothing but trouble twelve years ago, and now she's got you mixed up in a murder investigation."

Jonas took a deep breath and focused on his parents' hideous kitchen wallpaper. Patience was what he needed, and patience was what he sorely lacked. "It's not Olivia's fault someone murdered Gant."

"Why was I left to discover your involvement with Olivia in the *Ballybeg Chronicle*? I'm too embarrassed to show my face outside the house." Mam's hands fluttered to her throat. "Who'll look after Luca when you go to prison? Me and your dad? We're not getting any younger."

He stared at his fingertips. Deep, cleansing breaths were doing nothing to keep his temper in check. "Mam, I am not going to prison. I was brought in for questioning, not arrested."

"Sure and it's only a matter of time." His mother tugged on the crucifix around her neck. "I saw the way those Dublin detectives stared at you when they dropped you home on Saturday. Oh, why can't you do the right thing for once in your life? If you're not dropping out of college, you're getting girls pregnant. When is it going to stop?"

Jonas counted to ten before replying. "First, I never dropped out of university. I switched from an engineering degree to one in journalism– which I completed with first-class honors. Second, Susanne is the only girl I ever got pregnant, and I took responsibility for Luca. We've been over this a thousand times."

"But you didn't *marry* the girl," his mother insisted. "You should have gotten *married*."

"The girl, as you call her, didn't want to marry me," he said tersely. "As it turned out, she didn't even want Luca."

"What sort of example are you setting for Niall?" Her mouth opened and closed in a silent prayer.

Jonas thought of his little brother, away at university, blithely ignoring his studies in favor of partying. "I doubt Niall needs my help in learning to misbehave," he said dryly. "Besides, I work hard to support my son. How is that setting a bad example? As for Susanne, I don't see what difference a marriage certificate would have made to our relationship. We'd have broken up either way."

If his mother tugged any harder on her necklace, she'd strangle herself. "I'm only saying what other people think. If you hadn't gone and punched Gant on the beach a few months ago, no one would suspect you of murder."

He shoved his chair back and stood. He'd had enough of this crap. "Let them think what they like. I know I had nothing to do with Gant's death, and that's all that matters."

His father lumbered into the kitchen, clad in his work clothes, Luca by his side. "That's enough, Nuala. Leave the boy in peace."

"You always stand up for him, Liam," she said bitterly. "You won't hear a word said against him."

"Of course I always stand up for him," Liam said gruffly, meeting Jonas's eye. "That's what dads do." He gave Luca a gentle shove toward Jonas.

Jonas took the hint. "And this dad is going to take this boy home to bed. Thanks for looking after him this afternoon."

"Ah, he was no bother. Great little lad, he is." He nodded to Jonas. "Come on. I'll walk you two to the car."

Outside the house, Luca ran to the car and got into the back seat. Jonas made to go after him, but his father laid a hand on his arm. "Don't mind your mother. She has a sharp tongue at times, but she loves you. She's out of her mind with worry."

"Doesn't she realize I'm worried, too?" Jonas said in exasperation. "And not just for myself. If those clowns from Dublin cobble up enough so-called evidence to charge Olivia with murder, there's no guarantee a jury will find her innocent."

"I know, son." Liam's graying eyebrows were drawn together. "But you're doing Olivia no good by worrying yourself into a fret."

Jonas plucked a stray leaf off a garden bush. "Let's face it– Mam's saying what you both think. I know you have no time for Olivia."

"Don't put words into my mouth or my mind," Liam said in a gruff tone. "I won't deny I've said negative things about Olivia in the past, but she was good to Luca while your mother was away, and she was a pleasure to work with during the café renovation. Besides, I never had time for Aidan Gant. A nasty, sly weasel of a man."

"Wow. I had no idea you disliked him so intensely."

Liam snorted. "Why wouldn't I? He swanned around Ballybeg like he owned the place and every woman in it."

"His affairs were common knowledge?" His voice rose in a question. "I had no idea he was unfaithful until Olivia mentioned it."

"Oh, yeah. He was discreet, but word gets round. I assumed Olivia put up with it for the money."

The idea of anyone, let alone strong, feisty Olivia, being brought so low as to feel they had to tolerate such treatment set his teeth on edge. "I think she felt trapped."

"If she did, it was a trap of her own making." His father waggled bushy eyebrows in disapproval. "Mind you, it's no wonder her priorities are skewed. That family of hers is a bad lot, particularly the mother.

Neither she nor her husband pay any attention to their children."

Jonas grimaced. "Olivia's mother was never my greatest fan."

"Of course not. You don't fawn over her overexposed cleavage and crappy art."

"Now, now, Dad," he said with a laugh. "Your claws are showing."

Liam snorted. "If I were the police, I'd look in a different direction for Aidan's killer."

His eyebrows shot up. "What do you mean? Do you know something?"

"I know nothing," he said, his mouth forming a belligerent line. "But I'm in and out of houses in Ballybeg every week for work. I can't help but hear snippets of gossip or see things I'm not supposed to."

"If you have any idea who did this, you have to talk to the police."

His father sighed and shook his head. "Son, if I had proof, I would. They're not going to listen to a hunch, now are they?"

"Probably not," he conceded. "But for feck's sake, don't go around telling people you know who did it. I don't want you to be the next victim."

His father crossed his arms and gave him That Look that had scared the bejaysus out of him as a child. "I'm not a fool, Jonas. If the person I suspect is the guilty one, I wouldn't dare get on their bad side."

CHAPTER TWENTY-NINE

Olivia stared numbly at the coffin. None of it seemed real. The mass of people milling around– even more than at Aidan's wake – was an exercise in torture.

A lot had happened in the four days since the incident at the café. The police had questioned her again, this time with her new lawyer present. She'd told them everything she knew, including a list of Aidan's girlfriends, people he'd argued with over politics, and former investors in the shopping center project. Once again, Connelly had dismissed her story about Aidan's proposed settlement. No evidence of a draft had been found on Aidan's computers, and his divorce lawyer claimed ignorance.

The forensic pathologist had finished her work a couple of days previously, and the body had been released to the family for burial. During an awkward conversation with Patricia, she gave her mother-in-law formal permission to organize the funeral as she saw fit.

And now here Olivia was, sitting stiff-backed in a church pew, the hard wood uncompromising and uncomfortable as the accusatory stares from the congregation.

She shifted on the hard bench, grateful for her brothers sitting on either side of her. Their parents and grandfather also sat in the front pew on one side of the church; Aidan's mother and her few relatives were on the other. Patricia was regal in her dramatic black gown, complete with a veiled hat. Olivia fingered her beige cardigan. The hypocrisy of wearing relentless black revolted her. She'd compromised by choosing subdued colors. Her eyes flitted over the tall stained-glass window at the front of the church. She avoided looking in Patricia's direction. The one cold glance she'd caught from her had been hard as flint.

Her nostrils twitched from the cloying scent of incense. Thank goodness she wasn't expected to do a reading. Father Fagin droned on, as he was wont to do, making the mass seem interminable. Father Fagin was ancient and had known Aidan since his christening. He relayed every small incident from Aidan's life, all highly embellished. Olivia remembered the vicious jokes Aidan used to make at the elderly priest's expense. He obviously hadn't envisioned the elderly priest officiating at his funeral.

At last the bells tolled, and the procession from the altar to the graveyard commenced. Her grandfather linked arms with her as they followed the coffin. The younger members of the town council carried it to the hearse along with a couple of men from the Gnome Appreciation Society. Try as she might, the only emotion Olivia could muster when she stared at the rich mahogany casket was a numb sense of regret. Partly for Aidan, partly for herself, and partly for the entire sorry situation. How had this happened? A few weeks ago, she'd been happy. For the first time in years, she'd felt at peace, light, carefree. Now it was all smashed to smithereens.

At the graveyard, the crowd surrounding Aidan's plot brought out her inner claustrophobic. In typical Irish fashion, the whole town had turned out for the funeral. Those who couldn't squeeze into the church had made sure to storm the graveyard. Aidan had been a well-respected member of the town council and solicitor to many of Ballybeg's inhabitants. The fact that he'd been murdered merely added to the allure of his funeral. She shuddered. People were sick.

On the other side of the plot, she registered Jonas's tall form, standing toward the back of the crowd with Luca and his parents. Liam gave her a nod, but Nuala merely pursed her lips and looked away.

Julie Jobson and her family were there, snobby and aloof. The look of sheer hatred in Julie's eyes gave Olivia the shivers.

She shifted her attention to her own family. Resplendent in black velvet, Victoria's eyes were red-rimmed and downcast. Beside her, Dad shifted uncomfortably in his ill-fitting suit. Despite all that had happened, Aidan had been their friend once upon a time.

When the coffin was finally lowered into the ground and the requisite prayers intoned, the crowd began to disperse. Olivia had taken a few tentative steps toward the car park when she someone grabbed her arm. Sharp nails dug into her skin. The cloud of Elizabeth Arden's Youth Dew tipped her off before she turned.

"You're a disgrace," hissed her mother-in-law. "I told Aidan not to marry you. I warned him no good would come of it. But even I didn't foresee you stooping to murder. You and that...that...fornicator."

Fornicator? Seriously? Who used that term in this day and age? This was fast descending into a third-rate comedy, only Olivia wasn't laughing. She yanked her arm free. Whatever fragile hold she'd had over her emotions splintered. "Shut your mouth, Patricia. I didn't kill Aidan, and neither did Jonas. Let the police do their job before casting aspersions."

"Oh, I'll let them do their job all right." Patricia mouth trembled. "I'll help them in any way I can. Anything to get you and that murdering thug locked up. We're not safe in our beds with you at large."

"Oh, for feck's sake. Get a grip. We lived under the same roof for the best part of eight years. In all that time, did I give you any reason to be afraid of me?"

Patricia sniffed. "I always knew there was something off about you. I told Aidan. I warned him." She heaved a sob. "And look what's come to pass."

Seán Mackey approached with purposeful gait. "Anything the matter, ladies?"

"I want this creature to leave." Patricia's voice broke on a sob. "I don't want her anywhere near my son's funeral."

She gestured to the dispersing crowd. "In case you hadn't noticed, the funeral is over. I wasn't planning on coming back to your place for sandwiches."

"Come on, Olivia." Seán took her arm gently. "Let me drive you home."

"Home is where I was headed before Patricia ambushed me." She huffed in frustration. "But I refuse to slink off letting people point fingers and assume I have something to be ashamed of. After all, Aidan slept with half the women here. Anyone with a scrap of intuition knows our marriage was a farce."

Patricia made a choking sound.

"Olivia," Seán murmured, a pained expression on his face, "is this the moment?"

"No, of course it's not. But I'm fed up with people judging me when they don't know what my married life was like." She faced Patricia. "I didn't kill your son, and I didn't wish him dead, but I'm not sorry he's out of my life."

Seán's eyes darted around the crowd. "Christ, Olivia. Shut up for your own sake. Connelly's itching to arrest you. Don't give him an excuse."

She put her hands on her hips. "Do you have proof against me?"

"You know we have nothing concrete, or else we'd have come calling long ago."

"So I can say what I like." Hot tears spilled down her cheeks, and she rubbed them away hastily.

Seán ran an agitated hand through his tightly cropped hair. "Come on. I'll take you back to the cottage."

"No need," said a familiar deep voice from behind her. "I'll drive her home."

Seán's blue eyes clashed with Jonas's dark ones. Olivia suppressed a groan. Now was not the moment for them to have a macho power struggle.

Thankfully, Seán shrugged, conceding defeat. "Fine. Just make sure she stays clear of Patricia."

Jonas nodded gravely and took Olivia's arm. She allowed him to lead her through the curious crowd toward the graveyard car park.

"Was that wise?" she whispered as they approached Jonas's car. "If the gossips hadn't already guessed there was something between us, you've confirmed it now. I'm beyond caring, but your parents will be upset."

"My parents already know I'm seeing you," he said and pressed the automatic car key. He held the passenger door open for Olivia before getting into the driver's seat.

Her jaw slid south. "You told them about us? Are they upset?"

"I didn't have to tell them. They read about it in the local rag like everyone else." He grimaced. "They're not thrilled, but they'll get over it. Dad rather likes you in his grudging fashion. Mam brought up Bry again, but I cut her off. It's high time she accepts his death was an accident and stops blaming you." He pulled out into the road and drove in the direction of their street. "Speaking of grieving mothers, you're going to have to learn to hold your temper around Patricia Gant. In her current mood, she'll do anything to prove you killed her son."

Olivia's stomach sank. "She can't prove what didn't happen."

He cocked an eyebrow. "Are you sure? She was in no hurry to support your story about the settlement. If part of it would have been her money, she must have known about it."

"Yet she denied all knowledge of it to the police," Olivia said with a sigh. "Yeah, I see where you're coming from, but Patricia needs someone to blame and I'm an obvious target."

"So avoid her."

She gave a little laugh. "Easier said than done in a town this size. Plus I'll see her tomorrow at the reading of the will."

"That won't be pleasant."

"Quite the understatement." She groaned and put her face in her hands. "I was obsessed about becoming financially independent from Aidan. The very idea of inheriting his money is nauseating."

"It might give you enough to get a house large enough for you and your brothers."

"I know. It's what I've been working toward for ages. I feel awful profiting from Aidan's murder."

Jonas turned into their road and eased the car into his parking space. "Could you go away for a few weeks after the will's read? Did the police say you had to stay put while they conduct the investigation?"

"They haven't confiscated my passport, if that's what you mean. But Detective Inspector Connelly"– she made a face– "'strongly suggested' I not go anywhere."

He cupped her chin in his hand. "I worry about you, Olivia. Those shadows under your eyes tell me you haven't been sleeping. A break might do you good."

"Perhaps. But I have the café to run. Besides, if I was going anywhere, I'd rather it be with you." She leaned forward close enough to smell peppermint on his breath. "Daft as it sounds, I'm glad you're next door. It helps knowing you're nearby."

"You know you can call round at any time, right?" He dropped a kiss onto her forehead. "I haven't pushed myself forward since Aidan's death because I sensed you needed the space. If that's no longer the case, please tell me."

Olivia put a hand on his thigh, feeling the now-familiar thrill of awareness course through her veins. "I don't want to push you away and don't want to wreck what we've started. But my emotions are all over the place. I'm not sure I'd make good company at the moment."

"So?" He gave a laugh. "I live with Luca, remember? He's not exactly Mr. Sociable. Call over anytime, or text me if you want us to come next door."

"Thanks, Jonas. I will." She opened the car door, then paused before getting out. "Are you coming inside, or do you need to collect Luca?"

"I need to collect him. My mother has a doctor appointment in an hour, and Dad has work. Will you be all right on your own?"

"I'll be fine. I'm going to give Fiona a call to see if she can come by."

"You do that." He leaned over and gave her a feather-light kiss on the lips. "Now get inside and pour yourself a large whiskey. After the morning you've had, you deserve it."

She watched him drive off and then fumbled through her bag for her key. *Why can't life be a little less complicated?* she thought as she climbed the ladder to her loft apartment. Why couldn't everything run smoothly from Point A to Point B without meandering detours and unexpected forks in the road? At twenty, she'd been sure of her path in life. Even a couple of months ago, she could see her way. Now everything was thick with foggy indecision and uncertainty. And fear. If the Cork detectives charged her and Jonas with murder, would a jury find them guilty?

CHAPTER THIRTY

Olivia's hand froze over the cake, the knife suspended in the air. Was she hearing right? "You don't want to move in with me?" she repeated dumbly. The walls of her grandfather's kitchen closed in on her.

Ronan and Kyle exchanged uneasy glances. "Why did you think we would?"

"I...," she stammered, "I just thought you two were keen to escape our parents."

Ronan flushed and stuck his hands in his pockets. "I said I couldn't wait to move out of home. I never said I wanted to move in with you."

"No offense, Sis," Kyle said with a grin, "but I don't think I'd like living under your regime. Mum and Dad let us do pretty much whatever we want."

She wrung her hands in exasperation. "That's precisely the problem." Had she wasted all this worry over their home situation for nothing?

Kyle jerked a thumb toward their grandfather's living room. "What do you think of my new girlfriend?"

"Serena seems a nice girl," replied Olivia cautiously.

Kyle's grin widened. "In other words, you hate her."

"I didn't say that."

Ronan cocked an eyebrow. "Why would any of us be interested in your girlfriend? You'll have a new one by next week."

Kyle ignored his brother and yanked open the fridge "Serena wants a diet cola. I'd better bring it in to her. Want one, Ro?"

"Yeah," Ronan said. Kyle tossed him the drink, and both boys disappeared back into the living room.

After they left with the drinks, Olivia poured herself a large glass of water and massaged her throbbing temples. In an attempt to restore family harmony, her grandfather had gathered the clan for lunch on the Sunday after the funeral. The reading of Aidan's will had revealed that while Aidan had very little money in his own name, the small holiday house he owned in Cobh was mortgage-free and now belonged to Olivia. She couldn't do anything with it until probate ended. Once that occurred, she'd planned to sell the house and use the money to buy another in Ballybeg, one large enough to accommodate her brothers, should they wish to live with her. Which, apparently, they did not.

Her grandfather slipped into the kitchen and closed the door. "Not exactly the Sunday lunch I'd envisioned. Too soon after the funeral?"

Olivia bent down to pet Jasper and give him some leftovers. These he consumed with gusto. "Perhaps."

"I take it the boys didn't respond well to your offer of an alternative home."

"No. I was sure they'd be delighted." Her stomach twisted at the memory of their mockery. "I thought I was rescuing them, but it turns out they don't want to be rescued."

"They're teenagers. Jim and Victoria aren't the most responsible, but they're not mistreating the boys. The boys, I suspect, rather enjoy the freedom that comes with having absent-minded and self-absorbed parents."

"I was certain they'd jump at the chance to live with me. It was part of my plan to escape Aidan."

"I know I'm just a doddery old man, but I've lived a long while."

"Hardly doddery, Granddad. You're fit as a fiddle. I want you to stay that way for many more years."

"I hope so, my dear," he said with a small smile. "As for your brothers, don't you think you used the idea of the boys needing rescuing to motivate yourself to leave Aidan? It's often easier to fight for those we love than for ourselves."

"Perhaps you're right." She gave a little laugh. "You should have become a psychologist, Granddad."

"I have no patience. I'm much better at barking orders at people. The army was perfect for me." He regarded her with concern in his eyes. "How are you coping at the café? With the rumors, I mean."

She shrugged. "There's little I can do to stop them. Until and unless the police arrest someone for the murder, they'll continue. I heard what you did, by the way. Sticking up for me in the supermarket. Bridie mentioned it to Fiona."

"Ah." A faint pink tinged his cheeks.

"Thanks, Granddad, but don't feel you need to defend me every time some eejit makes a remark."

" A *disparaging* remark, Olivia. You're my granddaughter. I will always defend you against vicious rumors and vile accusations."

His words brought tears to her eyes. On impulse, she kissed his warm, wrinkled cheek. "I love you."

"I love you, too, my dear." He paused in his task of polishing the wine glasses. "There are a couple of topics I've been meaning to discuss with you." He fished in his trousers' pockets before extracting a neatly folded piece of paper. "First, here's the number of a barrister in Cork. He specializes in criminal cases. I think you should give him a call and make an appointment. If there are any fees to be paid, send me the bill. You deserve the best legal representation money can buy."

"It's kind of you, but don't you think you're jumping the gun? I have a solicitor, and she seems to be doing her job."

"I wish I could be as optimistic," he said grimly. Then, catching her stricken expression, "No, I know you didn't do it, dear, but the justice system doesn't always favor the innocent. I think you should talk to this man before the police come knocking on your door. Know your rights ahead of time."

Tears stung her eyes, making her blink. "The police aren't even looking for anyone other than me and Jonas. That's what frustrates me the most. They've already decided we're guilty, and now they're just trying to figure out how they can stitch us up." The longer the police focused on them as the sole suspects, the harder it was to envisage a future with Jonas. Over the past few months, she'd grown used to having him next door, had enjoyed rekindling their former friendship and reigniting the spark between them. For the first time in years, she was happy. The idea of that happiness evaporating terrified her.

"I'm sure the police are exploring many roads of enquiry," her grandfather said. "If they weren't, they'd have arrested you and Jonas by now."

"In that case, wouldn't talking to a barrister be like tempting fate? My solicitor hasn't mentioned it yet."

"Nonsense. It's the sensible thing to do. If the worst should happen, you'll have someone familiar with the case whom you can call." He pushed the piece of paper toward her. "Now, come. Take the number and use it."

She took the piece of paper reluctantly, rubbing the quality paper between her fingertips. Moleskine, she'd bet. Her preference was for Claire Fontaine. And by dwelling on stationery, she was trying to distract herself. Sometimes her sharp self-perception was a bitch.

"I hope you're right," she said. "I don't want to go to prison for a crime I didn't commit. Much as I despised Aidan, he deserves justice. If they pin it on us, the real murderer will never be found." She'd seen the way Connelly and his team looked at her. They were convinced of her guilt. They were merely biding their time on the arrest until they had more concrete evidence, whatever that might be. She knew her DNA would be all over Aidan's house. How could it not be? She'd lived there up until a few months ago. But she highly doubted her fingerprints were on the gnome that had been used as a weapon. "Okay, I'll ring the barrister tomorrow."

Granddad squeezed her arm. "That's my girl."

"What was the second thing you wanted to talk to me about?"

Her grandfather's face grew grave. "A person rather than a thing. Jonas."

She took a shuddery breath. "You think I should stop seeing him, don't you?"

"Please don't misunderstand. I'm fond of Jonas. I think he'd be good for you under different circumstances." He laid a hand on her arm. "But whatever happens with the murder investigation, your continuing involvement with Jonas will do you no good in the eyes of the town. You depend on the people of Ballybeg for your business."

"And Jonas has Luca to think of." She stared out the kitchen window and the sea. "I hear what you're saying, and I know what I have to do. It's just seems unfair. For the first time in years, life was working out for me."

She glanced in the direction of the closed kitchen door. “I suppose we’d better serve the coffee and cake.”

He grimaced. “I suppose we’d better.”

Conversation flowed no more freely over dessert than it had during dinner. The Major made several remarks designed to be conversation openers, after which everyone lapsed into silence once more.

Olivia brooded, avoiding thinking about Jonas by turning the facts of the case over in her mind. Aidan didn’t have many friends, but the list of people who actively hated him was short. Apart from herself and Jonas, there were, of course, her parents. Hate might be too strong a word to apply, but they certainly had reason to resent him. He’d bailed them out of financial difficulties, but at a price. There was Moira Keating, Aidan’s last mistress. If the rumor mill were to be believed, she was fairly bitter about being thrown over in favor of a younger, blonder replacement in the weeks prior to Aidan’s death.

Then there was the landscape architect who claimed Aidan had stiffed him on a bill a couple of summers ago. He seemed an unlikely candidate, but one never knew. If only she had access to Aidan’s private files, perhaps she’d find some irregularities in his dealings with clients.

Clutching at straws, but what else could she do? Sit and wait while the homicide team gathered evidence to support their theory that she and Jonas murdered Aidan? She didn’t want to go to prison. And she certainly didn't want to go to prison for a crime she didn't commit.

When the family gathering finally drew to an end, Olivia gave her grandfather a quick hug. "Thanks, Granddad. For everything."

"Chin up, old girl," he whispered into her ear. "It'll turn out all right in the end."

She certainly hoped so.

Her family's good-byes were awkward, with only Ronan taking the time to address her personally. "Cheer up, sis," he said with a slight smile, unconsciously reiterating their grandfather's message. "Once they lock up whoever killed Aidan, tongues will stop wagging."

Olivia was getting into her car when an idea struck her. Her parents were in a good position to know of anyone who had a grudge against Aidan. Perhaps they had a few names she hadn't thought of. On impulse, she leapt back out of the car and strode over to her mother. "Mum? Can I have a word? In private, preferably."

If Victoria was surprised, she hid it well. "Why don't you call around tomorrow?" she said airily. "Your dad and the boys will be out in the afternoon."

"All right. I'll call you before I leave the café."

In Victoria's case, calling in advance was essential, preferably no more than five minutes before arriving. She was apt to forget arrangements and never bothered to cancel if something better cropped up. When it came to a visit from her daughter, something better *always* materialized.

Now for the task she'd been putting off since the morning in the Ashbourne hotel– breaking up with Jonas.

CHAPTER THIRTY-ONE

"Dad? Are you going away?" A lone tear ran down Luca's cheek.

If someone had punched Jonas in the gut, it wouldn't have hurt as much. He held a mental middle finger up at all the autism experts who insisted autistic kids couldn't emote. He'd never found that to be true in Luca's case, although part of him wished it were today. If he could absorb Luca's pain, he'd do so in a hot second. But he was powerless to shield Luca from hurt. Instead, he knelt down in front of his little son and held out his arms. After a moment's hesitation, Luca took a tentative step toward him.

"Please don't cry," he said gently, taking his son into his arms. "I'm not going anywhere."

"Tommy Daly said you were going to prison," Luca said with a hiccup.

Damn Tommy Daly. And damn whatever adult had mentioned the murder investigation within his hearing. He stroked Luca's cheek, wiping away his tears. "Tommy is wrong. The police are investigating a serious crime. They need to talk to lots of different people to find out what happened, including me and Olivia."

"But they think you did it," Luca insisted. "If they think you did it, they'll lock you up."

Luca looked small and vulnerable in the oversized dinosaur sweatshirt Gavin had bought him for his last birthday. A lump formed in Jonas's throat. He could lie to the kid, but it wouldn't be fair. "At the moment, maybe the police do think that. Olivia and I are hoping to convince them otherwise."

"And if you can't?"

"Well...we'll just have to hope for the best and see what happens."

"You can't promise you won't go to prison?"

Jonas bit back a groan. Luca needed reassurance. How could he promise the child something he couldn't guarantee? "If the police do arrest me, there'll be a trial before they decide to send me to prison. I'll get a good lawyer, and he or she will try to make sure I don't go to prison."

Luca was clearly not satisfied with this response. "Can I sleep in your bed tonight? I'm scared."

"Yeah, go on," Jonas dropped a kiss onto the little boy's tumble of dark curls. "Just don't hog the quilt this time."

"I never hog the quilt," replied Luca in indignation.

"Hmm...," Jonas said teasingly. "That's not how I remember it. Go on and get your teddy."

Luca disappeared into his bedroom, soon returning with his dino encyclopedia and a well-loved bear.

"I'll read you a story before you go to sleep. Then I have to get a bit of work done. I'll be in after that."

It didn't take Luca long to travel to the land of slumber. As Jonas watched the small, sleeping form, his temple began to throb. Would that he could take Luca's worries away. But Luca voiced the same concerns that were plaguing him. He was terrified of being sent down for something he didn't do and leaving Luca all alone. Yeah, his parents would help out, but that wasn't what he wanted for his son. Luca belonged with him.

His mother's absence had been an eye-opener. He'd loved spending more time with Luca and getting to know the little guy better. He'd also loved watching Luca interact with Olivia. Somehow, seeing her be sweet with his son had resurrected all the feelings he'd suppressed for years. Yes, they'd been lovers for a brief and intense couple of weeks, but they'd been friends long before that. The sooner this damn murder investigation was over, the better. The longer it dragged on, the less likely it seemed that he and Olivia would be able to make their relationship work.

Despite his brave face, he worried that they'd charge Olivia. His writing research meant he knew far too much about life inside an Irish prison to regard a sojourn there with anything but horror. Tucking the covers around Luca, he bent down and placed a kiss on his forehead. He closed the bedroom door behind him quietly and padded down the hallway to his home office. After his extravagant promise to hire the best legal representation money could buy, he'd best get cracking on his manuscript.

The cursor blinked on the monitor. His heart raced. Jonas took a deep breath and began to type.

He'd finished three pages when the doorbell rang. A glance at the clock told him it was late for callers, especially ones he wasn't expecting. Then he remembered the text message he'd heard come through earlier but had forgotten to read. He grabbed his mobile phone. Sure enough, there was a brief message from Olivia, asking if he had time that evening to talk. Without a moment's hesitation, he bounded to his feet and strode toward the front door.

Olivia looked pale and tense in her stylish blue jacket, her long red hair uncharacteristically wild.

A ball of panic formed in his stomach. "What's wrong? What's happened?" He took her hand and tugged her over the threshold and into his arms.

"Did you get my message?" The bags under her eyes indicated she'd passed another sleepless night.

"Just this instant." He moved aside to let her pass. "Come on in."

She looked past him dubiously. "Are you sure it's okay? I don't want to disturb Luca if he's sleeping."

"Don't worry about it." He took her jacket and hung it by the door. "Luca's insomnia never starts before midnight. Come on through to the kitchen."

He led her toward the kitchen and put on the kettle. It was too late for coffee, but Olivia was fond of a cup of hot tea before bed.

She cradled the steaming mug in her hands, a haunted expression on her face. Just as it had with Luca, seeing her this stressed physically hurt. He reached for her hand. "What's up?"

"Ever since the morning at the Ashbourne," she began, her eyes downcast, "We've been skirting this topic. I think it's best we stop seeing each other. I know we said we'd keep our distance, but we haven't been very good on following through. The more we're seen together, the more the police will focus on us as the suspects."

Her words slashed him like a dagger, the ball of panic turning to bile. He opened his mouth to protest, but she held up a hand.

"Please, Jonas. Just hear me out. I've started doing a little digging around of my own. Maybe I can come up with an idea of who killed Aidan. Until I do, or until the police make an arrest, I'm going to stay away from you."

He opened his mouth to protest, but she held up a hand to stop him. "For Luca's sake, if for nothing else. Remember the story you told me about selling your motorbike because Luca was having panic attacks? You gave up something you loved because you love your son more. That's what a good father does. Now it's time to give up me."

He wanted to contradict her, say it didn't matter to him what the police thought. Then a vision of Luca's worried face danced before his eyes. If he were sent down, how would he earn the money necessary to pay for Luca's therapies? Even if his father labored until he was seventy, he'd never have enough to pay those sorts of sums. Jonas squeezed his eyes shut and uttered an oath. His number one priority was supporting his son. It had to be. No matter how much he cared about Olivia, Luca's welfare came first.

"I fecking hate this." He slammed a fist on the table. "If those incompetents from Dublin would concentrate on doing some actual detecting, we wouldn't have this threat hanging over us.

"I know." Her eyes were wet, her voice thick with emotion. "The police seem fixated on the idea of us scheming together to kill Aidan. But if we're seen less together, perhaps they'll consider other options."

He came round to her side of the table and slipped his arms around her. "This isn't over, Olivia. We're not over. The moment the police find the killer, I'll come knocking on your door."

"I'll be waiting." She leaned up and kissed his cheek, her lips skimming past the edge of his mouth. He had to resist the urge to grab her and kiss her the way she deserved to be kissed.

She stepped back and moved to the coat stand. "I'm glad we've at least put some of our ghosts to rest over the past few months. I cared deeply for Bry. I hated you thinking I'd ever harm him, either willfully or through negligence."

"I know that, Olivia. I've always known it."

She shrugged into her jacket and reached for the door handle.

"Wait." He spun her around and took her in his arms. "Promise me that if you do come up with any ideas as to who could have killed Aidan, you'll go straight to the police. Don't put yourself in unnecessary danger."

Her eyes were haunted and bloodshot from tears, shed and unshed. "If I have even a hint of a clue, I'll tell Seán Mackey."

"That's my girl." With a final bittersweet kiss, he released her. "I guess this is good-bye."

"I prefer *slán go fóill*," she said, blinking through her tears.

He swallowed past the painful lump in his throat. "Good-bye for now it is."

CHAPTER THIRTY-TWO

Fiona was in full outraged mode. "This is madness. How can you throw away a perfectly good man because you're afraid of screwing up a second relationship? For heaven's sake, we all screw up multiple relationships before we find The One. Even then, some of us screw that up as well. Look at me and Gavin."

Olivia stopped kneading dough and faced her friend. "You and Gavin weren't the chief suspects in a murder case."

"*But you didn't do it*. The police have to know that."

She shook a ridiculous amount of flour on the kitchen counter and attacked the dough. "I don't know what they know, Fee, but that's not the point. It's not that I'm afraid of another relationship. One crappy marriage has left me with scars, true, but I still believe in happiness, and I know I'll find it someday. And I hope the person I find it with will be Jonas. But the timing is all types of wrong. We both have baggage, and now there's this investigation hanging over us..." She swallowed hard. "The best thing I can do for both our sakes is to keep my distance."

Fiona threw her arms up in exasperation. "You're determined to play the martyr, aren't you? We all have baggage, Liv. You have baggage. Show me someone pushing thirty who doesn't have baggage, and I'll show you the *really* screwed-up person in the room. Jonas has a kid. Check. Jonas has an ex who may or may not show up at some point and cause trouble. Check. His mother holds you responsible for his brother's death. Check. But if he's willing to give it a go despite all that plus take on all *your* baggage, surely you can do the same for him? I know you love him."

Olivia wiped flour from her brow and washed her hands in the kitchen sink. "Yes, I love him. And I know he feels something for me, but I don't know if it's love." Her voice caught. "He never mentioned love, not even after we slept together."

Fiona's face crinkled in amusement. "Hate to bring it up, but your Morning After was rather dramatic. I doubt whispering sweet nothings were at the forefront of his mind."

"Point taken," Olivia said, wiping her hands dry. "But I know I've made the right decision. Jonas and I have no future together."

Fiona raised a pierced eyebrow. "Are you trying to convince me or yourself?"

"Do you want a list of reasons why the timing is craptastic?"

Her friend crossed her arms. "Go on then."

Olivia tossed the towel on the counter. "First, his mother hates me for what happened to Bry. I know Jonas says it wasn't my fault, but I can't imagine Nuala will ever accept that."

"So what if she doesn't?" Fiona scoffed. "You want to be with Jonas, not her. Most in-law situations have their tensions. Just be true to yourself and live life to the full. Jonas's parents will either accept you, or they won't. Frankly, they're Jonas's problem, not yours."

"Secondly, Jonas has Luca, and I have the promise I made to offer my brothers a home. We both have responsibilities to other people."

Fiona rolled her eyes. "Oh, please. You're brilliant with Luca, and he obviously adores you. I don't see him being an obstacle. As for your brothers, they turned down your offer. I don't think they'll change their minds. Let it go, Liv."

"Whatever about Kyle, I was certain Ronan would jump at the chance to escape Mum."

Fiona shook her head. "I don't know about that. Ronan's angst seems standard teenage fodder. I doubt it would be any different if he lived with you."

"But I'd have them in a routine. I'd make sure they ate healthily, did their homework, and went to bed at a decent hour."

Fiona grimaced. "Sounds like Teenage Me's idea of hell."

Olivia blinked. "I'd have loved more stability growing up."

Fiona grinned. "Are you certain?"

"I...well..." Olivia broke off, flummoxed, and pinched the skin above her nose. "If business in the café continues to decline, offering a home to the boys might be a moot point."

Fiona's brow creased in concern. "Are things that bad?"

"Not quite, but they will be unless trade picks up. Business stress is yet another reason that it's crappy timing for me to start a relationship with Jonas, not to mention the oh-so-small matter of us being the prime suspects in a murder enquiry."

Fiona paused. "That part is unfortunate, I'll admit."

Olivia exhaled sharply. "It's a bit more than 'unfortunate.' It's a flipping disaster. Every time we're seen together in public, speculation increases. The best thing I can do for all of us is keep my distance."

"What about Luca? Are you going to ignore him, too?"

"Don't be daft. He's a child. I'd never snub him." Actually, she missed the little guy terribly. After a thorny start, they'd grown fond of one another.

"Why don't you offer to look after him for an afternoon?" Fiona persisted. "After all, you've built up a relationship with the kid. Seems cruel to cut contact with him when he's gotten used to having you around."

"I have no intention of cutting contact with him. I'm not heartless. Actually, I was going to offer to take him to play in the woods."

Fiona gave a sly grin. "An excellent idea."

"You're a relentless matchmaker," Olivia said dryly. She slid the loaves of bread into the oven and set the timer. Her first port of call in her quest to do a bit of private sleuthing was her parent's house. The very notion of facing her mother filled her with dread. She removed her apron and smoothed down her hair. "Right. I'm off to see Mum. Walk out with me?"

In the main room of the café, Jill was sipping a latte and flicking through a glossy magazine.

"Hey," Fiona said, "did you get that job you interviewed for in Dublin?"

A wide smile spread across Jill's face. "Yes. I start the first week of August."

"Congratulations. You'll be working at the Sports Day next Saturday?"

Jill laughed. "For my sins. Will you be there?"

"Alas, yes." Fiona made a gagging motion. "Bridie is on the organizing committee, and I've been roped into serving drinks."

"In that case, I'll see you Saturday."

"Will you be okay on your own until I get back?" Olivia asked.

"Sure," Jill said. "Take your time. It's not like we're rushed off our feet with customers these days."

No, they weren't. The initial macabre curiosity after the murder had waned, and many of the café's regular customers were staying away. All the more reason to get to the bottom of the mystery. She couldn't afford for the business to go belly-up, especially with Jill departing for her new job in Dublin in a few weeks.

Outside the café, she pulled her car keys from her handbag. “If I don’t see you before Saturday, have a good week.”

“Thanks. You too.” Fiona gave her a bear hug. “Take good care of yourself. Please think about what I said.”

“I will.”

Her friend strode off in the direction of the Book Mark, and Olivia climbed into her car. A quick check in the rearview mirror told her that her makeup was perfect. She added an extra layer of lipstick just in case. Spending an hour or two in her mother’s company was her idea of hell, but she needed to find out what Victoria knew. If the police weren’t going to find Aidan’s killer, she would. Olivia gunned the engine.

***

Victoria flicked ash into an overflowing ashtray and took a sip from her wine glass. “I don’t know why you keep going on about it. Aidan didn’t confide in me.”

Olivia wrinkled her nose with distaste. She despised cigarettes and disapproved of anyone drinking alcohol this early on a weekday. A lifetime of dealing with her parents had given her a healthy disdain for all forms of substance abuse. She was aware of her hypocrisy in this regard. She was allergic to people passing judgment on her, yet she had no problem judging her parents.

“Mum,” she continued calmly, “I was just asking if you knew anyone other than us with a particular grudge against Aidan. Maybe Dad knows something. He was friends with Aidan for decades, after all, and he might have been more privy to his business dealings than I was."

Victoria's eyes narrowed. She took another drag on her cigarette. "Leave your dad out of this. Isn't it bad enough he's lost his livelihood?"

"Has he started looking for another job?" asked Olivia. The question was perfunctory. She knew her father had neither the gumption nor the professional reputation to find another position.

"He's been to the job center," said Victoria with a sniff, "but they have nothing suitable to offer."

"What do they have that would be unsuitable?"

"Don't be cheeky. You know very well your dad can't turn his hand to manual labor, especially not at his age."

Olivia winced at the notion. She'd seen Dad wield a hammer. The results weren't pretty. "Fine. I know it's hard to find a job these days. Is he eligible for unemployment benefits?"

"For goodness sake. Stop with the questions. I don't know, and I don't want to know." Victoria sloshed another dollop of wine into her glass, not bothering to offer any to Olivia. "Besides, once you come into your money, we'll be fine."

Olivia's heart lurched against her ribs. "What do you mean?"

"What do you think I mean? You'll help us out, surely."

Oh, feck. She should have anticipated this. "No, Mum. I have no intention of giving you any money."

Victoria's expression turned glacial. "What about your brothers? Do you want them to be homeless? Patricia is threatening to throw us out of the house."

"Cut the dramatics. If I can afford a place large enough, I'm happy to offer them a home. Supporting you and dad is out of the question. And as I'm hardly in a position to take over Aidan's law practice, I can't exactly offer Dad a job." She gave a sly grin. "Now if either one of you are interested in helping out at the café, I'll see what I can arrange."

Victoria's face went pale then red with rage. "You'd have me work as a waitress?"

"No. I was thinking of someone to help kitchen staff. If that goes well, we could see about you working out front."

"I'd be nothing more than a kitchen skivvy?" Victoria's lower lip quivered. "Surely you owe me better than that."

"I don't *owe* you anything, Mother," Olivia replied coldly. "Whatever you think I'm inheriting from Aidan, I can guarantee you it won't be as much as you expect. He took a hit when the shopping center plan imploded, remember? Besides, he kept most of his money tied up and under his mother's name, hence Patricia inheriting your IOU. Frankly, I'd have been better off financially if he'd lived long enough to divorce me. He was prepared to make me a settlement, which included money from his mother."

Victoria blanched. "How much?"

"It's a moot point now, isn't it?" Olivia shrugged. "The sum he suggested was in the region of a half a million euros. A large chunk of that would have been his mother's contribution, so I know I'll be entitled to far less now."

She watched the wheels in her mother's head turn. Victoria was an odd bird. At times, she wore her emotions like a vibrant dress. At others, she was utterly inscrutable.

"What about life insurance?" Victoria demanded. "Surely he had a policy?"

"Why would he? We didn't own property with a mortgage attached, and we had no children. There was no reason for Aidan to take out life insurance." Olivia stood to leave. "Frankly, I can't see how any of this concerns you."

Victoria's hands began to shake. "I can't believe it," she said, her voice brittle. "You're telling me you're worse off with him dead than alive?"

"That's about the size of it." Olivia grabbed her jacket from the back of the kitchen chair and slipped it on. "Unfortunately for me, Aidan never got round to sending a copy of the proposed settlement to my solicitor. As far as the police are concerned, they only have my word for it that any such settlement was in the offing. I can only hope they find some record of it on his computer or among his files."

Victoria made an odd choking sound.

Olivia ignored it and moved toward the door. "Give my regards to Dad and the boys. If you or Dad can think of anyone who might have borne a grudge against Aidan, please tell me. Better still, tell the police."

With trembling hands, Victoria reached for her cigarette packet. She shook one free and lit up. "If I were you," she said between drags, "I'd keep my nose well out of it. Leave the investigation to the police."

CHAPTER THIRTY-THREE

The annual Ballybeg Sports Day was a disgrace to sporting events nationwide. With the notable exception of a few hardened runners and ardent swimmers, the people of the town equated sport with an alcohol-fueled three-legged race along the beach. Food and nonalcoholic beverages were provided for children, pets, and– presumably– homicide detectives.

Jonas scowled across the sand at Detective Inspector Connelly and his lackeys. "Do they seriously think they're going to solve Aidan Gant's murder at this shindig?"

"Wait for it," Gavin said. "All will be revealed during the three-legged race."

Jonas surveyed the beach. "We're screwed, mate. We're not drunk enough to win this thing. No surprise John-Joe Fitzgerald and Buck MacCarthy win every year."

His friend snapped the pull top off his can and squinted at their competitors. "Sure we'll be grand once we have another beer."

"Speak for yourself. I'm staying sober. I have to collect Luca later."

"Looks like he's getting on great with Olivia." Gavin nodded to the cake stand where Luca was gorging on cream cake and Wiggly Poo was scarfing doggie treats.

"Yeah, he misses her. I don't think he's as fond of his new babysitter."

"Nor are you, I'd imagine," Gavin said with a sly grin.

Jonas ignored him and picked his way across the sand to his son.

"Hey, Dad."

"Hey, yourself." He tweaked the little boy's nose, making him squeal.

A string of customers were keeping Olivia busy. She looked elegant in an old-fashioned tea dress. The rosy tinge to her cheeks when she caught sight of him sent his heart rate soaring.

Luca tugged at his sleeve. "I wanna do the men's three-legged race with Wiggly Poo."

"No can do, kiddo. Dogs aren't allowed."

"That's discrimination." The boy crossed his arms over his skinny chest. "Wiggly Poo should be allowed to take part if he wants to."

Jonas eyed the curly-furred canine, currently hacking up an unidentifiable substance. "I don't see Wiggly Poo submitting to having his legs bound."

"Aw. It's not fair."

"Welcome to real life, mate." He flipped open his wallet and pulled out a tenner. "This should keep you and the mutt fed and watered for a while. Stay with Fiona and Olivia. I'll be back to collect you right after we finish."

Brian Glenn, the young policeman from the local station, was organizing the three-legged race. "Come on, lads," he bellowed into the megaphone. "Take your places at the starting line."

"Five months spent training for this farce"– Jonas bent down to help Gavin with their bindings– "and you're too drunk to run."

"All part of the fun," his friend slurred. "Sure look at John-Joe and Buck. They can never see straight, yet they always win."

"As I recall, Buck only has one eye."

"Maybe that's our problem. We need three eyes to win a three-legged race."

"Up with you." Jonas hauled his friend to his feet, and they staggered to the starting line.

Suddenly Gavin clutched his arm. "Jaysus. Please tell me it's the beer. Is John-Joe Fitzgerald wearing a thong?"

Sure enough, John-Joe Fitzgerald, Ballybeg's resident Elvis impersonator, was naked save a very small, very tight pair of leopard-print swimming trunks. "I'm doing the swimming competition after this race," he called, catching sight of their horrified expressions. "No time to change between events."

"I need eye bleach," Jonas muttered. "I did not know it was possible to have an arse that hairy."

"On your marks, get set, and...go." Brian Glenn blew his whistle, and they were off.

The first few meters passed in a blur of flying sand and sweaty men. Jonas and Gavin had sufficient practice to maintain a decent and synchronized pace...until disaster struck.

"Woof!" Wiggly Poo darted into the throng and hurled himself at his master.

Gavin staggered backward, dragging Jonas down with him. "Go away, you daft dog."

The labradoodle, deciding his master was in imminent danger, pawed their leg binding with intent and whimpered.

"It's fine, Wiggly Poo," Jonas said through a mouthful of sand. "Leave it alone."

The dog threw his head back a let out an unholy howl. Within seconds, other dogs in the vicinity took Wiggly Poo's hint. The cacophony that followed would shatter glass.

"Would someone shut that hound up?" yelled an elderly man with a cane. "I can't hear the race commentary."

Jonas looked at Gavin. "Race commentary? What are we? Greyhounds?"

Fiona appeared above them, hands on hips. "No. You're two overgrown eejits running a race usually reserved for children. I hate to break it to you, lads, but in addition to causing total mayhem, you came dead last."

"John-Joe and Buck won again?" asked Jonas.

Fiona grinned. "Yup."

"Next year, we need three eyes," Gavin said mournfully.

His wife's grin widened. "Or matching leopard-print swimming trunks."

***

All afternoon, Olivia served cakes with a plastered-on smile and forced small talk with customers. In truth, her mind was elsewhere. Ever since her visit with Victoria, she'd felt unsettled. She was probably being fanciful, but something about the way her mother had spoken about Aidan's murder set alarm bells off in her head. Her mother was ruthless and could be hard as nails when she wanted to be, but surely she wouldn't stoop to murder. Or would she?

A shiver ran down her spine. The memory of her mother's cold eyes, the color eerily reminiscent of her own when she stood before the mirror, but with a calculating and inscrutable edge to them, gave her the creeps. Her mind was a jumble of thoughts both incoherent and unpalatable.

"Go on home, Liv." Fiona was packing the last of the unused paper plates into a crate. "I can take it from here."

The offer was tempting. A walk along the seafront followed by a piping hot shower would clear her head. "Are you sure?"

"Of course. Gavin and Jonas will be here in a minute to help me pack up the car. In the meantime, I have two handsome males to keep me company. Don't I, boys?"

Wiggly Poo gave a bark of acknowledgement, but Luca appeared distracted.

Olivia dropped a kiss onto the little boy's forehead. He didn't acknowledge her, his gaze fixed on some point out at sea. "Everything okay, little guy?"

"The beach is covered in rubbish. People need to clean it up. The tide's coming in."

"Don't worry, Mr. Neat Freak. A cleaning crew is on the case." Olivia grabbed her cardigan from underneath the makeshift counter and slung her bag over her shoulder. "See you soon, Luca. Bye, Fee."

Although she wasn't fond of the beach itself– working the sports day cake stand had required significant will power– there was nothing like a stroll in the Atlantic wind to blow off the cobwebs. She took the stone steps up to the promenade.

Glancing at her phone, she read a quick text from Jill assuring her that all was well at the café. She had a little time before she needed to get back.

Her pace was brisk, and the wind was strong. She drew the salty air into her lungs with relish. She rarely looked out over the sea, but for some reason her eyes were drawn today to the spot where Bry drowned. A small boy played in the spray, fully clothed and clutching a red object. Olivia put a hand to her forehead to hold back her hair and get a better look. She squinted. The child looked very like Luca. But surely he wouldn't be in the water unattended?

She watched as the boy waded further into the water. He'd best be careful not to go too far out. The current could be treacherous here, and the tide was on its way in. The waves crashed, but the child ignored them, seemingly intent on reaching a floating object. Suddenly, a large wave crashed against the shore, knocking the boy off his feet. Another followed in quick succession, followed by yet another.

At this point, Olivia ceased to think. Dumping her bag and cardigan, she vaulted the stone wall and fell to the sand below. She kicked off her shoes the instant she hit the ground. Then she ran like she'd never run before.

By the time she caught up with the boy, he was face down in the water, struggling to regain his footing.

"Luca!" Her banshee screech was lost in the wind.

Her heart hammered in her chest as she waded into the water. She grasped under his arms and dragged him up. The tide was strong, making keeping her balance a struggle. She was already knee-deep in water. A vague notion she should feel panic flitted through her mind, but she crushed it. This was not the time to freak out.

Hauling Luca, she struggled toward the shore. She dragged him a few meters away from the water before collapsing onto the sand.

Luca coughed and spluttered but seemed otherwise none the worse from swallowing a bucketful of seawater. When she was sure he was okay, she lost her cool.

"What on earth were you doing? You know not to wander off on the beach alone, let alone wade into the water." The pounding of her heart rang in her ears. She hadn't been this close to the sea in ages. It had taken her the best part of five years after Bry's death to screw up the courage to walk along the beach, and even that she did while steadfastly refusing to look out at the crashing waves.

"I wanted to clean up the rubbish before the tide came in." Luca's cheeks grew red with embarrassment. "The cleaning crew wasn't working fast enough."

"So you decided to go by yourself?" She shivered. Her wet clothes clung to her body. She was soaked from head to foot and shaking from cold and terror.

The little boy was suddenly finding his soggy shoes of intense interest.

She modulated her tone. "You know how dangerous the beach can be without an adult. Even adults have to be careful around the water. You know what happened to your Uncle Bry."

Luca hung his head in shame. "Nana talks about him when we go to mass. We always light a candle for him. Seems silly to me. It's not like he can see it."

"It's a symbolic gesture, and it obviously means a lot to your grandmother. Now come on. Let's find your father." She took his small hand in hers, and he squelched along beside her as they trudged over the sand. "Why on earth didn't you take off your shoes and socks before you went for a dip?"

"I didn't have my flip-flops with me. I don't like walking on stones."

Typical Luca logic. "Your dad must be frantic."

As if on cue, Jonas came pounding down the steps, an expression of sheer terror on his face. Gavin followed close behind, looking equally rattled. At Gavin's heels was Wiggly Poo. Of the three, Wiggly Poo was the only one delighted to be there.

"My god, Luca," Jonas cried, his voice breaking with emotion. "I thought I'd lost you."

Luca ran to his father, and Jonas caught him up in a bear hug. They looked so damn sweet together that her breath caught.

"One second, you were helping us load up the car. The next, you were gone." Jonas stroked his son's wet hair. "Promise me you'll never run off like that again. Don't go near the sea without an adult."

"I promise," Luca said between sobs. "Am I in trouble?"

"Yes." His father hugged him close. "But not today. We'll figure out a suitable punishment tomorrow. For now, I just want to get you home and into a hot bath."

Gavin hovered in the background. "Should I come back with you to Curzon Street?"

"No, I can manage. Go help Fiona pack up the stand. I'll give you a ring tomorrow."

"Okay. I'm relieved the little guy is all right."

"All thanks to Olivia." Jonas's smile brought heat to her cheeks and a stab of lust to her groin.

"It was nothing," she murmured, dabbing at her wet face, conscious of her wet and bedraggled appearance.

"Bollocks." Jonas's eyes shone with emotion. "You saved my son's life. I know how you feel about the sea. It was a huge deal for you to go into the water."

"Luca's safety is more important than my phobia," she said through chattering teeth.

"Are you heading back to your cottage?"

She nodded. "I need to change out of these wet clothes."

"Then let's walk back together." He reached for Luca's hand. The little boy gave a sneeze and a shudder.

"We'd best get a move on," Olivia said. "Luca is turning blue."

During their trudge to Curzon Street, they drew curious stares from passersby.

"I'm sorry for what I said the other day. About us keeping our distance. I was panicking, thinking I was being noble."

His eyes twinkled with mischief. "The mighty Olivia admitting she was a tad rash?"

She scrunched up her nose, then sneezed violently. "Oh, rub it in, why don't you?"

"Sorry." He grinned, looking not the least bit repentant. "I couldn't resist. I've missed you terribly, as has this little guy." He patted Luca's shoulder.

The little boy gave her a slow smile. "I miss your scones."

She laughed and bent to kiss his soggy hair. "I've missed your endless dinosaur stories."

When they reached their road, Jonas turned to her. "Will you come by our house later?"

"Sure. I'm going to get dried and changed, then help Jill close up the café. I should be round in a couple of hours."

"Excellent. I wanted to ask you about what you mentioned the other day. About you doing a bit of sleuthing on your own. Please tell me you weren't serious."

"I was deadly serious. If the police aren't following up any other leads– assuming they even have any– then it's up to me to clear my name. If I clear my name, I clear yours."

He shook his head. "I don't quite follow your logic. Don't go haring around looking for trouble. Someone had no qualms about bashing Aidan's brains in with that gnome."

Olivia flinched. "Thanks for that visual."

"Sorry, but it's true." He quirked an eyebrow. "Do you want a similar fate?"

"Of course not."

"Then be sensible and leave it to the police. And if you do know something, talk to Sergeant Mackey. He might not be in charge of the case, but he's got more sense than that fool from Dublin."

"So far, I have nothing to tell. I only wish I did." Her mother's hard expression from earlier danced before her eyes. She blinked it into oblivion and shivered.

They reached their respective cottages.

"You'd better get out of those wet clothes. Thank you for saving Luca," Jonas said solemnly. "I'll never forget what you've done for us."

Tears sprang to her eyes, and she blinked them away. Expressing emotions didn't come naturally to her. She wasn't used to feeling overwrought, and she wasn't sure she liked it. She focused her attention on little Luca. "Make sure you behave for your Dad."

"I will," Luca promised before disappearing into the house behind his father.

Olivia had a quick shower and changed in her loft bedroom, grateful for the dry clothes. She was shaky with shock. The enormity of what had happened– and what could have happened– was dawning. If Luca had been in deeper water, would she have remembered how to swim? As a child, she'd swam like a fish, so much so that her grandfather had called her his Little Mermaid. There wasn't a swimming trophy in the county she hadn't won, even making it as far as the Munster championships. But after that fateful night with Bry, she'd thrown every swimsuit she'd owned into the bin and relegated her swimming days to history.

The exhilaration she'd once experienced when she looked out at the crashing waves was no more. The terror of the first couple of years had been gradually replaced by a cautious respect for the power of the tides. It still made her nervous when her brothers swam, but she swallowed her anxiety and plastered a smile upon her face.

It did no good to dwell on the past. Bry was gone. Not everyone who waded out to sea disappeared beneath the waves forever. If today proved anything, it was that she could face the water in a crisis. She regarded her pale reflection in the bathroom mirror. She straightened her shoulders. Maybe she should think about going to the swimming complex in Clonakilty. They had a shallow pool she could try before venturing into the deep end. It was time to face her demons.

CHAPTER THIRTY-FOUR

Luca splashed in the bath as if nothing extraordinary had occurred. Jonas vacillated between the urge to shake the little guy and to hug him.

"I like Olivia. I wish she came round more like she used to."

Jonas wished she did too. He missed her. Missed the belligerent tilt of her jaw when she was digging her heels in over something or other; missed her lively green eyes; and most of all, he missed talking to her. This part surprised him. He'd never had many female friends, and his conversation with former girlfriends had been limited to certain topics. With Olivia, he could talk about anything. And then, of course, there was the sex...

"What happened to Uncle Bry? Everyone whispers about it but no one says what happened."

"He drowned."

"I know that. But why do Granny and Granddad say it was Olivia's fault?"

"Because she went swimming with him. He drowned. She didn't." Dark memories surfaced in all their unedited horror. "Olivia was...She and I had just started going out."

"She was your girlfriend?"

"Yeah. I was studying journalism in Dublin at the time, so we only saw each other every second weekend. The evening Bry died, there was a beach party. I was meant to be there, but the train from Dublin was delayed. Bry, Olivia, and I often had swimming contests. I guess they decided to go ahead without me. By the time I got to the beach, Olivia was wet and hysterical and Bry was missing."

"Do you think it was her fault?"

He shook his head. "No way. They were both drunk and foolish to ignore the warning flag, but it was nothing the three of us hadn't done on countless occasions before."

"Can I have hot chocolate?" Luca asked, effectively derailing the conversation. He had the info he'd wanted and had no interest in hearing anything else.

"Sure." Jonas scrubbed the boy's hair with a towel and helped him into a pair of clean cotton pajamas.

"Olivia makes great hot chocolate." Luca perched on the kitchen counter and watched his father dissolve chocolate powder in hot milk. "But yours isn't too bad... except when you burn it and it gets a gross skin at the top."

"I'll try my best to avoid gross skins."

Once they finished the chocolate, he brushed his son's teeth and tucked him into bed. "Sweet dreams, little guy."

But Luca was already asleep. Jonas dropped a kiss onto the boy's soft cheek and tiptoed out of the room.

In the hallway, a soft rap of knuckles on glass drew his attention to the front door. A red-haired blur was visible through the frosted panes. “Hey,” he said when he opened. “Come on in.”

Olivia stepped into the narrow hallway. “I didn’t want to ring the doorbell in case Luca was asleep.

“Today’s adventure appears to have worn him out. He was asleep before I’d finished reading the first page of his bedtime story.”

She poked the tip of her tongue between her teeth. “Let me guess...dinosaur-themed?”

“Shockingly, no. I persuaded him to borrow a space adventure story from the library.”

“Good job, Dad.” She raised a questioning eyebrow. “Self-preservation?”

“Ab-so-lutely.” He tugged her into the living room and drew the curtains. “Shall I open a bottle of wine?”

Olivia touched a finger to her red-rimmed mouth, then traced a line from her bottom lip to the top button of her blouse. “No wine. The only taste I want tonight is you.”

His arousal began the instant she unbuttoned the first pearly disc. By the time the silky garment slid off her shoulders to reveal her braless-state, Jonas was rock hard. “Whoa.”

“I didn’t bother with underwear. I didn’t think I’d need any.” She took a step forward and lowered her voice to a husky whisper. “Was I wrong?”

“Hell, no.”

Her dirty laugh set his blood humming. "I didn't think so." Touching his jaw, she drew her fingernails through his stubble. "Take off your T-Shirt."

He obeyed, his mouth parched. She ran her palms over his chest, tweaking his nipples, massaging the planes of his torso. Tracing the bulge in his jeans, she flashed an impish grin and slid to her knees.

***

Olivia took Jonas's erection into her mouth, relishing each centimeter of taut, silky flesh. When she reached the tip, she danced her tongue in circular motions, making him groan. "Not good?" she teased.

"Too good."

He found the zip of her skirt and pulled the garment over her hips, revealing the bare skin beneath. The sight of the cheeky little leprechaun on her left buttock made him growl. Picking her up, he carried her to the sofa. He ran his hands up her inner thighs and stroked the flesh between her legs.

She was already slick with need, hot with desire. "Condom?"

"Here." He produced a foil wrapper with a flourish and winked at her. "I took it out of my wallet before my jeans hit the floor."

"Clever boy." She leaned into him, and his lips claimed hers in a passionate kiss. He smelled of hot chocolate and shampoo. Utterly delectable. She pulled him closer, needing, wanting more.

When he entered her, she adjusted her hips to accommodate his size. And then she ceased to think, each thrust bringing her closer to release. She ran her hands over his shoulders and down his back, kneaded his buttocks, and drew him deeper inside. Her orgasm hit like a tsunami of pleasure. She cried out, and he muffled her scream with a kiss seconds before his own climax.

Afterward, gasping, sweaty, and utterly satiated, they collapsed on the sofa.

"I am never letting you go again," she murmured into his ear. "No matter what happens, you're stuck with me."

Jonas's deep laugh tickled her neck. "Just as well you think so, because I'm not letting you go." He gazed into her eyes, suddenly serious. "I love you, Olivia. I always have. Let's put the past behind us and make a future together."

She opened her mouth to respond but was silenced by the shrill ring of the doorbell. Jonas drew back, frown lines marring his otherwise smooth forehead. "Rather late for a social call."

The implication of his words dawned. Their gazes locked. In his eyes, she read fear, and her sense of foreboding quadrupled.

Jonas leaped to his feet and threw on jeans and a T-shirt. Olivia followed suit, her fingers fumbling over the tiny buttons of her blouse.

Out in the hallway, she discerned dark shapes through the frosted glass panes of the wooden front door. Panic twisted her stomach into knots, and she grabbed his arm. "Don't open it."

The piercing ring of the doorbell echoed for the third time, shrill and insistent. Luca appeared in the hallway, rubbing sleep from his eyes. "What's all the noise?"

"Go back to bed, mate. Nothing to worry about." The tremor in Jonas's voice belied his reassurances.

The little boy ignored his father and took a step toward Olivia. She put an arm around him and hugged him close. "You'd better open up, Jonas. They won't go away."

As his hand reached for the latch, Olivia's heart rate accelerated.

Detective Inspector Connelly loomed in the doorframe, a coldly satisfied look on his craggy face. Seán Mackey stood beside him, his expression closed.

Connelly broke the silence. "Jonas O'Mahony, I'm arresting you on the suspicion of murdering Aidan Gant on the twenty-first of June this year. You are not obliged to say anything unless you wish to do so, but whatever you say will be taken down in writing and may be given in evidence. Do you understand?"

Jonas swayed, then steadied himself. "I've used the official arrest caution of *An Garda Síochána* so many times in my books that I can repeat it in my sleep."

"Excellent. Then you know you'll need to accompany us to the station."

"Olivia." Jonas's voice was deceptively calm. "Can you look after Luca? And maybe call my parents?"

The boy whimpered and huddled against her. "Of course," she said. "Whatever you need me to do."

She longed to slap the self-congratulatory smirk off Connelly's face. "I told you we'd get you in the end, O'Mahony," he crowed.

"Whatever it is you think you've got on me won't hold up in court," Jonas ground out. "I didn't kill Aidan Gant."

"You've been cautioned, remember? Surely you've written enough detective novels to know your best bet is to keep your trap shut until your lawyer arrives."

Jonas opened his mouth but shut it again when Olivia shot him a warning look. Connelly was right. He needed to keep his cool and do things by the book. "I'll call Karen McCormack." She shot a glare at Connelly. "You're making a mistake, Detective Inspector."

"We'll see," Connelly's beady eyes hardened. "It'll be interesting to see what the interview turns up about *you*."

Jonas gave Luca a quick kiss on the cheek, then met Olivia's haunted gaze. Before she could speak, his mouth claimed hers in a passionate kiss.

"Come on, now," snapped Detective Inspector Connelly. "We need to get going. We'll have to handcuff you, O'Mahony."

"Is that necessary?" Seán protested. "I doubt he's a flight risk."

Connelly glared at his subordinate. "It's standard procedure when arresting someone suspected of murder,

Sergeant Mackey. We can't bend the rules just because he's a local boy."

Jonas held out his wrists. "It's fine, Mackey. Do what you have to do."

The snap of metal set Olivia's teeth on edge. Cuffs in place, Seán led Jonas down the garden path to a waiting police car. Before he got into the vehicle, Jonas turned to look at her and Luca one last time. "I love you," he called as Connelly stepped forward and shoved him into the backseat. "Both of you."

"We love you, too," she whispered as the car door slammed and they sped off into the distance.

***

The next few hours passed in a sleepless nightmare. Jonas's parents were out at a dinner party and didn't answer their phone until well past midnight. Given the lateness of the hour, it was decided that Olivia would spend the night with Luca, and his grandparents would collect him after breakfast.

The two of them lay in Jonas's double bed. The sheets held a hint of his spicy scent. Luca tossed and turned but mostly lay awake shaking in terror. Olivia tried everything she could think of to distract him from telling stories to singing songs. It was past dawn when he finally fell asleep. Waking him for breakfast seemed cruel, but his grandfather was due any minute.

She prepared the food in a daze. This was all her fault. If Jonas hadn't gotten mixed up with her, he'd be safe at home spending the morning with his son.

Luca was sitting on a kitchen chair, his expression curiously blank. After getting acquainted with him over the past few months, Olivia knew this meant he was overloaded with emotions and was having difficulty processing them. She stroked his soft curls. Patience was key. "I made your favorite. French toast with maple syrup."

He made no response, but she dished out a generous portion for him anyway.

After going through the motions of pushing food around their plates, Olivia helped Luca pack a small bag of clothes, books, and toys. She looked around for his dog-eared dinosaur encyclopedia and eventually located it over the fireplace under Jonas's wallet. He must have forgotten it in the drama of last night.

The piercing ring of the doorbell made her jump. It would be either Liam O'Mahony come to collect his grandson, or Seán Mackey looking for Jonas's wallet. She grabbed the wallet from the mantelpiece just in case.

But the shape through the glass was too small to be either Liam or Seán. With a hesitant hand and a newfound hatred of doors and doorbells, Olivia undid the latch.

Luca sidled up to her and peered at the glamorous woman standing on the faded welcome mat. His grip on Olivia's hand tightened. "Mummy?"

CHAPTER THIRTY-FIVE

Jonas's ex-girlfriend was fashion model stunning. By Ballybeg's standards, Olivia was stylish. In comparison to Susanne, she was downright dowdy. Given Jonas's off-hand response when she'd asked him what his ex looked like, she'd formed a mental image of a spray-tanned bottle blond with large breasts. The woman on the doorstep was rail-thin and elegant from the top of her raven chignon to the toes of her designer shoes.

"Hello, Luca." Susanne's gaze rested briefly on her son before she proffered an expertly manicured hand to Olivia. "You must be Jonas's girlfriend."

"Well, I...yes," she stammered, uncomfortably aware of her short, unvarnished nails and despising herself for her vanity. Cooking and baking all day didn't exactly lend themselves to maintaining the perfect manicure. "My name's Olivia."

Susanne's handshake was firm and assured. "May I come in?"

"Jonas isn't home. I don't think..."

"I know he's been arrested," Susanne said calmly. "That's why I'm here."

Her accent was posh south Dublin, either the result of attending the "right" schools or artificially acquired in adulthood.

Olivia dithered, but only for a second. The woman was Luca's mother, after all, and she wasn't sure what sort of custodial rights she still had over the child. For the first time in her life, she wished Liam– or even Nuala– O'Mahony would show up and come to her rescue. *Oh, the irony*.

"Can I offer you a coffee?"

"No, thanks." Susanne took a seat at the small kitchen table. "But I'd like a glass of water."

By the time they were settled, Olivia had regained her composure. Luca was on edge but didn't seem negatively disposed toward his mother. Indifferent was the more accurate description. Poor kid was stressed enough over his father's arrest. He didn't need more upheaval today. She placed a hand on his shoulder. "Why don't you go read a book in your room? I'll come get you in a few minutes, okay?"

He nodded and beat a hasty retreat. His mother didn't warrant so much as a backward glance.

Olivia regarded the woman across from her. There was no point in beating about the bush. "I understood you had no contact with Jonas and Luca."

"That's correct."

Susanne didn't blink. She seemed as indifferent to her son as he was to her. If he were Olivia's kid and she hadn't seen him in ages, she wouldn't be able take her eyes off him. But it was a moot point. If he were her kid, she'd never have abandoned him in the first place.

"How did you get to Ballybeg so quickly? It's only nine o'clock. Even if you heard about the arrest on the morning news, you can't have had enough time to drive down from Dublin."

"Sergeant Mackey called my husband late last night."

Olivia pinched the bridge of her nose. "Okay, I haven't slept and I'm confused. Why would Seán call your husband? Why are you even *here*?"

"Mackey was one of the investigating officers in a murder case my husband defended a couple of years back. I don't know the particulars, but Barry thinks highly of him and is aware of my connection to Jonas."

"Giving birth to Jonas's child definitely counts as a connection." The woman's ice-queen act was pissing her off.

Susanne appeared to be impervious to sarcasm. "I'm here to see if I can help."

"Help with Luca?"

That elicited a small smile. "No. As you've likely been informed, I'm not the maternal type. I do, however, care for my son's welfare. Having a father in prison is hardly in his best interests."

Despite exhaustion and stress, the dots were connecting. "Your husband is willing to have a look at the case against Jonas?"

"Yes. He's a barrister specializing in criminal law. His name is Barry Brennan." Another tepid smile. "You might have heard of him."

Indeed. Barry Brennan had successfully defended a number of high-profile criminal cases over the past decade. "I thought you hated Jonas's guts."

"God, no." The woman's pale blue eyes widened in surprise. "Although I daresay he hates mine."

"I don't know about *hate,* but I get the impression you're not on his list of favorite people."

Susanne quirked a pencil-thin eyebrow. "Diplomatically put. My relationship with Jonas failed because we're too different. The only reason we stayed together was my pregnancy, and I'm the first to admit that having Luca was a mistake."

Olivia flinched. "Harsh words indeed.

The other woman sighed. "You despise me, don't you? Look, not every woman is cut out to be a mother. Clearly, I fall under that category. I carried Luca for nine months and gave birth to him, yet I've never felt the remotest connection to him. How would it have been better for any of us if I'd stayed?"

Olivia made no response. What could she say to that? The emotional part of her recoiled from Susanne. The intellectually curious part wondered if the woman might also be on the autism spectrum. Her bluntness and apparent lack of emotion indicated something atypical. Or was she merely judging Susanne's actions according to society's view of a mother's role? How many fathers who walked out on their families were dismissed as deadbeat dads but not accorded intrinsic evil?

A flicker of genuine emotion passed over Susanne's face, the first Olivia had observed since her arrival. "I'm saying what many women think but are too afraid to say out loud. From day one, Jonas was a better parent than I was. I know he doubts himself, but it's all nonsense."

"Jonas is a wonderful father."

"Absolutely. That's why I'd never dream of taking Luca away from him. What can I offer the boy? More money? I don't think that's going to make up for having an emotionally distant parent, do you? No, he's far better off staying with his father."

For the briefest moment, Olivia pitied her. She was missing out on so much by not having her son in her life. "Did you not wonder if you had postnatal depression? That combined with the stress of Luca's diagnosis might made bonding with the baby difficult."

The woman's gaze shifted toward the window. "Oh, I've been down the counseling route, but there's no way to prettify it. I would like to keep in touch with my son, if Jonas permits it. And contribute financially. But that's where it ends. I want to lead a different lifestyle than I'd have if I went back to Jonas and tried to make it work with him and Luca. Besides, assuming he ever loved me, that ship sailed long ago." She eyed Olivia shrewdly. "I'm betting the only woman he has eyes for now is you."

"How would you know that?"

Susanne's lips curved into a sly smile. "The newspapers say so. For once, I think they've got it right."

Olivia's cheeks grew warm. "I care for Jonas and Luca."

"Then let me help you fight the system and get Jonas home."

She exhaled. "All right. What do you need from me?"

"At the moment, your phone number. Beyond that, I'm not sure, exactly. That's Barry's department. He's going to do some digging this morning, and I'm sure he'll be in touch with questions."

"Whatever I can do to get the charges dropped, I'll do it gladly." Olivia scribbled her mobile number on a Post-it note and gave it to Susanne.

"Excellent." Susanne stood and extended her hand. Olivia shook it hesitantly. While she admired the woman's candidness, it was hard to look in the eye someone who'd rejected her own child. And yes, she'd say the same if Susanne were a man. But right now, Jonas needed a miracle. If Barry the Barrister could enact it, then so be it.

***

Jonas was lying on the narrow cot in his cell, staring at the cracked paint on the ceiling and plotting his next mystery. Not, perhaps, the most sensible occupation for a man accused of murder, but "sensible" was hardly his middle name. Besides, making Detective Inspector Connelly the victim of a gruesome crime was affording him no end of pleasure.

The interrogation had been brutal. Given Connelly's volatility and obvious frustration with the responses he received, Jonas was inclined to believe that the arrest was a desperate attempt to trick him into incriminating himself and providing the homicide detectives with sufficient material to bring formal charges. Thankfully, even Connelly had to eat on occasion, leaving Jonas to enjoy a brief respite before the grilling continued.

The door creaked open to reveal a harassed-looking Sergeant Mackey. "Your mum's here. You'll have to make the visit quick, mind. I'm only supposed to let you have one visitor apart from your lawyer, and Olivia is due soon."

Jonas swung his legs over the side of the cot and heaved himself to his feet. The room rotated briefly, then his balance settled. "I'm relying on you to keep the visit brief, Mackey. Once my mother starts off on one of her harangues, only a divine intervention can stop her."

A grin broke through the police sergeant's serious expression. "I doubt I count as divine, but I'll do my best."

Mam was sitting in one of the interrogation rooms, looking tired and stressed. Her plump cheeks appeared sunken and drawn. Guilt gnawed at his gut. If it weren't for him, she wouldn't have this stress, and she wouldn't have the added responsibility of caring for Luca.

"Son." Even her voice sounded tired.

He kissed her on the cheek and took the chair opposite. "How's Luca?"

"Fine. Quiet. Your dad collected him from Olivia this morning."

"I'm sorry," he said. "For all this."

"Sure there's no need to apologize."

"There is, though. Before you went on your cruise, I relied too much on you and Dad. While you were away, I realized I could cope on my own, even if having extra help eased the load."

"And now?"

"And now I'm afraid I'll lose the little guy altogether." His voice broke as he spoke, raw emotion filtering through the cracks. "I couldn't wait to foist him off on other people, then escape to my office and immerse myself in my writing. It was easier than dealing with the fear I felt every time I looked at Luca. The fear is still there, but I've learned to see past it and focus on the wonderful little boy I have rather than the hypothetical 'normal' child I don't have."

His mother squeezed his hand. "You'll be home with him soon. The police will come to their senses."

"I'm not so sure. Detective Inspector Connelly and his team are fools."

"If the police screw up, the courts will set it right."

"Would that I had your faith in the Irish justice system."

"Would that you did. In more ways than one. A bit of prayer helps in times like these." She extracted rosary beads from her purse and pressed them into his hands.

He shoved them away. "No offense, Mam, but they're not my thing."

"They were blessed at Knock," she said, as if this would make all the difference. "Father Malachy sends his regards. I've asked him to pray for you."

His mouth twisted in distaste. "Father Malachy can go f– "

"Jonas!"

"He's a sanctimonious prig. Not to mention a hypocrite." The priest was one of Jonas and Gavin's former teachers. Although Ireland had banned corporal punishment in the classroom a few years before they'd begun primary school, Father Malachy hadn't gotten that memo. Jonas had always despised the man, preferring the gentle if doddery parish priest, Father Fagin.

Nuala clutched her rosary beads. "Just know that we're all praying for you."

"Thanks, Mam. If my solicitor is correct, they don't have enough evidence to make charges stick."

"Of course they don't," Mam said in outraged indignation. "I reared you better than for you to go round killing people."

If the situation weren't desperate, he'd laugh out loud.

"Even if you were guilty," she said incongruously, "I'm sure you'd have had a good reason."

"For feck's sake. I didn't kill Aidan Gant. Surely you know me better than that."

"Love can drive men to do things they'd never dream of otherwise." Mam dropped her voice to a stage whisper. "Like cover up for others."

"Olivia is not a murderer."

"I won't deny she's been good to Luca, but she's a bad influence on you."

"You said the same years ago when she was friends with me and Bry."

"So I did," she said severely. "And look what happened to *him*."

"Ah, Mam. Get over your hang-up about Olivia being responsible for Bry's death. Losing a child is the worst thing that can happen to a parent, but blaming someone for a tragic accident isn't fair. Besides, it's the height of hypocrisy to come in here complaining about Olivia when you had no problem letting her babysit Luca overnight."

"If it weren't for her, you'd be at home with your son."

He leaned back in his cheap plastic chair and supported the back of his head with his palms. "Is your purpose in visiting to bitch about my girlfriend and pray for my soul? If so, you can take your complaints and prayers elsewhere."

His mother made a moue of disapproval. "Believe it or not, I'm trying to help."

"But you're *not* helping." He leaned forward and gave his mother an imploring look. "I love Olivia. Once I get out of here, I want to build a future with her and Luca. Do you want every family event to be fraught with tension? I know I don't, but you being rude to her isn't something I'm prepared to tolerate."

Mam's mouth opened and closed, her lips forming unspoken words. Finally, her shoulders slumped in defeat. "If you're in a relationship with Olivia, I'll cope."

He raised an eyebrow. "Cope? Does that mean you'll be polite to her?"

She gave a grudging nod. "I want you to be happy. I can't deny I'd rather you'd kept your distance and not gotten embroiled in this sordid business, but if you're serious about Olivia, then she's welcome in my home."

"Thanks, Mam. It means a lot to hear you say that."

Sergeant Mackey knocked on the door. "Time's up."

Mam muttered something indecipherable as she reached for her coat. It was her Sunday best. Why she deemed a visit to a son in a police interrogation room worthy of her Sunday best, he'd never fathom.

His chair scraped against the floor. "Thanks for the visit. Give my regards to Dad and a kiss to Luca."

An envelope materialized from the depths of her enormous handbag. She tossed it on the table before him. "You'll be wanting these," she said defiantly. The rosary beads followed. "And you'll be needing those."

His fingered the envelope. It contained a ballpoint pen and crosswords, both the regular and cryptic varieties, neatly cut out from the past few days' *Irish Independent*. N o *Irish Times* in their household. His parents' politics leaned heavily toward the conservative with more than a dash of nationalistic fervor.

He cracked a reluctant smile. "Thanks."

She gave a stiff nod. The air of the martyr hung about her shoulders like a well-worn shawl.

The door clanged shut, and the bolt slid into place. Jonas fingered the envelope. He hated crosswords. He was a man of words but despised puzzles of all kinds. However, the pen would be confiscated at the earliest opportunity, and he might as well put it to good use. He uncapped it and contemplated three across. Ten letters. Solution: Redemption. He grinned to himself. Good old Mam.

CHAPTER THIRTY-SIX

The crosswords occupied him until Sergeant Mackey announced another visitor– Olivia. She looked beautiful, if sleep-deprived– hair mussed, dark circles under her eyes. He leaped up to greet her, the languid stiffness in his limbs miraculously disappearing.

"Jonas!" She ran to his arms and kissed him. She smelled damn fine.

In the background, Mackey cleared his throat. "I'm not supposed to leave you two alone, given the identity of the murder victim...Ah, feck it. If I lock the pair of you in, it should be fine." He shook a warning finger. "No monkey business. I'll have to chuck you out the moment Connelly gets back."

"Thanks, Seán," Olivia said with a smile. "We'll behave ourselves."

The metal door clanged shut.

Still holding hands, Jonas maneuvered himself into the seat opposite. "How are you?"

"Bearing up. More to the point, how are *you*?"

"Surviving. My guess? Connelly is stalling on the questioning to let me 'stew.' Then he'll apply for one extension after another until he's legally obliged to charge or release me." He rubbed a hand across his unshaven jaw. "He'll find some reason to charge me, even if it won't hold up in court."

"What evidence do they think they have against you?"

"Gant's security camera picked up images of a man entering the house through the back door. Unfortunately for me, the cameras rotate. While they recorded the man arriving, there's no record of him leaving."

"To think I laughed at Aidan's pretension when he installed those cameras last year." She shook her head. "Go on. I assume the police think that man was you."

"That's what they'd like me to admit. Connelly was apoplectic when he learned I'd sold my Harley a few months ago. Apparently Aidan's mysterious visitor arrived on the same model as the one I used to own. Fake plates, though."

"Okay, you said the cameras picked up images of a man *entering* through the back door. As in 'breaking and entering?'"

"No. That's the unusual part. Apparently the man pushed open the door and strolled on in. No fiddling with locks necessary."

Olivia frowned. "Now that *is* odd. Aidan was vigilant about setting the alarm after dark, even if he was at home and awake."

"Could his mother have forgotten to switch it on?"

"I doubt it. As you may have noticed, Patricia is of a dramatic bent. All Aidan had to do to make sure she wasn't scatty about setting the alarm was to tell her he might be in danger coming up to the election."

"Do you think he was genuinely afraid?"

"Something was bothering him in the months before I left, but I assumed it was financial stress after the shopping center project collapsed." She leaned forward and bit her lip. "Listen, there's something I need to tell you. I– or rather, you– had a visitor just after breakfast."

He frowned. "Who?"

She stared at him, chewing on her lower lip. "Luca's mother."

His heart rate shot up. "Susanne?" *Feck.* His hand flew to his forehead. He supposed she'd heard the news. The papers would be having a field day over his arrest. Bestselling murder mystery author arrested on suspicion of murder? Yeah. He could imagine the lurid headlines. "What the hell did she want? To gloat?"

Olivia recoiled at his aggressive tone. "To help."

"She what?" Was he hearing right? Susanne actually gave a shit whether or not he went to prison? Realization dawned. *Of course.* If he were incarcerated, she'd be expected to make decisions for Luca's future. He ground his teeth. No wonder she was worried.

Olivia stroked his hand. "Susanne offered to have her husband look into your case. He specializes in criminal law, and apparently he knows Seán Mackey. I accepted on your behalf."

"I don't need Barry Brennan's help." A film of perspiration formed on his forehead. The last thing he wanted was his ex reinserting herself in his life, and she and Barry came as a package deal. The last thing he wanted for Luca was contact with the mother who'd rejected him.

"Don't panic," Olivia said, as if reading his thoughts. "Susanne says she's only here to help get the case against you dismissed. She's not looking for custody of Luca."

He gave a raucous laugh. "'Help' and 'Susanne' are two contradictory terms."

"I think she's serious. Let's hear what Barry the Barrister has to say when he's done 'calling in his contacts.'"

"Did she ask to see Luca again?"

"No, but she offered money toward his upkeep."

"I don't want her stinking money," he growled.

"Haven't you heard the saying 'Pride cometh before a fall?'"

"I do well enough to support me and Luca." Or at least he would as long as he wasn't convicted.

"Why not let her pay into a savings scheme for Luca? You don't have to touch the capital if you don't want to, but at least it's there for when he's older."

"I suppose," he grunted. She was right, of course. Olivia usually was.

"You sound *so* enthusiastic."

He gave a reluctant laugh. "I resent Susanne swanning back as if nothing happened and offering to throw money at me. She can't buy back the time she's lost with Luca."

"No, and I don't think she wants to. But she is his mother. Let her contribute something toward his future."

He ran a finger over her delicate skin. "You're more reasonable than I am."

"Naturally. I have less emotion invested. It's easier for me to see both sides, even if I'll never understand how she could walk away from that gorgeous little boy."

He leaned over and gave her a kiss. "I meant what I said yesterday. I love you, Olivia."

The look of fear and exhaustion on her face vanished. "I love you too. So very much."

He squeezed her hand tighter. "Whatever I have to do to keep out of prison, I'll do it– for all our sakes. So yeah, if that means accepting Barry the Barrister's offer of help, I guess that's what I'll do."

She smiled, and an expression of relief flickered across her face. "Thank you for being sensible."

"Not a trait I'm normally accused of having." He ran a hand through his overly long hair. It was in need of a trim. If they sent him to prison, no doubt he'd be treated to a buzz cut. "Is Susanne staying in Ballybeg?"

Olivia shot him an impish grin. "She and her designer luggage are putting up at Clonmore Castle Hotel."

That made him laugh. He kissed her softly, aching to run his hands down her body and take her here and now, regardless of Seán maintaining a discreet presence on the other side of the door. He settled for a second kiss.

Olivia stroked his wrist and dropped a kiss onto his pulse, sending a stab of awareness down to his groin. "I'm due to join them for coffee at their hotel later this afternoon. Barry thinks he'll have news by then."

Jonas frowned. "He's down here as well? I wouldn't have thought Ballybeg would be his scene."

"Ah." Olivia gave a mischievous grin. "Clonmore House Hotel has a golf course, remember?"

"That figures." While he'd attended a couple of weddings there, the luxury hotel was way outside his price range.

He drummed his fingertips on the table separating them, his mind racing. Olivia massaged the thumb of his other hand. His cock stirred in response. *Jaysus.* He shouldn't be feeling turned on at a time like this. She smiled, and his heart skipped a beat. If he went to prison, he'd lose not only Luca and his freedom, but also the chance at a future with Olivia. He swallowed hard. He couldn't bear the thought.

"Are you sure you're okay with Barry looking into your case?" Her forehead was creased with concern. "Susanne caught me unawares, and I didn't know how to react. She seemed...reasonable...so I thought it couldn't do any harm to let him see what he'd turn up. Did I do wrong?"

"No." He gave her hands a reassuring squeeze. "I can do with all the help I can get. Barry's got a fearsome reputation in the courts. I doubt he got it without reason. Let his minions find out what they can."

Her relief was palpable. "Thank goodness. I was afraid you'd be angry with me."

"Hardly. You're one of the few people on my side. That Susanne is another is a turn-up for the books, I'll admit."

"I don't like her." Her direct gaze met his. "But I realize I'm prejudiced. I can understand not wanting children. Aidan and I decided against it, and I have no regrets. But to have a child and then reject it...it turns my stomach."

"Fathers do it all the time," Jonas said gently. "Society judges them less harshly."

Olivia's laugh was bitter. "That was Susanne's defense."

"Whatever her reasoning, I'm determined to make up for her absence and give Luca the best upbringing I can provide. That's why I need to get out of here."

"You will." Olivia leaned in and touched her mouth to his. He pulled her head closer and deepened the kiss.

A rapping at the door reminded them of Seán's presence. "Time's up, folks. Connelly and his team just pulled into the car park."

He dropped a last kiss onto her silky soft hair. "Thanks for visiting."

"It's the least I could do. You're in here because of me."

"Don't say that," he said in a hoarse voice. "And don't think it. I'm in here because the cops screwed up. They had their eye on us from the start and were too lazy to look elsewhere."

They both looked up when Seán strode into the room and cleared his throat.

Olivia gave Jonas a last lingering kiss. He could feel the tingling on his lips long after she left.

CHAPTER THIRTY-SEVEN

Olivia's eyes bugged. So this was the suave barrister who'd stolen Susanne away from his son. For the life of her, she couldn't see the appeal. Barry Brennan was short and squat. The bristly black hair covering his ball-shaped head owed its vibrancy to Grecian 2000. However, his jovial features did not bespeak the grumpy barrister she'd envisaged from the newspaper articles.

Susanne sat next to him, resplendent in a cream tailored suit. They should have been caricatures of the aging wealthy man and his much younger trophy wife. To Olivia's amazement, Susanne seemed as smitten with Barry as he was with her. Could theirs be a love match? Well, Olivia had hooked up with Jonas against all the odds, so who was she to say *anything* against Cupid's mysterious machinations?

They were seated in the lobby café in Clonmore Castle Hotel. Its five-star splendor put even the Ashbourne to shame. The chain that had converted the house into a premier hotel had spared no expense. They'd retained the old-fashioned feel of the house while bestowing it with every modern convenience. In its heyday, the Clonmore estate had been famous for its beautiful gardens. They'd fallen into disarray in the early twentieth century but were now restored to their former glory. Most of the farmland belonging to the original estate had been sold off, but the hotel retained a sizeable plot that had been turned into a golf course.

Olivia could recall precisely three occasions on which she'd visited Clonmore Castle Hotel. This was the third. People often asked her if it felt strange to drive past the imposing gates and know the house and gardens had belonged to her family for generations. In fact, she had no extraordinary connection to the estate except to admire its beauty. The days of the wealthy Protestant landowners had ended well before her birth. Even her mother had never lived at the house. She was glad it was preserved as a part of Irish history, but it held no personal significance. Thankfully, Barry and Susanne were unaware of her link to the old estate, sparing her from questions about its history and architecture that she wouldn't have been able to answer.

After the initial awkward small talk, a crisply uniformed waitress brought their coffees. Barry heaped sugar into his black coffee and then withdrew a slim leather folder from his briefcase. "As far as I can tell," he said in his rich baritone, "the case against Jonas is flimsy at best. First, forensics indicate Aidan was most likely killed by a right-handed person. Jonas is left-handed."

Olivia frowned. "Surely they shouldn't have arrested him if they knew that. Isn't that a basic fact to check out?"

Barry shook his head, once again drawing Olivia's attention to the unlikely color of his hair. "It's not quite as simple as that. Real-life crime investigation isn't like it is on TV. While the forensics experts concluded that the person wielding the fatal weapon was probably right-handed by nature, it's not impossible for someone to fake it."

He flicked through his folder and removed a piece of paper. "More compelling is this– we got hold of CCTV footage from the Ashbourne. From the time of his arrival until the following day, Jonas doesn't leave the hotel via the main or rear entrances. Witnesses saw him at the hotel bar and dance club well after midnight. In order to make their accusations stick, the police are asking us to believe that Jonas shimmied down a drain pipe from the third floor of the hotel without anyone noticing him– and this in Dublin, the city that never sleeps– drove to Ballybeg at breakneck speed in an as-of-yet unlocated vehicle, killed Aidan Gant, drove back to the Ashbourne, somehow reentered the hotel without anyone noticing him, and was back in his room by the time Seán Mackey showed up looking for you. Timewise, it's possible, but barely. He'd have had to break every speed limit on the way down to and back from Ballybeg. On a six-hundred-kilometer stretch, that he wasn't picked up by control radar anywhere is possible but adds yet another unlikelihood to a long list of improbabilities."

"Why did the police never mention the CCTV footage from the hotel?"

"Because it wasn't found during their initial search. The relevant recording was damaged, and it took a while to locate the backup."

"But you found it?" asked Olivia with a raised eyebrow.

"My people did, yes."

Impressive. Olivia stirred her latte and thought. She'd compiled a list of relevant questions for Barry, but the most pertinent ones hardly needed her to consult a piece of paper.

"What about my conversation with Aidan about the settlement? I told two of my friends about it. They can back me up."

"All they can do is to confirm what you told them of the conversation after it happened. They weren't at the café when Aidan arrived and can't say firsthand what was discussed. From a legal point of view, we only have your word that Aidan ever contemplated granting you a financial settlement substantially higher than what you'll now receive as his widow."

"Damn."

"Damn, indeed," agreed Barry. "Aidan's solicitor knows nothing about a settlement, and his mother is denying they ever discussed it. The police examined his various computers to see if they contained a draft, but found nothing."

Olivia frowned. "It's odd he didn't mention it to Patricia. I was under the impression she'd agreed to let him give me some of her money."

"Mrs. Gant is adamant she knows nothing about it. I don't believe her for an instant. She's determined you and Jonas be found guilty."

"You'd think she'd want the real killer to be found," Olivia said bitterly.

Barry gave her a long look. Despite his uninspiring appearance, his eyes were shrewd and intelligent. "Perhaps she genuinely believes you murdered her son. Or that Jonas did so on your behalf."

She flinched. His words acted like the lash of a whip, yet she knew them to be true. Fiddling with the sugar cubes, she blinked back tears. While she'd never seen eye to eye with her mother-in-law, the extent of Patricia's hatred weighed heavily. She gave herself a mental shake and snapped to attention. This was not the time to indulge in frivolous sentiment. "You mentioned police had checked Aidan's home and work computers. What about the laptop he kept at the summer house in Cobh?"

Barry consulted his notes. "I have no mention of a property in Cobh."

"I assume police searched it. Aidan bought the house as a rental property, but over the past couple of years, he spent at least one weekend a month there. Twenty-four Sandy Lane." The address was burned into her memory, and for all the wrong reasons. It was the place she'd first discovered Aidan in bed with another woman. It was also the setting for the first time he'd hit her. She exhaled sharply, the memories stirring up emotions she'd rather suppress. It had taken her weeks after his death to realize that in spite of their dysfunctional relationship, there was a small part of her that mourned him. Whether it was regret at all the things she hadn't said or done to stand up for herself, she couldn't tell.

Barry retrieved his mobile phone from his briefcase. "One moment. I'll call Connelly." He tapped out a number and held the device to his ear. "Detective Inspector Connelly? Barry Brennan here." A pause, followed by a wink at Olivia. "Yes, *that* Barry Brennan. I'm interested in the Gant case. Did you check the laptop that he kept at his summer house in Cobh? Hmm...okay. Thanks for the information. I'll be in touch if I have more questions."

"What did he say?" Olivia asked after Barry rang off. "Another dead end?"

"I wouldn't discount it as that just yet. Connelly says they didn't find a laptop at the summer house. Might be worth having a look ourselves."

"Are we allowed inside? I know it's not the crime scene, but it's not really mine to access until probate is over. The solicitor hasn't even given me the keys yet. "

"That probably has more to do with the murder investigation than probate. The police will want access to the house. I'm sure they have a set of keys." Barry's eyes twinkled. "And we have a connection at Ballybeg Garda Station."

"Seán Mackey."

"Exactly. I'll phone him and see what can be arranged. Do you have plans for later? Or for tomorrow morning?"

"I run a café but a friend took over my shift for today. I'll need to work tomorrow, though."

"In that case, I'll see if Mackey can meet us in Cobh in a couple of hours. I'll text you with the details." Barry rose to his feet. "In the meantime, I promised Susanne a quick round of golf."

"Thanks, Barry. I appreciate everything you've done."

"My pleasure. Jonas means a lot to Susanne, and she means the world to me." The affection with which he regarded his wife warmed Olivia's cynical heart. They looked at one another as if the rest of the world had ceased to exist.

Love...Not long ago, it had been an alien concept. Now it was all she could think of. It motivated her to get out of bed in the morning, to put one tired foot in front of the other. The timing was crap, but for the first time in her life, she had a shot at happiness. She'd be damned before she'd waste it.

***

Detective Inspector Connolly wrapped up the afternoon round of Twenty Questions with obvious reluctance. Jonas's solicitor, Karen McCormack, was making the most of Ireland's spanking new law that permitted a suspect to have their solicitor present at all times during questioning. A law that– in Jonas's opinion– brought Ireland in line with most other civilized countries.

"He's entitled to a dinner break," Karen was saying to the fuming inspector, "and he's entitled to consult with me in private."

"Fine," Connelly growled. "I'll give you ten minutes and not a second more."

He stomped out of the room and slammed the door.

Karen shoved her mobile phone at Jonas. "Better make it quick."

Startled, he took the phone. "Hello?"

"It's me," Olivia said. "I have news. I met Barry and Susanne at their hotel. We're going to search Aidan's holiday home in Cobh. The police haven't found the laptop he kept there."

"I suppose Barry is going to want to talk to me at some point," Jonas said gloomily.

"Definitely. He's not a bad guy, you know."

He laughed. "That's what I'm afraid of."

She sounded amused. "You want Susanne to be unhappy?"

"Yes. No. Hell, I don't know." He stared at the gray-speckled sky visible through the tiny window. "I appreciate her getting Barry to take up my case."

"The man has clout. No denying that. He's also keenly intelligent. If he's made a success of his legal career, I suspect it's well deserved."

"Please tell me he has a toupee?"

Karen snorted into her banana, then feigned deep concentration on her notes.

Olivia chuckled. "Nope."

"A comb-over?"

"Again, negative."

"Ah, well." He sighed. "I can always imagine."

"Will a mop of bristly black Grecian 2000'd hair do?"

"If it's the best you have to offer, I'll take it."

She blew him a kiss down the telephone. "I'll let you know what we find. In the meantime, behave yourself and resist the temptation to strangle Connelly."

"I love you."

"Love you too."

CHAPTER THIRTY-EIGHT

Barry wasted no time in contacting Seán. By six o'clock that evening, the four of them were assembled outside the door of Aidan's two-story holiday home in the seaport town of Cobh, wearing hopeful expressions and latex gloves.

Seán pulled a set of keys out of his jacket pocket and inserted one into the lock.

"Does Connelly know you're here?" Olivia asked.

He grinned. "Hell, no. I'm off the clock."

"You really don't like the Detective Inspector, do you?"

Seán exchanged a furtive glance with Barry. "No, I don't."

"You're not going to tell me why?"

"Let's just say it has to do with a case we both worked on in Dublin."

"The same case that led you to meet Barry?"

Again the shifty look. "Yes."

"Did this lead to your demotion?"

"You ask a lot of questions, Olivia. I'd prefer to concentrate on the case against Jonas."

She stuck her tongue out at him. "Fair enough. I'll get the story out of you eventually."

Inside the cottage, Olivia gave them a brief tour. "Let's split up. Susanne and Barry can search downstairs while Seán and I do the upstairs rooms."

Seán scratched his head. "The whole place has already been thoroughly searched. I don't know what you're expecting to find."

"Given its size, finding the laptop is probably a stretch, but there a couple of places you might not have thought to look."

The police sergeant checked his watch. "Okay. I'm back on duty at eight, so I need to leave before seven thirty."

"Then we'd better get a move on."

As predicted, the laptop was nowhere in evidence. After an hour rooting through drawers and boxes, the search party was on the verge of calling it quits.

Olivia paced around the kitchen like a caged panther. "We can't give up yet. Jonas is depending on us."

"But we've looked everywhere at least twice," Susanne said, not unreasonably. "The house isn't big."

"We're not even sure the missing laptop contains relevant material," Barry interjected, "and we haven't found anything useful during our search."

Olivia pivoted on her heel and headed for the stairs. "I'm going to have one last look in Aidan's office. It's been a while since I was last in this house, but it hasn't changed much. And yet I have a nagging feeling there's something I've missed."

Seán followed her up the tartan-patterned stairs. "Why don't you try a trick we were taught at police academy? Stand in the door of the office and close your eyes. Visualize the room as it was when you were last here. Take your time. Sift through each detail in turn. Then open your eyes and tell me the first thing you see."

"Okay," she said dubiously. "It's worth a shot."

She squeezed her eyes shut and conjured an image of the office as it had been two years ago. In stark contrast to Aidan's work office, it was crammed with furniture. Drawers stuffed with papers. Bookshelves filled with an eclectic mix of dry legal tomes and popular fiction. An upholstered chair that Aidan never used. A leather chair behind an antique wooden desk.

She knew the answer before she opened her eyes. "The rug. The rug under the desk. That's new."

Seán moved to the desk and crouched down to examine the gray woolen material. "We looked under the rug when we did the police search. I know because I helped one of Connelly's men heave the desk, and it nearly killed our backs."

"Let's look again."

Seán nodded, then went to the top of the stairs. "Barry? Can you give me a hand up here?"

Barry bounded up the stairs two at a time, spritely for a man pushing sixty. Susanne followed at a more sedate pace.

On the count of three, the men lifted the desk off the rug. Olivia darted forward and yanked the rug aside. The sight of the oak rectangles beneath was a bitter disappointment. "Nothing."

"Not so fast." Seán knelt beside her and removed a slim penknife from his jeans. Gently, he inserted the blade between the wooden slats. "I helped move the desk. Connelly's men conducted the search. I don't recall them doing more than tapping on the flooring."

One of the slats came loose. Lifting it to the side, Seán shone a flashlight into the opening. "There's a box in here. Can you get it out? Your hands are smaller than mine."

Olivia reached into the gap, and her fingers wrapped around a hard handle. She pulled her prize up and out. It was a green metal box with an old-fashioned padlock. "How good are you at picking locks?"

"Bollocks to that." Seán smashed the padlock with the butt of his penknife and flipped open the lid.

Barry leaned over Olivia's shoulder. "Well, well."

It was a British passport made out to one William Brent. Aidan's smug face stared up at them, his arrogance immortalized by the forger's camera. Underneath the fake passport was an equally fake driver's license and credit card. Last but definitely not least, Seán withdrew a wad of colorful– and genuine– bank notes. "While this doesn't exonerate Jonas, it certainly raises questions about other potential motives for Gant's murder."

Olivia reached for the money. "May I?" She flipped through the banknotes, then froze. "I was right. See here? On the edge? That's paint. I know that shade of blue. It looks like one of the paints Aidan used to touch up his gnomes. I might be stretching, but I don't think so."

"And a gnome was smashed over Gant's head."

They looked at one another for a long moment before Barry's sonorous baritone broke the silence. "I'd rather like to meet these infamous garden gnomes."

***

An hour later, Seán's police car and Barry's Audi crunched up the gravel drive and parked in front of the Gant residence. Olivia stepped out of the police car and shivered in spite of the warm weather. Memories of her last visit loomed large.

Susanne was staring at the gnomes, her mouth agape. "They're hideous. I'd have nightmares if I had to live with them."

Olivia gave her a wry smile. "Frankly, they were less of a nightmare than their owner."

Barry, phone pressed to his ear, hauled himself out of the Audi and narrowly missed falling over one of Patricia's cats. "Excellent work, Smith. I'll be in touch."

"Did Smith have news?" his wife asked.

"Indeed he did. Remember that fellow on the motorcycle who visited Gant the night he was killed?"

They all nodded, ears pricked with curiosity.

"One of my people sniffed him out. It was Lar Delaney." He waggled his eyebrows in animation. "You remember him, don't you Mackey?"

Seán's expression was grim. "Indeed I do. Delaney works for Ray Greer. On the surface, Greer is a respectable businessman. Underneath, he's a crook and a swindler. We suspect he has a finger in every dirty little pie in Dublin, but we've never been able to make charges stick."

Barry shook his head. "This time won't be the exception. Delaney says he delivered money to Gant at around eleven o'clock on the night of the murder and left ten minutes after. This ties in with the evidence from the house's surveillance camera. He claims he was paid to deliver a package to Aidan Gant by a stranger he met in a pub. He denies all knowledge of the contents of the package and insists that Gant was alive when he left. Unfortunately for us, he was able to prove he was halfway to Dublin at the time the pathologist estimates Gant was killed. There's CCTV footage of him at a gas station that gives a clear visual of Delaney without his helmet and the number on the bike."

Seán's nostrils flared. "The stranger-in-a-pub story is total bollocks. Greer sent him with the money. But why?"

Olivia stepped toward one of the gnomes. "Why don't we ask this creature?" In one fluid motion, she smashed the gnome against the ground. It broke open to reveal... nothing. "Feck."

"Don't give up so quickly," Susanne said. "Let's smash a few more before admitting defeat."

They struck gold with the fourth gnome. Olivia shoved her hand into the headless garden decoration and pulled out a wad of cash bound with an elastic band. "There must be around ten thousand euros here. What on earth was Aidan up to?"

A screech drew their attention to the house. Patricia Gant wobbled down the front steps, clutching Olivia's mother's arm. "Is that you, Sergeant Mackey? What are you doing to my son's gnome collection?" She stopped short at the sight of her daughter-in-law. "What is that woman doing on my property? I want her to leave *at once*."

"Calm down," Olivia said to her former mother-in-law. The old woman was frail and had aged a decade since her son's death. "Believe it or not, I'm here to help. Why are you here, Mum?"

"Patricia is staying with friends in Ballybeg. Your dad drove us out to the house to get her more clothes. He's due to collect us any minute." Victoria paled when she registered the smashed gnomes on the ground and the cash in her daughter's hand. "So that's where he– " She broke off, wild-eyed.

"Mum, do you know why Aidan was hiding large sums of cash in his gnomes?"

"No, of course not." She was about as convincing as an ad for antiaging products.

"If you know something– anything– about this money, you need to tell us. I know Dad was running mysterious errands for Aidan that had nothing to do with the election campaign."

At the mention of her husband, Victoria snapped to attention. "Jim had nothing to do with this. Absolutely nothing. All right, I'll tell you what I know. When the property market took a hit, Bernard Byrne and some of the other shopping center investors lost money."

"Including Aidan?"

"Including Aidan. At the time, they were convinced it was a minor blip, but they were short of funds, so they accepted a loan from a Dublin property developer."

"Does this Dublin property developer have a name?" Seán asked dryly.

"Jack Bowes."

The policeman whistled. "Jack Bowes is one of Ray Greer's sidekicks. The loan was really from Greer?"

Olivia's mother nodded. "Bernard and Aidan only discovered that later."

"When the proverbial shite hit the fan and the shopping center development was in its death throes, Bernard absconded with whatever money he could lay his greedy paws on and left Aidan to deal with the fallout?"

"Exactly. Greer's been putting the screws on him ever since."

The gears shifted in Olivia's brain. "Aidan smuggled cash out of the country for Greer. He made a few trips abroad during the last year we were together, and they were all– wait for it– to gnome exhibitions."

"I knew Aidan was smuggling cash," Victoria said with a frown, "but I didn't know he was hiding it in his gnomes."

Olivia let out a bark of laughter. "I figured as much. If *you'd* known where the cash was hidden, you'd have nicked it after Aidan died."

"Well, I never," said her mother. "Do you really have such a low opinion of me?"

"Do you really want me to answer that question? Were your recent trips to art exhibits to do with these shenanigans?"

"Yes. I transported cash in my canvases."

"What was your husband's involvement?" Seán asked. "He was employed as Aidan's lackey, after all."

Her eyes darted from side to side. "Jim had nothing to do with this. It was all me."

Seán pinned Victoria with an accusatory stare. "Did you kill Aidan Gant?"

"Yes." Her voice broke on a sob. "I killed him. I– "

She clammed up at the sight of a beat up VW van weaving its way toward them.

Olivia's father stuck his graying head out of the driver's window. "What's all this? Did you forget to invite me to the party?" When he noticed the broken gnomes, he turned chalky white. He tumbled out of the van, belatedly remembering the handbrake. "Don't listen to a word she says, Mackey. It was me. I killed Aidan. Victoria is innocent."

"No, you fool," his wife said through gritted teeth, "I killed him and *you're* innocent."

Husband and wife stared at one another for a beat, comprehension dawning.

"You didn't kill Aidan?" Victoria whispered.

"*You* didn't kill him?" Jim scratched behind an ear. "Well if it wasn't *you* and it wasn't *me*, who was it?

"Oh for God's sake, would the pair of you ever shut up," screamed Patricia. "It was me!"

CHAPTER THIRTY-NINE

There was a collective gasp. Olivia's world revolved at lightning speed. Her parents and the others faded into the background of her consciousness, leaving Patricia in the spotlight. "You killed Aidan? Why would you kill your own son?"

Tears ran down the grooves of Patricia's wrinkled face. "He was going to leave me. Don't you understand? He was going to leave me all alone."

"What happened?" Olivia demanded. "Tell us everything."

The old woman took a deep breath and began her tale. "I was aware Aidan was in some sort of trouble, but he never confided in me. He'd always been on the reckless side. I'd hoped marriage to you would calm him. For a while, it worked. Then everything started to fall apart. Over the past year, he's been acting shifty, his behavior moody and erratic. The gnomes turned from a hobby into an obsession." She toed a piece of broken pottery and gave a bitter laugh. "It was bad before you separated and grew much worse after. I don't know how he managed to keep up appearances at work and on the town council."

"What happened on the night he died?"

Underneath the thick layer of makeup, Patricia's skin was gray-tinged and waxy. Without bothering to wipe the tears from her face, she shook a cigarette free from her pack and lit up. "I found a packed suitcase in his room," she said between shaky puffs. "I wasn't in the habit of rooting through my son's things, but he'd behaved strangely over dinner, and he hadn't said a word about going away. So I peeked inside. I found a plane ticket to Singapore for a person named William Brent plus a significant quantity of cash."

"You confronted him?"

"Yes." Patricia took a deep drag. "He was playing with one of those damn gnomes in his office and had a stack of banknotes on the desk. I showed him the plane ticket and demanded to know what was going on. He said he was leaving and wouldn't be back. He'd gotten into a spot of bother with an investor in the shopping center project. He'd hoped he could fix the problem, but had failed. Since Bernard Byrne did a runner with money from the project, a journalist had been sniffing around, digging for dirt. Plus a bunch of Dublin gangsters were breathing down his neck." She broke into an hysterical laugh. "It all sounded absurd, just like one of the tall tales he told as a little boy."

"How did this conversation lead to murder?"

Another cigarette puff, followed by a rattling cough so violent Olivia thought her former mother-in-law would collapse. When Patricia recovered, she drew her shoulders back and regarded the assembled company with an air of defiance. "It was a moment of madness. I couldn't believe my son would abandon me, especially when he knew I was ill."

"You're sick? What's wrong with you?"

"Lung cancer." Patricia gave a wan smile. "You were right to nag me about these cigarettes, but there's no point in stopping now." She took a last drag before discarding the butt on the ground. "I suppose I lost my mind. I picked up the gnome and hit him. I hit him again, and again, and again. I felt detached from my body, as if someone else was doing the hitting and I was merely looking down on the action from above. Afterward, I went to bed, had an excellent night's sleep, and phoned the police in the morning."

"Why were you willing to let Jonas take the blame?"

Patricia shrugged. "He took you away from Aidan. If you'd stayed, none of this would have happened."

Olivia recoiled from the older woman's hateful words, but soon pulled herself together. She needed to focus and get as much information out of Patricia before she lawyered up. "Do you have the missing laptop?"

A tired half-smile. "Of course. It's among the luggage that I left at my friend Colette's house. I don't use computers, but I know Aidan used it to type up a draft of the settlement proposal."

"There's one point I don't understand. Why did Aidan offer me a settlement if he knew he was running away? Why bother gagging me if he wasn't going to be around for the mayoral election?"

Patricia finally swiped the back of her hand across her damp face. "I believe he'd had an escape plan in place for some time, but the decision to leave that night came after the visit from the fellow on the motorcycle. When Aidan approached me about contributing money to your settlement, he said it was his way of making amends for how he'd treated you."

Too little, too late. No amount of money could compensate for Aidan's behavior. Olivia knew that now. The price she'd paid for "marrying money" had been extortionate.

Seán Mackey cleared his throat. "I'll have to take you into custody, Mrs. Gant. And I'll need statements from Mr. and Mrs. Dunne."

Victoria clutched her throat. "Will we go to prison?"

"I don't know. You might be able to strike a deal. We're more interested in Ray Greer and his cohorts." The police sergeant took Patricia's arm. "Do you want to call someone before I caution you and take you to the station?"

The old woman shook her head. "Who can I call apart from my solicitor? My friends will be appalled at what I've done."

No one could think of anything to say to that.

***

If Connelly didn't stop smirking, Jonas was going to lose his temper. And losing his temper was the last thing he should do during a police interview.

"Olivia Gant is an attractive woman. Easy to see why a man would fall for her." The detective leaned closer, treating Jonas and his solicitor to the unfiltered effect of halitosis. "Tell me, O'Mahony. Did she have sex with you as a reward for killing her husband?"

Karen McCormack, the solicitor, gave a little cough. He'd noticed she did this whenever Connelly posed an obnoxious question. It served as a warning to him and an irritation to the detective.

He started to respond but was interrupted by a knock on the door. Connelly whirled around just as Brian Glenn stuck his red head into the interrogation room.

"Message for you, sir. Looks important."

Swearing, Connelly snatched the note from the young policeman. "It better be bloody important to justify interrupting an interview with a murder suspect."

Brian winked at Jonas. "I think you'll find it worth your time."

While the detective read the note, his face underwent a series of transformations. "Is this your idea of a joke, Garda Glenn?"

"No joke, sir. Sergeant Mackey has a signed confession. Patricia Gant killed her son."

Jonas's jaw dropped. *What the hell? Patricia Gant?* It didn't make sense.

Karen McCormack pushed back her chair. "If that's the case, you no longer need to detain my client."

Connelly's mouth opened and closed, fishlike.

Jonas followed his solicitor to the door, still reeling from shock over the identity of the killer and the abrupt end to his incarceration. "Thanks for the real life experience of a murder interrogation, Detective Inspector. I'll be sure to include your technique in my next book."

The detective emitted a sound that might have been a moan.

Out in the police station lobby, Jonas scanned the crowd for Olivia. Instead, his gaze settled on a face he hadn't expected to see.

Susanne looked radiant. *Damn her.* Couldn't she have the good grace to look miserable? Or at least exude some sort of regret that she'd abandoned her son?

She stood when he approached. "It's good to see you, Jonas. It's been too long."

"Your choice, not mine." He wasn't prepared to give her an inch.

"Yes, but Luca is better off with you. We both know that."

For an instant, he saw a shadow of regret flicker across her delicate features. It was gone so fast he might have imagined it.

"I owe Barry for all he's done for my case."

"It's the least we can do. You're Luca's father after all."

And his sole acting parent. It wouldn't do for him to go to prison, leaving Susanne in the uncomfortable position of possibly having to care for her own child, now would it?

He regarded his ex-girlfriend from the corner of his eye. She exuded an aura of contentment. Obviously, life as Mrs. Barry Brennan suited her. Perhaps in a few years, he'd be glad for her, but he couldn't quite bring himself to feel entirely at peace with her just yet.

A short man of sixty with improbably dark hair emerged from a room with Sergeant Mackey. When the stranger spotted Jonas, he extended a hand. "Barry Brennan, Susanne's husband. Pleased to meet you at last."

Flummoxed, Jonas returned the handshake. "Thank you for all you've done."

"In truth, I did very little. Olivia and Sergeant Mackey found the evidence, and the confession that came in consequence took us all by surprise."

"Regardless, I owe you one."

Brennan gave a small smile. "No, I owed you one. I think we're even." He looked over at his wife, who was darting impatient glances at the exit. "Enjoy your freedom, O'Mahony. Don't waste your chance with that fine young woman."

Then it was Seán Mackey's turn to shake his hand. "We're completing the paperwork for your release. Should be done in a few minutes. Once that's done, you're free to go."

"Thanks, Mackey. I appreciate you following your instinct."

"All part of the job." The police sergeant nodded over his shoulder. "There are two people very keen to see you. Best not leave them waiting."

In the doorframe of the Ballybeg Garda Station stood Olivia and Luca, hand in hand. They both broke into huge grins when they saw him.

He grabbed Luca up into his arms and swung him around. "I have missed you so much, little guy."

"Put me down, Dad. You're making me dizzy."

Laughing, Jonas set his son back on his feet and turned to Olivia. She hurled herself into his arms. "I'm delighted to see you outside that horrible room."

"Sounds like you've had quite an adventure this evening. How bad was it?"

She shuddered. "Horrendous. I've spent weeks hoping the police would find the murderer and let us get on with our lives. Never in my wildest imaginings did I picture Patricia as the killer."

"Why did she do it?"

"The 'Reader's Digest' condensed version: Aidan planned to do a runner and Patricia freaked. Given her state of health, Barry doubts she'll stand trial." She cuddled closer. "Trust me. The story is more convoluted than the cleverest of your plots."

"You can fill me in on all the lurid details over wine. I think we deserve dinner at a fancy restaurant tonight. What do you think, Luca?"

"As long as they serve white food, I'm good."

Jonas looked questioningly at Olivia.

"He's on a white-food kick," she explained. "It started this morning."

He ruffled his son's hair. "In that case let's go find some white food."

Putting an arm around each of his two favorite people, Jonas steered them out of the police station and down the steps to the car park.

"By the way, Dad," Luca said with deceptive casualness, "I've asked Olivia to move in with us."

"Have you, now?" He roared with laughter. "Cheeky sod. And what did she say?"

Olivia smiled up at him, a wicked twinkle in her eye. "She said yes."

EPILOGUE

FIVE MONTHS LATER

From: livlongandprosper@imail.ie
To: jillbekele@web.ie

Hi Jill,

Hope life in the Big Smoke is treating you well. Are you managing to avoid Ratfink? Any hot men on the scene?

Life in Ballybeg is as crazy as ever. The Cottage Café is doing a roaring trade. I've hired a second girl to help out a couple of days a week. Ever since the murder investigation, Jonas's book sales have soared. The television production team brought the filming of his new miniseries forward to cash in on his notoriety. People are ghoulish, aren't they?

I'm guessing you've seen the newspapers. With Patricia dead, there won't be a trial. Mum and Dad took this as their cue to clam up and deny all knowledge of Ray Greer and the money laundering shenanigans. If the police don't manage to link the money back to Greer, my parents might very well be in the clear. Not sure how I feel about that. My emotions are all over the place.

In more positive news, Luca is doing great! He adores his teacher. We moved him permanently to the school in Cork City. In theory, keeping him at the local primary school for part of the week was a nice idea, but it wasn't helping him integrate in either place. Despite the expense, the private school is the better choice.

Ooh, I have gossip! Remember Brian Glenn, the cute young policeman? Word is that he's hooked up with Sharon MacCarthy, Ruairí's little sister. A cop and a shoplifter? I'm curious to see how that relationship develops.

Speaking of gossip, I have some of my own! Yeah, I'm saving the best for last. Have you any plans for New Year's Eve? If not, will you be my bridesmaid? Sorry for the short notice, but we decided spontaneously on Luca's birthday. It won't be a fancy affair. I've done the big white dress wedding once in my life, and I don't need that again. Bridie Byrne is finally making an honest man of my grandfather, and we thought it would be a laugh to make it a double wedding. We've hired a reception room at Clonmore Castle Hotel. The café will provide the desserts, and the hotel kitchen will take care of the rest of the catering. Let me know if you can make it. Fingers and toes crossed! Let's make this the best wedding ever!

Love and Kisses from Ballybeg,

Olivia xx

THANK YOU!

Thanks for reading *Love and Leprechauns*. I hope you enjoyed it!

Love and Leprechauns is the third book in the Ballybeg series. All the stories are designed to stand alone–Happy Ever Afters guaranteed! However, you might prefer to read them in order of publication to follow the development of the secondary characters and happenings in the town.

To find out what's next, or to sign up to my new release mailing list, check out my author website at:

http://zarakeane.com

You can also turn the page to read a blurb and excerpt from my Christmas novella *Love and Mistletoe* (Ballybeg, #4).

LOVE AND MISTLETOE

(BALLYBEG #4 – NOVELLA)

Kissed by Christmas...
Policeman Brian Glenn wants a promotion. Studying for a degree in criminology is the first step. When a member of Ballybeg's most notorious family struts into his forensic psychology class, his hopes for a peaceful semester vanish. Sharon MacCarthy is the last woman he should get involved with, however hot and bothered she makes him get under his police uniform. Can he survive the semester without succumbing to her charms?

...Loved by New Year.
Sharon's had a rough few months. She knows her future job prospects depend on finally finishing her degree. When she's paired with her secret crush for the semester project, she sees a chance for happiness. Can she persuade Brian that there's more to her than sequins, high heels, and a rap sheet?

OUT NOW!
Turn the page for an excerpt.

EXCERPT FROM
LOVE AND MISTLETOE

BALLYBEG, COUNTY CORK, IRELAND

Location: The MacCarthy Farm

Time: 21:06

There were many places Garda Brian Glenn would rather spend his Saturday night. Dry places. Warm places. Places that didn't stink of cow shite. Wrinkling his nose, he hunched down behind a bush and squinted through his police-issue night-vision binoculars. "They've finished unloading the car."

Sergeant Seán Mackey shifted on the grass beside him, the sudden snap of a twig serving as a timely reminder to keep the volume down. "Are you sure about this?" His breath floated through the damp night air in smokelike wisps. "Because if you're not, we're trespassing on private property. Not to mention freezing our balls off. Trust you to pick the first cold night in September to go on a flaming stakeout."

Brian lowered his binoculars and grinned through the dark at his partner and superior officer. "Speak for yourself. I had the good sense to wear thermals. Seriously, man. My intel is solid. The MacCarthys are definitely up to their old tricks. I overheard Sharon discussing it with Naomi Bekele in the pub. Brazen as brass."

The police sergeant grumbled and tugged his hat lower, presumably to shield his ears from the harsh wind. *His perfectly flat ears...*Seán was film-star handsome with a deep Dublin baritone that made the women of Ballybeg swoon– a far cry from Brian's sing-song Donegal lilt and sticky-out ears. If his new partner weren't a decent bloke and a fine cop, he'd have resented him.

"Come on, Seán. Sure what else would we be doing this evening? At least a stakeout is more exciting than breaking up a fight at MacCarthy's pub."

"Who are you trying to convince? Me or yourself?"

"This is the first interesting lead I've got on, well, anything in ages. Not much happens in Ballybeg." And when it did, the local police weren't left in charge for long. At the rate Brian's career was going, he'd be stagnating in uniform until retirement. He needed something– anything– to impress the higher-ups.

"I realize Sharon hasn't been the most law-abiding of citizens," Seán said, "but I can't see her manufacturing drugs in her own kitchen."

"Why is it so hard to believe?" Brian forced himself to keep his irritation no louder than a whisper. "You haven't been down here long enough to know the full story about that family. Apart from the father being a regular fixture at Cork Prison, one of the brothers was convicted of drug dealing a couple of years ago, and a second was done for possession."

"Yeah..." The older man drew out the word, giving it a wealth of meaning, "but Sharon's previous infractions include shoplifting, speeding, and drunk and disorderly behavior. And all her priors are at least a couple of years old."

He stared at his partner, slack-jawed. "How the hell do you know all that?"

Seán gave a low chuckle. "The MacCarthy files were among the first to cross my desk when I started working at Ballybeg Garda Station. I've read everything we have on the entire clan, including the fact that Sharon has cleaned up her act since she started university."

"Do you really think attending college has magically transformed her character?" Brian snorted in disgust. "Come off it, man. Think of all the students who are busted for dealing. Being clever enough to get into uni doesn't mean you're smart enough to stay on the right side of the law."

"All right. Don't get your thermals in a twist. We'll check out whatever is going on in the house. I just hope we don't end up making tits of ourselves in the process."

"Apart from not landing face first in cow shite, my main concern is avoiding a close encounter with one of Colm MacCarthy's hellhounds."

"Jaysus. Don't tell me he's still involved with the dog fights?" Seán's mouth curled in disgust. "I knew the judge should have given more than a fine the last time he was up in court. That man's more of an animal than the ones he breeds."

"Agreed. I've nothing concrete about Colm and the dogs, but I could have sworn I heard one bark earlier. Did you hear it?"

“Can’t say I did, but it’s hard to hear anything over this wind.”

Brian hunkered down in the shadows and peered through his binoculars. Shapes moved against lit windows, but he couldn’t identify who they were. “Vicious dog or no, we need to get closer to the house. I can’t see anything from this distance.”

“Me neither. Pity the station’s budget can’t cover more powerful binoculars.”

“The station’s budget doesn’t cover roof repairs, never mind binoculars,” Brian said dryly. “I can’t move in my office without tripping over a bucket. It’s been like that since I was first sent to Ballybeg. We’re always being promised more men, better equipment, and a new station building. It’ll never happen.”

Seán hung his binoculars around his neck and turned up the collar of his coat. “Come on, then. Let’s go.”

They crept through the field as silently as they could manage, the house and farm buildings looming closer with each step.

“Wait!” Seán grabbed Brian’s arm. “Do they have motion-detector lighting over the yard?”

He considered before answering. “I don’t think so. No lights came on while they were unloading the car. Either they’d deliberately switched them off, or they don’t exist.”

“All right. Go on.”

Moving stealthily, they covered the last few meters of the field and took up their position behind an ancient water trough.

Seán rubbed his hands together to keep them warm. "I'm frozen. I'd kill for a cup of coffee right now."

"I've a thermos in my pack." Brian slid his rucksack off his back and extracted a metal can. "It's tea, not coffee."

His partner gave an exaggerated shudder. "How did you make it through training college without having the shite beaten out of you? Everyone knows cops drink coffee."

"Everyone knows cops drink *bad* coffee." Brian unscrewed the top of his thermos and poured piping-hot tea into the lid. It burned his tongue when he took a sip, but he relished the warmth wending its way from his mouth to his stomach. He held the cup out to his partner. "Sure you won't take a swig?"

Brian couldn't see Seán's face clearly in the dark, but he could sense the indecision flickering over his features. "Ah, go on, then. I'm desperate." The other man had the cup halfway to his lips when a sharp bark hacked through the silence. The cup of the thermos shot out of his hand and ricocheted off the metal trough, knocking against a rusty bucket in the process. "Feck." Seán cradled his hand. "I'm after scalding myself."

"That was definitely a dog." Brian craned his neck to see over the trough. Lights went on in the room nearest the back door. A human-shaped shadow flitted across the window. "Someone's coming. Duck."

Voices floated out the open door, the occasional word decipherable. Voices from a house that was likely to be a lot drier and warmer than Brian and Seán's current location. The dog barked again followed by a high-pitched whine. Footsteps rang over the cobblestones, and light from a flashlight bobbed in a drunken dance. A woman wearing high heels. *Sharon.* Brian would bet his police badge he was right.

He pictured her in his mind: medium height, medium build, generous bust, and a high, tight arse that begged to be pinched. *Jaysus.* Where had that notion sprung from? He couldn't stand Sharon MacCarthy. She unnerved him, seemed to take a devilish delight in taunting him at every opportunity. She was no beauty– not in the classical sense– but there was something about her that caused men to look twice. He crouched down and waited for her and the dog to go back inside.

Minutes dragged by. Finally, right at the point Brian was ready to scream from holding still for so long, a door creaked shut, and the clickety-clack of the heels moved back across the cobblestoned yard to the house.

When the lights in the room nearest the back door went out, his tense muscles slackened.

"Whatever eejit of a hound Colm's got now is a useless guard dog," Seán whispered. "Why didn't it pick up our scent?"

Brian shrugged. "Dunno. No sense of smell? Maybe he got it cheap."

"No sense of smell or not, it sounds vicious." Seán shifted restlessly. "We're going to have to try to get a look in the window. Without proof that they're up to something they shouldn't be, we've no business being here."

"You go, and I'll shadow you?"

Seán laughed, a low rumble. "Nice try. This stakeout was *your* idea. *You* get to do the honors."

"Fair enough."

"You can leave the thermos with me."

Brian tossed it to him with a wry smile. "Changed your mind about hating tea?"

"Nah. More like not changed my mind about being cold. At least the can will keep me warm."

After giving the yard a quick scan to check for prowling animals and lurking humans, Brian emerged from behind the trough and half crept, half ran to take up his position beneath a windowsill. Cautiously, he unfurled enough to be able to peer in the glass. The sight that assaulted him was enough to give a man heart failure. A furry face was pressed to the window, lips drawn back to reveal sharp fangs.

***

Location: The MacCarthy Farm

Time: 21:06

Sharon surveyed the ingredients lined up on the kitchen counter: Epsom salts, coarse sea salt, baking soda, corn starch, citric acid, essential oils, and food coloring. Everything they needed to make fabulous homemade bath products. "The Ballybeg Christmas Bazaar won't know what hit it. We'll make a fortune."

Naomi paused in the act of unpacking a selection of cupcake-sized baking molds in a variety of shapes and sizes. "I don't know about making a fortune. Personally, I'd settle for making our money back." She fingered a little bottle of lavender oil. "Did you have to go and spend so much on the ingredients?"

"There's no point in bothering if we're going to use shite ingredients. Decent essential oils don't come cheap." Sharon patted her friend on the back. "Don't stress. Not only will we break even, but we'll make enough profit to afford the rental deposit on a decent-sized flat."

Naomi's expression was dubious. "I certainly hope so. This has wiped out the last of my savings."

"It'll be no problem, Nomes," Sharon said cheerily. "Trust me."

Rummaging through a cupboard, she located the kitchen scales behind a broken toaster and her brother's bong. She stood and stretched her back like a cat. "Hey, if our bath product range takes off, we might persuade a couple of shops in town to stock them. I know Olivia sells stuff like that at the Cottage Café."

"Don't jump the gun." Worry lines creased Naomi's normally smooth forehead. "We haven't made our first batch yet. It might be a disaster."

"Such pessimism! Relax. It'll all be grand. What you need is a large glass of vino before we get to work." She wrenched open the fridge and assessed its contents. Beer, beer, and more beer. Sausages, bacon, and moldy cheese. She extracted a carton of milk and sniffed. *Holy mother.* When had it gone off? A shudder of revulsion ran through her body. Thank God she rarely ate at home. Standards in the MacCarthy household had never been high. Since Ma died, they'd plummeted to a record low.

Slamming the fridge door shut, she pivoted on her platform heels and almost tripped over a mobile bundle of fur. "Well, hey there, Wiggly Poo. Did you have a nice snooze?" She bent down to stroke the dog's curly fur. He wagged his tail and gave her a generous lick. "Buttering me up, eh? At least one male in my life loves me enough to kiss me. What's it you're after? Food?"

The labradoodle darted to his bowl and waited, panting and tongue lolling in expectation. Sharon rooted through her bag and found the tin of dog food that her boss, Bridie Byrne, had given her earlier in the day. She emptied it into the bowl, and the dog consumed the foul-smelling substance with gusto.

Naomi switched the oven on to preheat for the bath bombs. "How long are you dog-sitting?"

"Just for this evening. Bridie's minding him while Fiona and Gavin are off on a romantic weekend, but she didn't want to leave him alone in her house while she was out at bingo. He's a little on the wild side and has a penchant for ornaments."

Naomi laughed. "Sounds like you and he are a matched pair."

"Get away with you." Sharon uncorked the wine and poured two generous glasses. "I've cleaned up my act since Ma got sick. I promised her I'd get my psychology degree, and get it I will." She scrunched up her nose. "Concentrating on my studies would be a whole lot easier if I didn't have to live with Da. The second I can afford a place of my own, I'm out of this dump."

Naomi raised her glass. "Then let's hope the bath product plan bears fruit."

"*Sláinte.*" They clinked glasses, and Sharon took a sip of wine, relishing the tart taste on her tongue.

A crash outside in the farmyard made her choke midswig.

"What was that?" she spluttered. She raced to the kitchen window and yanked back the frayed net curtains. Through the dark mist, she could perceive only the pitch black of the night.

Naomi moved to her side, craning to see. "Did one of the cows get out, do you think?"

"Dunno." Sharon was already moving toward the mudroom and the door to the yard. She snagged her jacket from its peg and grabbed her scarf.

"Are you sure you want to go out there alone?" Naomi pulled her cardigan tight around her thin body. "It's creepy when it's this dark."

"I'll be grand. It's probably just one of the animals. Besides," she said with a grin, "I don't see you offering to join me."

Her friend shuddered. "I don't like the dark at the best of times. Out on a farm with wild animals roaming? Nuh-uh."

Sharon laughed. "*Domesticated* animals, you eejit. You'd swear we had lions prowling the property."

"All the same, I'm staying put."

"Suit yourself." Grabbing a flashlight, Sharon ventured out into the dark.

Rain fell in heavy sheets, forcing her to yank up her hood. Up until a couple of months ago, they'd had floodlights that came on when they sensed movement. When they broke, Da hadn't bothered to fix them, insisting a flashlight would suffice and was a hell of a lot cheaper. Sharon shivered in the damp chill air, cursing herself for not wearing a heavier coat.

"Woof!"

She whirled round to see Wiggly Poo slip out the door and dance at her feet. "Daft dog." She petted him and buried her nose in his curly fur. He was a crap guard dog, but she was glad to have his company. Despite her bravado, the dark farmyard was kind of creepy. She shivered beneath her thin jacket. The weird sensation of being watched sent prickles down her spine. If only Da would fix the damn floodlights.

Picking her way carefully over the cobblestones, she headed toward the cowshed. All quiet, save for the odd moo. It was a similar story in the sheep's enclosure and in the henhouse. The familiar sounds and smells were bittersweet. When she was little, they'd had a farm full of animals. Now they were down to six cows, eight sheep, and four hens. Times had changed on the MacCarthy farm, and not for the better.

She closed the door of the henhouse. Whatever had caused the crash wasn't apparent out here. "Come on, Wiggly Poo. Let's get back inside before we're soaked through."

Back in the kitchen, Naomi had started weighing and mixing the ingredients to make bath salts. "No luck?" she asked, raising an eyebrow when Sharon and Wiggly Poo returned from their outside adventure, wet and bedraggled.

"I don't know what caused the noise. The animals all seem fine." She leaned over her friend's shoulder and sniffed the air. "Divine. What scent combo are you making?"

"Lemongrass and lavender. We can add a little purple food dye to give it an appealing color."

"Sounds good. I'll get started on the bath bombs."

"Woof!" Wiggly Poo was on the alert, racing to the window and jumping up to press his paws against the glass. "Woof!"

"What's up with him?" Naomi asked. "I didn't hear anything."

Sharon's shoulders slumped. "Feck. I hope it's not Da. He said he wouldn't be home until late tonight."

The labradoodle was growling now, the menacing sound mitigated by his cute and fluffy appearance.

Naomi's dark eyes widened. "Do you think there's a pervert out there? I told you I thought someone was watching us when we were unloading the car."

"A wanker? He'd need to be seriously desperate to venture out on a night like this." Wiggly Poo was growling at the window. "Oh, for feck's sake." Sharon marched to the window and threw it open.

A pale face loomed before her, light blue eyes darting from side to side, panicked. "You were right, Nomes. It *is* a pervert." Sharon crossed her arms over her bosom and grinned. "Hello, Garda Glenn."

OUT NOW!

OTHER BOOKS BY ZARA

1. *Love and Shenanigans* (novel)
2. *Love and Blarney* (novella)
3. *Love and Leprechauns* (novel)
4. *Love and Mistletoe* (novella)
5. *Love and Shamrocks* (novel – out 2015)

ACKNOWLEDGEMENTS

Love and Leprechauns touches on an issue close to my heart: parenting a child on the autistic spectrum. I wrote the first draft in 2010, the year my son was diagnosed. I soon realized that I wasn't in the right frame of mind to do justice to the Luca storyline because I was living the raw reality of the diagnosis. So my first thanks go to all the therapists, teachers, and healthcare professionals who have helped my little boy make such impressive progress over the past few years.

Many thanks are also due to my wonderful critique partner, Magdalen Braden, for keeping me sane during the writing of this book; to Karina Bliss for her insightful critique of the first three chapters of a very early draft; Rhonda Helms, editor extraordinaire, for working her magic on the manuscript; to Trish Slattery and April Weigele for beta reading the final draft; and to Anne and Linda at Victory Editing for the thorough proofread.

Finally, thank you to my family for being unique, quirky, and wonderful. I love you guys!

ABOUT ZARA KEANE

Zara Keane grew up in Dublin, Ireland, but spent her summers in a small town very similar to the fictitious Ballybeg.

She currently lives in Switzerland with her family. When she's not writing or wrestling small people, she drinks far too much coffee, and tries– with occasional success – to resist the siren call of Swiss chocolate.

zarakeane.com

Printed in Great Britain
by Amazon